HUSBAND ON APPROVAL

Was she still in love with him or was she merely in love with all he had once stood for? Arden, confronted with the husband who had divorced her, was forced to ask herself this question. But there was one, also, which she found still more pressing. What was the indefinable power which drew her towards Lance Ashton, the distinguished novelist? This deeply absorbing romantic novel tells the story of Arden's relationship with three men: with Derek, the husband whom she had once loved and to whom she longed to return; with Lance, the brilliant and fascinating author whom she finds so compelling; and with Brian, the faithful friend who has been her devoted admirer for so long. The novel is set against a vivid and interesting background, for Arden is a commercial artist, commissioned to design the jacket for one of Lance's novels. The story of a beautiful and passionate woman who at last, after suffering the bitterness of disillusionment, finds true love. This book will be regarded as one of Sonia Deane's most enthralling novels.

HUSBAND ON APPROVAL

SONIA DEANE

THE ROMANCE BOOK CLUB
121 CHARING CROSS ROAD
LONDON W.C.2.

Made and printed in Great Britain by
Taylor Garnett Evans & Co. Ltd
Watford, Hertfordshire

For

My god-daughter

MARGARET

with my love

CHAPTER I

ARDEN'S gaze travelled to the calendar. It was exactly a year ago that her marriage to Derek had been dissolved.

She sat motionless at her desk, her luminous dark eyes sightless as memory blurred her vision, making her oblivious of her surroundings. Emotion, disturbing and destructive, swirled her thoughts from the book jacket she was sketching and suspended her in a world remote from reality. Her life suddenly revealed itself in all its sterile unfulfilment, its empty purposelessness. Restlessness crept upon her, sliding into a mind which, thus far, had resisted its temptation. Was she still in love with him, or was she merely in love with the idea of all he had once stood for? Habit, she told herself contemptuously, died hard. Live with a man for five years and you could not expect to erase him from your thoughts as though he were a mere acquaintance.

She moved from the desk and went to the windows which gave a view over the garden of her small, country cottage. The stillness of dusk added to the enchantment, the magic, of the summer night. Loneliness stabbed like the blade of a knife thrust into her heart. She doubted, in that moment, the wisdom of choosing a home five miles from the nearest village and a mile from the next habitation. Seclusion, absolute isolation—which she had been determined to secure—was hers, for the two acres of ground that surrounded her was either walled in, or fenced in, concealing her property even from the lane by which it was approached. She knew, suddenly and starkly, the anguish of being alone—in spirit, mind and body.

Fiercely, she switched on the light and pulled the cord which drew the curtains, shutting out the beauty of a night that stirred longings she had struggled valiantly to suppress. Back at her desk she looked down critically at the "rough" she had done, her lips twisting bitterly as the title leered up at her: *If You Can Dream . . .*

Kipling's words flashed through her mind: *"If you can dream and not make dreams your master."* Tears stung her eyes and she dashed them away, impatient of her own weakness.

And in the silence the door bell rang startlingly, making

her jump in fear. Instinctively she glanced at the clock: ten minutes past nine. She was not expecting anyone and felt disinclined to answer it. With a sigh, however, she went out into the hall and lifted the latch, opening the door with a certain apprehension. She thought cynically that in this highly progressive and civilized age one never knew just when one was going to have one's head battered in.

A man's voice asked:

"I'm looking for the home of Mrs. Rayne. . . . I wonder——" A startled exclamation, then: "Arden! So *this* is the cottage! I've been knocking on doors for miles around during the past hour."

Arden's legs lost their strength, her heart almost choked her with its sudden, wild beating.

"Derek! *You!*"

He stepped into the hall without waiting to be asked inside.

Arden squared her shoulders, took a deep breath and tried to sound casual.

"You—you want to see me?"

A trace of his old cynicism flashed as he answered:

"I should hardly be here otherwise—should I?" He atoned for that swiftly, by adding: "I've wanted to see you for a very long while."

She led the way into the study and he glanced around him, aware instantly of the unmistakable touches of home which stamped her personality upon the room.

"You certainly have a retreat here," he commented. "No one had ever heard of a Mrs. Rayne."

She managed to meet his gaze with coolness and poise.

"That could be because I am known solely by my professional one. Arden Marchly." She was losing her confidence before his steady scrutiny.

He said slowly:

"I haven't forgotten your name. In fact I haven't forgotten anything."

Arden studied him, trying to be dispassionate.

Derek Rayne was tall, well built and good-looking. He had an air of supreme confidence which his friends regarded as forceful and his enemies as arrogant. At thirty-five he was manager of a highly successful advertising agency and resolute

8

in his determination eventually to gain for himself a seat on the Board. Failure in any aspect of life offended him. He regarded it as a personal affront.

Arden's thoughts and emotions were chaotic. Tension mounted in the wake of suspense as she said:

"Even so, I do not quite see why you are here."

"No?" He walked with slow, deliberate movements to her desk and drew her gaze so that it travelled with his to the calendar. "A year ago to-day," he added briefly.

Arden's resistance was waning. As she looked at him all the memories of happier days flooded back, wiping out not only the year that had elapsed since their divorce, but the shadows that had, from time to time, enveloped their marriage. Retrospect held all the magic of illusion, scorning reality.

"I remember," she said huskily.

He glanced at the sketch on which she was working. Without saying anything she knew that he was not impressed by it. Then:

"I've been waiting to hear of your marriage to Brian." His gaze was suddenly direct and penetrating. "What went wrong, Arden?"

Faint colour mounted her cheeks. Before she could speak he had added, "It seems fashionable these days for co-respondents to back out of their obligations once the case is over." His tone changed. "I'm sorry."

Arden's voice held a sudden, warning calm. "Since Brian and I were never lovers there was no earthly reason why we should marry."

Derek sighed as he studied her.

"Strange," he said softly, "how little any of that matters now I've found you again. . . . You're lovelier than ever, my darling. I never realized quite how dark your eyes were, or how deep was the gold of your hair. It shines like silk as you stand there. . . . Arden——"

She cried, "I don't understand. A year ago you wouldn't listen to me; you hated me. Nothing has happened to change all that." She was struggling against the treachery of emotions that would, she knew, betray her; aware that already her heart was thudding, her body tensing as excitement tore through her body, mocking the former loneliness and misery of her life.

He answered, *"I've* changed, Arden. I've forgiven the past——"

"There was nothing to forgive."

"Forgotten, then," he corrected.

She paled and stepped back as though she would prevent any precipitate move that might so easily lead to greater heart-ache. The room was suddenly deathly in its silence; the atmosphere filled with suspense, with the drama of memories and shattered hopes. She said, bewildered, "This doesn't seem real, Derek."

He reached her side and, leaning forward, took her into his arms, looking down into her startled eyes with a mocking light of conquest as he lowered his lips to hers. Then, drawing back, he asked softly, "Is *that* real?"

Arden's cheeks were flushed, her eyes suddenly bright. She was hardly conscious of anything that had been said, so great was the tumult within her. Had Fate conspired with Derek Rayne he could not have selected a more propitious time for his visit, or one when she was more vulnerable. It was as though in that second he stood for life itself, against the sombre background of soul-destroying existence.

Her murmur was inarticulate and she felt again the pressure of his arms around her, the passion of his mouth on hers. The ecstasy of the past surged back to plead its own cause. Desolation vanished, hope speared the future. Yet the faint voice of sanity prompted her to say finally, as she released herself from his embrace, "Emotion is illogical and unreasonable, Derek. To be fooled by it would be absurd."

"It would be equally absurd to disregard it," he exclaimed.

Again there was a heavy and uneasy silence which she broke by saying deliberately, "Have you come here to ask me to remarry you?"

He met her gaze levelly.

"And if I had?"

She trembled and sat down rather unsteadily. Then:

"I should have to be very sure that you'd undergone a change of heart, Derek, and that you believed in my innocence so far as Brian was concerned. Anything less would be a travesty." She waited tense and apprehensive for his answer.

"Doesn't my being here prove my sincerity?"

"No," she replied boldly. "Some spark of—of affection or

even nostalgia might have prompted you. Or, as you said, you could have forgiven me." Her eyes hardened. "I do not want forgiveness, but vindication."

"Then you already have it," he replied quietly. "I'm sorry, Arden, but you must admit that the evidence seemed irrefutable."

"Circumstantial evidence always does. Perhaps the greatest irony lay in the fact that of all the men I'd ever met, Brian appealed to me least of all in that way."

"Jealousy can goad any man to madness," Derek exclaimed ruefully. "I'm ready to admit that it has always been a weakness of mine. You're hardly the type of woman to allay it, my sweet. I'm very sure that Brian's interest in you was not that of mere friendship."

Arden didn't employ subterfuge.

"That's true, but I didn't know it until after the divorce."

"You make it sound very convincing," he said swiftly.

Instantly she flashed, "Are you doubting my word again?"

He shook his head and flicked the ash from his cigarette.

"You're twice as attractive when you're angry and your eyes flash. Of course I'm not doubting you."

Arden relaxed. It was balm to be understood. She watched him carefully. Derek, she thought swiftly, was a man of curious reserves and inscrutability and his words, on occasion, could lack the conviction of their text.

"I've often wondered how I should feel if anything like this happened," she mused.

"And now that it has?" He paused, then: "We are still in love with each other, Arden."

She sighed and glanced down at her hands which were ringless.

"Love." There was faint cynicism in the echo. "It can be a very abused word, Derek. I'm not sure of anything any more. When I married you I believed that it was for ever; that nothing could ever part or come between us. And what happened?"

"I behaved like a fool," he admitted with an honesty that both startled and disarmed her. "Marriages can often be strengthened by mistakes."

"Even after divorce?" she inquired. "You speak almost as if we were still married."

"Possibly because I could never feel that we were not."
He studied her intently. "You look as though every word I say strikes you as being quite incredible or unbelievable."

Arden took a deep breath.

"Perhaps I may be forgiven for my natural scepticism, Derek. When one has been badly hurt once——" She paused.

"Ah," he exclaimed with feeling.

She flashed at him:

"You hurt yourself."

She knew that it wasn't quite what he had expected and she was a little surprised by her own determination to defend herself against any further disillusionment.

Derek leaned forward in his chair and then got up restlessly.

"That can perhaps be the worst hurt of all, my dear."

She looked up at him.

"How could you possibly find this cottage—trace me at all, in fact?"

"Your sister-in-law told me vaguely where you were living while refusing to give me your actual address. All I got out of her was that the cottage was about five miles from Little Gaddesden in the Tring direction. She omitted the small detail of the name."

"Then," persisted Arden, "however *did* you find this place? It certainly cannot be seen from the road."

"The landlord of an old Inn about three miles from here said that there *was* a cottage—he couldn't say exactly *where*, but he'd heard tell of one——" Derek smiled at the recollection. "Quaint old character . . . I saw the chink of light through the trees and took a chance. You're certainly secluded here."

"I intended to be," she said a trifle grimly. Their eyes met and emotion surged between them. The intimacy of night wrapped around them, demanding decisions which Arden was loth to make. It was enough that suddenly she had come to life again and that after the bitter harvest of injustice had come this undreamed-of and unsought vindication. She said swiftly, "Can I get you anything? A drink?"

"I think the occasion calls for one—don't you?" He drew her to her feet and held her closely. "There's been no life without you, Arden—only a wilderness."

12

Her heart raced at his words and she looked up at him in swift, almost baffled inquiry.

"I cannot quite believe it is you talking," she murmured. "Even *now*."

He kissed her expertly and she relaxed in his arms, conscious of a thrill of passion, of desire re-awakening. The ice which had impacted her heart vanished and the blood seemed to heat in her veins, almost as though it, too, had been frozen in a sterile body.

He said softly, "You're still naïve, my darling."

She shook her head.

"On the contrary, Derek. I'm wary."

At that he smiled, a confident, almost challenging smile.

"I've a bottle of Bollinger with me in the car," he said calmly. "Wary or not, I've an idea you'll share it with me."

Arden laughed.

"Male conceit. I might have refused you admittance."

He eyed her contemplatively.

"In that case there would have been no need to mention it. Simple!" He moved to the door as he spoke.

Arden took the champagne glasses from the cocktail cabinet while he went out to the car. Her hands shook, the floor beneath her had lost its substance and she floated in some world of sweet enchantment. Already the room had come to life. Excitement took the place of apathy.

Derek called out to her, "You have a 'fridge?"

She went into the hall and showed him the way to the kitchen. He marched off completely at home. Returning, he caught her looking at herself in the wall mirror and said softly:

"It's a lovely picture, Arden. Everything about you is always so right. I like that blue dress . . . and your cool, clear skin." A pause. "You haven't changed. . . . I think I was a little afraid you might have done. I'm not speaking only of looks now."

She became suddenly serious. "Do we any of us know quite how much we have changed until our feelings are put to the test?" she asked suddenly.

His face clouded for a second, his expression grim as he answered: "True. One of the hazards of life. We surprise no one so much as ourselves."

She persisted, "You are as surprised at being here as I am that you *are* here. That's it—isn't it?"

He said, slowly and deliberately, "On the contrary. I've thought of nothing else for the past six months. I waited merely to satisfy a whim and to give you time really to miss me."

To miss me.

She struggled against confused, chaotic thoughts. Then she said weakly, "Oh, Derek! It's all been such a ghastly mistake, such a *waste*. If only you'd *trusted* me."

He murmured, persuasively, "It's over now . . . let's not look back. . . . The champagne will be chilled at least. I'll get it."

He did so, returned, uncorked the bottle and poured its bubbling amber contents into the glasses standing ready. He handed Arden hers and raised his own, then he said, his gaze holding hers, "To to-morrow, my darling—whatever we choose to do with it."

Arden drank and sat down limply on the arm of a chair, staring at him. An hour before she had been in limbo and now, suddenly, miraculously a new world had opened up before her. She said tensely:

"I'm not sure I want to think about to-morrow. Caution perhaps."

"Not, I hope, distrust of me."

A shadow crossed her face.

"No, Derek, merely the desire to make absolutely certain that the mistakes of yesterday are not repeated."

He looked down into his glass and then raised his gaze rather abruptly.

"You admit that there *were* mistakes?"

She sighed.

"Obviously; or we should never have reached a position where it was possible for you to doubt my word."

"Are you trying to apportion the blame, or exonerate yourself?" he asked seriously.

A tiny flame of anger whipped emotion to frenzy as she cried, "Neither! I'm trying to apply reason, Derek. One mistake is bad enough; two would be tragedy."

"So! Even were it possible to do so, you would not re-marry me to-night," he said sharply.

She got to her feet.

"No." The first, sharp impact of emotion, which she

14

recognized as more physical than mental, had died down. Self-preservation crept in to protect her from any impulsive or precipitate action.

Derek smiled. He knew, no matter what she might say, that he had won the first battle.

"Sensible woman," he agreed.

She glanced at the clock and reading her thoughts, he explained:

"I've already booked a room at the Bridgewater Arms, Little Gaddesden. I am on holiday for a week or so and thought it would give me plenty of time to find you!"

Arden basked for a second in a luxurious content. Why think ahead? Why analyse, or seek, explanation?

She said, softly, "I'm glad it didn't take you long."

He filled their glasses again.

"Do you go up to London each day?"

"No. Only when it is necessary to see an art editress or agency."

He said, with a faintly deprecating air, "That kind of stuff is hardly worthy of you, surely?"

"I take it as it comes, Derek. Actually, I have an interesting job on hand. The jacket for Lance Ashton's new novel."

"Ashton?" Derek showed appreciation. "Now he can write. Can't stand novels in the ordinary way, but his are different."

Arden said briefly, "He's accepted almost as a genius in his particular field. His keen perception, his knowledge of life and other countries—amazing. I believe he is a neighbour of mine."

"Probably completely eccentric and filthily conceited."

"They say not."

"Suppose he's made a fortune," Derek commented grudgingly.

Arden replied, "Naturally; his sales are fantastic. . . . I'm rather thrilled at being given the opportunity even of submitting a rough for anything of his."

"I suppose he could reject it."

"He most certainly could and probably will! But I think I know what he has in mind." Her smile was slow and provocative. "You wouldn't by any chance be hoping for me to fail?"

"Unashamedly. I want all your attention."

She said meaningly, "It was a very good thing I kept my

contacts after our marriage, Derek. Otherwise, a year ago, my financial outlook would have been rather bleak. The three hundred a year which Daddy left me would hardly have meant luxury."

Derek looked uncomfortable.

"Do you hold that against me?" His voice was low and appealing.

Arden was not the type to bear malice or a grudge and she said with impulsive generosity, "No; seeing that you believed I had betrayed you, it would have been ridiculous to suppose you would have any wish—and certainly no obligation—materially to provide for me."

His sigh was eloquent of relief. Then he asked, "Will you come out for the day with me to-morrow?"

She answered, reservedly, "To dinner. I must work until then."

"Ashton," he exclaimed in disgust.

"Yes."

"Look, Arden——"

"Dinner," she insisted firmly.

He caught her hand and held it, drawing her into his arms and saying fiercely, "This is so absurd. *Us*. I mean——"

"We cannot begin where we left off, Derek." Her voice was quiet and restrained and he looked at her half-fearfully.

"But we can start again," he persisted.

"That is entirely different."

He felt the purposefulness behind her attitude and exclaimed, "Your cold logic could be disheartening. A few moments ago you suggested that emotion disdained such attributes."

"Appreciating that fact can serve as a warning. Suffering brings a little wisdom."

He bent his lips to hers.

"Don't analyse it all out of existence, darling," he said tensely. "Isn't it enough that we both know we are still in love with each other?"

"Love was no insurance policy in our marriage before, Derek."

He looked at her very steadily, as he said, "True, Arden. But I'm not here to contemplate merely a friendly ex-husband-and-wife relationship. You know that."

Arden's heartbeats quickened as she replied, "I do not

16

deny that. Neither would I wish it. I just don't want to·rush into anything we might both regret afterwards."

A little of the first urgent rapture had given place to a caution normally foreign to her temperament. But the glow of happiness remained, the thrill of vindication after the bleak and embittering injustice that had surrounded her divorce.

He said suddenly, "Very well, my dear. You've earned the right to dictate terms."

She looked appealingly gentle.

"Not *dictate*, Derek. I want what is best for us both."

"I know you do. I know you are right. Call it masculine conceit, if you like. I just wanted to feel that I could sway you *beyond* reason."

She curved into his arms, her mouth raised invitingly.

"You probably will," she promised.

The clock struck eleven. He said as he raised his lips from hers, "I know . . . I must go." A sigh. "Are you sure you won't change your mind about to-morrow?"

"I can't," she answered honestly. "I must do the work on hand. After all, I didn't expect to see *you*!"

He smiled, quietly and enigmatically.

"No, my sweet," he murmured softly, "I'm sure you didn't, but you are going to see a very great deal of me from now on —I warn you."

Arden laughed spontaneously.

"That I can bear," she admitted.

Silence fell between them. A strangeness sharpened the edge of sudden, swift desire. Memories passed like a film clicking through a projector, holding them nostalgically. Derek said almost stiffly, "I'll come over for you to-morrow evening. Sixish?"

"Yes."

They walked out of the room into the hall. Derek opened the front door on a night bright with stars and a full moon which made the garden a giant etching. Arden's senses stirred and for a second a wild, impossible impulse wiped out reason and then died as she thought of the anguish of the past.

Derek turned then, his arms drawing her suffocatingly close, his kiss demanding and possessive.

Abruptly he released her and opened the door of his shining Jaguar.

"Good-night, my darling."

"Good-night, Derek," she said softly.

The car throbbed into the deep silence, winding its way down the narrow lane, its headlights throwing a golden beam upon trees and hedges, and then slanting and disappearing as the main road was reached.

Arden breathed deeply. The air was cool and filled with the perfume of roses and honeysuckle. Excitement churned within her as she went back into the house, which appeared suddenly to have changed its personality. She hardly knew what she was doing as she tidied her desk, cleared away the glasses and emptied the ash tray. Her movements were mechanical. She was like one in a trance in her absolute surrender to the happiness within her. Happiness . . . light in darkness; purpose in futility. Hope where, before, only resignation had existed.

Was this, she asked herself, love? Was this the fire and turbulence which once she had known, or an illusion created out of a passionate seeking, a loathing of barren unfulfilment? It seemed incredible to the point of fantasy that Derek should ever have returned. His doing so was completely out of character. Yet did not the very fact of her thinking along such lines prove how little she could have known him? Preconceived ideas, she argued, could destroy a relationship. Human emotions could not be expected to conform to any set pattern.

It was enough that he had come back and, above all, that he believed her word. Vindication was sweet.

She undressed and got into bed. There was something very intriguing about contemplating an association—no matter what form it might take—with an ex-husband. A little smile curved her lips. And this time she was in command.

CHAPTER II

THE next few weeks passed almost without incident as Arden and Derek gradually accepted the fact that they were bound by inexorable ties which no divorce could possibly sever.

Arden had given herself up to the happiness and solace of their reunion determined, at that stage, not to question or to invite controversy by looking ahead or trying to give their relationship any label.

It was a night when Derek had driven Arden to London where they had dined and danced at the Savoy, returning through the fragrance and cool stillness of deserted lanes to her cottage, that, removing her stole and turning her to face him, he said quietly, "You know we can't go on like this, Arden—don't you?"

She made no attempt to employ subterfuge.

"I know, Derek. I've drugged myself with blissful content during these weeks, pretending there were no problems, no issues."

"Mere friendship," he said tensely, "isn't possible between us." It was a statement of fact without embellishment and she did not question it. He looked at her very steadily. "And I have an idea that remarriage isn't what you want."

Faced with the problem, Arden realized that she had already made her decision.

"I would like it to be our ultimate goal, Derek. I want to remarry you; want it earnestly and sincerely, but the past inflicted too many wounds for me to be impulsive now."

He stiffened and a slightly defensive expression hardened his mouth.

"And until then?" His voice was smooth and cold.

She hesitated slightly before saying, "Would it be very revolutionary for a woman to ask her ex-husband to become her lover for a trial period?"

"*Arden!*" He gripped her shoulders. "Are you serious?"

"Perfectly." She raised her eyes to meet his passionate gaze.

"Is all this because you doubt my—my love, my sincerity?" His voice throbbed into the silence.

Arden tried to be scrupulously honest as she answered that question, without finding it easy. Her words came slowly and with great earnestness:

"Not doubt, Derek, so much as fear. Oh, I know that at the moment we are both emotionally stirred. The very nature of our relationship, and all that has gone before, makes that almost inevitable. But suppose all this were transient?"

He ridiculed the idea.

"Transient! After years of marriage? After being separated as we have?"

She moved away from him, without her expression being less serious.

"I know it probably sounds fantastic," she admitted, "and I hope more than anything that it is. All I ask is that we shall find each other—really find each other—and stay together for all time. Now we're both caught up in the spell of uncertainty —the glamour of re-discovery. I want more than that." She looked at him very levelly. "Are you quite sure in your heart that you *have* accepted my word about Brian? It might well be easy to delude yourself merely because you still desire me."

He stared at her faintly aghast.

"You seem full of deductions—amazing ones, too. Of course I believe you. Should I want to marry you again if I did not?"

She challenged him.

"And are you quite certain that you *do* want marriage?"

He gave a little low chuckle.

"Inquisition—eh? Darling, don't be absurd. Of course I want marriage. My being here——" He spread his hands in a gesture of appeal. "There's nothing more I can say to convince you."

She moved back within the circle of his arms.

"I will marry you again at the end of six months, Derek— if we both feel in the same mind as now. That is fair." She added, swiftly: "To both of us." As she spoke she looked up at him with great earnestness.

He smiled down into her eyes.

"That is one date I'll see you keep, my dear," he said hoarsely.

Arden's kiss was a promise, not a gift, but she was content that the problem was settled and their relationship stabilized. She had given a great deal of thought to the future, determined not to be precipitated into a passionate interlude on the crest of Derek's desire alone.

He said, teasingly, "Now I can understand your elusiveness, your provocative attitude." There was an imperceptible pause. "When did you decide to take me back—on approval?"

Arden's white teeth glistened as she smiled.

"I think that very first time you came here."

"Very calculated, surely."

"Calculation is better than blind folly. Before one has *been* married marriage can seem paradise—all the illusions are there, the romantic fantasies. When one discovers that hell can enter into it just as easily or even more easily——" A faint note of cynicism tinged her words. "It is only sane not to rush into the same mistake twice."

"It would," he said gravely, "be uncomfortably easy to persuade myself that you are not really in love with me, Arden."

"I distrust even those emotions I genuinely feel," she replied honestly. "I never intend wholly to be at their mercy again."

He laughed softly.

"Love cannot be so conveniently disciplined." His arms tightened about her. "There is no middle course—your heart tells you that."

She challenged him.

"For a man who has just expressed the fear lest I am not in love with him you are singularly confident!"

"Of course I am . . . I know you too well."

His words filled the silence with a strange tension. Both were reminded of how empty the statement was in the face of all that had happened.

Arden shut her mind against the problems, the past and even the future as she murmured, "That is what I want you to do, Derek—*know* me. . . . And now——" She stirred against him, her lips close to his. "Let's forget. . . ."

.   .   .   .   .

Arden threw aside the morning newspaper and glanced at Derek across the breakfast table. And although their being together was an inescapable fact it nevertheless held an element of fantasy because, after all that had happened, it didn't seem possible they could be sitting there, in harmony and content.

Derek said, "I can certainly see the virtue of no resident maids here!"

Arden smiled.

"It suits my purpose very well merely to have Mrs. Hawkins coming in as and when I send for her."

He held her gaze.

"But never I hope for quite the reason that it suits you —now."

Instantly, the smile went from her eyes.

"Never for that reason, Derek. Let there be no misunderstanding on that point." Her voice hardened. "I could not tolerate it."

He reached out across the table and grasped her hand.

"My darling, I was teasing." He sighed. "This is a lovely spot, you know." His gaze wandered over the old-world garden that lay in the peace and mellowness of a summer sun.

"I've loved it." She sighed. "It has been sanctuary and— loneliness."

"But no more loneliness," he hastened.

A glow touched her heart, warming her body. For the first time for well over a year she felt alive instead of merely a cardboard figure moving mechanically in a papier-mâché world.

"No, Derek—no more loneliness."

"That can be hell—sheer hell," he said tensely. "Everywhere I looked I saw your ghost. I hated even the bathroom because there were no pots and lotions and creams about—no fragrance. You'll never know how I missed you."

She was touched and thankful.

A clock struck ten, rather imperiously. She started and jumped to her feet.

"I've to see Lance Ashton this morning," she said breathlessly, remembering.

Derek said regretfully, "This *morning*? But it's Saturday." A pause. "You didn't mention it."

"I forgot," she confessed. "What would have been an event of major importance has become insignificant."

Derek said suddenly, "Give it all up, Arden. I want to feel——"

"No, Derek." She was firm and adamant.

"But——"

"I will give it up after we remarry," she promised. "Then I shall want a family and it will be immaterial whether or not I am financially independent." Her gaze held his. "You might not want to marry *me* at the end of six months. Then what? No, I must continue my work and Lance Ashton comes under that heading. He liked my idea for his book jacket and wants to discuss it with me."

Derek grunted.

"Why can't he discuss it with the publishers?"

"He can, but the art editress is wise enough to realize that he must not be displeased. And since he is prepared to deign to see me——"

"Deign!" He exploded. "I cannot have that. You——"

"My dear man, I might be a millionairess but, having taken on the job I have, then I must accept the conditions and discipline that go with it."

"How long will you be?"

"I haven't the faintest idea."

He lit a cigarette with impatient movements.

"I'd wanted to take you on the river to-day."

She laughed.

"There's plenty of time, surely?" She added whimsically: "And it might not be exactly a bad idea if, while I'm pandering to the vanity of Mr. Ashton, you went to your flat and filled a suitcase. Or have you forgotten that you can't wear evening dress all day—or that bath robe I managed to unearth for you!"

His mood changed as he laughed.

"Very well, my sweet. I'll go up to London and meet you after lunch. Ashton might want you to have lunch *with* him."

Arden laughed.

"That is most unlikely."

"How old is he?"

"I haven't the faintest idea—why?"

"No reason. Married?"

"That I don't know. He gives very little away about his private life and I understand that it is like drawing false teeth to get any biographical notes out of him. That, in itself, is unusual."

"Probably a line. You know—shunning publicity to get it."

"Quite probable. So long as he accepts my jacket I don't care if he has four legs and three heads," she said absurdly. "And now I must get bathed and dressed."

He gazed at her slender, yet voluptuous body, artistically concealed by a soft, diaphanous négligé.

"Seems a pity to disturb the picture which is quite entrancing." He moved and stood beside her chair. She leaned back and he bent his lips to hers.

Swiftly, she got up, her eyes dancing, her voice teasing. "And I mean *now*, or else!" She reached the door. "Mrs. Hawkins will be here in about an hour, so there's nothing to do in the house."

23

"She will *sense*——" Derek paused for want of the right words.

"Mrs. Hawkins," said Arden, "I suspect to be the type who, if she arrived and found a strange man in bed with me, would serve early tea, get another cup and behave as though strange men were a diet! She has an incredible indifference towards other people's business."

Derek chuckled.

"Not the result of long practice? Or do stray men litter the place?"

Arden laughed.

"You know I never could resist strays of any kind. . . . I must hurry."

"I'll shave while you bath."

"Do," she agreed naturally.

Arden went up to the bathroom. Derek joined her, glancing down at the perfect contour of her body, appraising her flawless skin glistening in the water.

"You're very beautiful, Arden." His voice was low and held a considered note.

She looked up at him and slid into a sitting position. Happiness touched her like fragrant velvet. She was a woman again—desired and desiring.

"And you have a very fine tan," she remarked, struck by the fact for the first time.

He continued to shave, using Arden's razor after having managed with some difficulty to get a lather with toilet soap. He didn't turn from the mirror above the hand basin.

"The credit for that goes to Capri. I'd had ten days there just before I found you, my dear."

Arden was rubbing herself with a bath towel.

"I thought England could not have managed to produce that. By the way, do you ever see anything of the Warners these days?"

Derek's head turned slightly. He smoothed his left hand down his left cheek and made a wry face at the result.

"Quite a bit. You knew that Rachel has recently lost her husband?"

Arden looked startled and shocked.

"No! But——"

"Car smash. Killed instantly. It was in all the papers."

Arden sprayed skin lotion over herself as she said quietly, "I'm afraid I am very much behind with general information. Poor Rachel. I always felt that marriage was essential to her."

"It improved her vastly," he agreed. "Ah well, now she's a rich widow and only about twenty-six. She'll soon find another husband. Mrs. Warner is taking her on a world tour, or rather an extensive tour. They are not due back until February or March of next year. . . . Where does Ashton live, by the way?"

"Between Whiteleaf and Princes Risborough."

"Rather vague."

"He has an old Manor House—known as The Manor—in the district."

"And, of course, will be news for miles around," came the faintly cynical retort. "These fellows get in my hair."

Arden shot at him, "I don't see why they should. The world would be a pretty dreary place without books and the kind that Lance Ashton writes will live."

"The literary giant! Adulation and all the rest of the tommy rot. Cocktail parties to launch the new masterpiece. Bah!" He dashed his face with cold water. "Ah well, rather you be going to see him than I. Don't invite him over here, my sweet, will you?"

Arden looked at him very steadily. A facet of his character was being spotlighted, reminding her that Derek had always resented the success of the other man, even though such resentment was, oddly enough, not built on his own failure but on some kink which made it impossible for him to be generous with his praise. She said, rather scornfully, "Lance Ashton's company is hard to come by, Derek. The literary giants as you call them would be honoured by his presence. He is hardly likely to single me out. This isn't a social call I'm making."

Derek scoffed.

"He's damned lucky to be seeing you. Now, if you were talking about D.H. I'd be inclined to agree with you. He *is* a genius."

"Donald Hambly? Chairman of your firm?" she cried aghast. "My dear Derek, Hambly is an illiterate who knows his job and can eat, sleep and drink advertising." She paused. "And I've no doubt but that even when you went to Capri he had you there on business, chasing *some* account or other!"

A dull flush spread over Derek's face, for a second his

temper flared. Then he said with a smile, "Suppose you're right, darling? I was trying to get the Marley account and may still get it. . . . I just dislike authors for no better reason that you've to go to see one on a Saturday morning," he finished stoutly.

Arden threw herself into his arms.

"Then I love you for it," she cried and gave herself up to his kiss.

When she was dressed in a smart tailored linen dress which shaded to ice blue and with which she wore navy accessories, Derek said gently, "You look perfect, Arden."

"Is that why you love me?" Her smile was warm and intimate.

"Who said I loved you?"

"Well, if you don't you've certainly given a very good imitation," she laughed.

"It's been wonderful . . . new, exciting and yet completely real."

She watched him as he spoke, thrilled by the depth and earnestness of his tone and the rich possibilities for the future. Out of disillusionment and heart-ache had come the splendour and reward of reunion. She trembled as she answered softly:

"It has to be, Derek. Not just for now—but for all time. I know I cannot accept less."

He reached out and clasped her hand and then watched her as she went from the cottage. A smile played about his lips as he waved to her.

Arden waved back. And her greatest joy lay in the fact that on her return he would be there . . . waiting. No longer would her key open a door into a wilderness of silence, of emptiness which wrapped around her like a cold, clammy blanket. No longer would loneliness eat into her soul as rust ate into metal. Miraculously, life rushed back; the blue and gold of the July day had a radiance that reached out and embraced her instead of mocking her. She was a part of it instead of merely an onlooker.

The stragglers ambling along the familiar roads suddenly became her friends. She wanted to smile at them and did. Her heart sang, her body felt light as air and her lips still burned from Derek's kisses, just as her face tingled slightly from the slight roughness of his cheek.

The Manor House? Her thoughts raced and she tried to sober down as she asked a villager the way. It would hardly do to visit Lance Ashton in a hilarious, excited mood. She expected that he would be ponderous and self-important, aware to the last degree of the importance of his position and the triviality of hers.

Her head went back in defiance. This was one occasion when no man on earth could intimidate, or frighten, her and if he didn't like her ideas then she had every intention of showing him that it was of no consequence to her whatsoever!

She slowed down at a poplar-lined drive and then swerved into it. And a little of her obstreperousness was lost in sudden appreciation of the beauty of the scene, of the peace and tranquillity of smooth lawns and clipped yews, of tall cedars and shady beeches . . . and of a bow-fronted, colonnaded Regency house that stood in the shadow of a past greatness.

Arden sighed. She was reminded that to meet this man had been an ambition, and to see her own work on a book of his almost an obsession. Now she was there. A tiny flame of fear, of nervousness, touched her as she got out of the car and mounted the four steps which led to the half-circular porch. Her small, gloved hand went out and pressed the bell.

CHAPTER III

ARDEN was handed from a smart parlourmaid to a secretary moulded on model lines whose black hair was upswept about a shapely head. She wore a severe, tailored grey dress, a choker necklace and had an air of elegant efficiency, together with a manner that was brisk, cold without unpleasantness and distinctly authoritative. Arden noticed that she had one of those pale creamy skins that seemed to be transparent. Only her eyes and lips were made-up.

"Miss Marchly?" Her brows arched. She subjected Arden to a piercing, critical gaze.

"Yes," said Arden without losing confidence. "I have an appointment with Mr. Ashton."

"I will tell him you are here."

"Thank you."

The militant figure retreated; the door shut. An impression

of vigilance remained. Arden thought irrelevantly: I could never like *that* woman.

She took stock of the room. Spacious, light, filled, but not to overflowing, with period pieces that were set upon a magnificent Chinese carpet of pale jade green that enhanced the golden glow of the parquet surrounds. Tall bowed windows looked out upon a scene of pastoral beauty, with velvet lawns merging into woodland and finally misting into distant farmlands. The razor edge of the Chilterns rose against a taut, blue sky, their hollows cradling woodland and grazing sheep. The muscles of her throat tightened; the scene was in harmony with her own emotions and now nostalgia had given place to the thrill of anticipation.

The door opened and she turned abruptly.

Lance Ashton came into the room. And any preconceived notions that Arden might have cherished vanished before the tremendous impact of his personality as, walking towards her, hand outstretched, he said, "I appreciate your coming, Miss Marchly. Especially on a Saturday morning."

His smile lit up a fine, scholarly face and his contemplation of her held interest without curiosity. There was no appraisal in it.

Arden felt suddenly limp and faintly nervous. She found herself watching him, unable wholly to concentrate on what was being said. She saw a man who in no way conformed to type or pattern, and although he was tall and it might well have been said that he was good-looking, neither assets mattered since it was in a vibrant, powerful personality that his charm lay. He was a man who attracted people as a magnet, inspiring within them confidence while yet able to be stern and commanding should the circumstances justify either. While he did not suffer fools gladly he was nevertheless tolerant and sympathetic. Humanity was his canvas. He had the inconsequential air of a man whose success mattered far less than the fulfilment of an inward craving for perfection. He appreciated, but was not swayed by, lavish praise, and was unmoved by adulation. And while he was friendly, there was a strange reserve about him that enabled him to withdraw into his private world where none might intrude.

Arden's voice was not very steady as she said, "I was more than happy to come."

28

"Thank you." His tone was business-like and he walked briskly to a desk on which Arden's rough for his book jacket had been placed. He picked it up and returned to her side. "I like this," he said with conviction. "It has imagination." A pause. "Do you happen to know Restronguet by any chance?"

Arden met his level gaze.

'I feel that I know it, Mr. Ashton. But that is because of your artistry with words. Otherwise—no." She hesitated before adding boldly: "I think this: *Full Circle* is finer even than any of your other books. There's just *something*—indefinable— but very impressive."

He studied her in silence for a second. She waited apprehensively. Then, "I think it a better book than the others. The critics and the public will probably prove me quite wrong."

"Do you mind?"

He laughed.

"Not in the least." He went back to the rough. "What I would like," he said, with a knowledge of his subject, "is a little less foliage and a little more river. I want breadth——"

Instantly Arden saw his point.

"The slopes less wooded."

"Exactly. There is just something about it as it stands that suggests an overcrowded room."

She knew he was right.

"I can very easily alter that."

"Otherwise, I'm more than pleased. I like the colour, the *life* of the scene. And you couldn't have been more accurate in getting that old Inn—The Pandora. No, that was what I wanted—with the reservations I've named. I'm amazed that you don't know your subject."

"Through you—I do. But I must certainly explore that part of Cornwall. I don't know its rivers."

"Then you have missed some of its greatest beauties. No matter where I go—to no matter what part of the world—I always return to those Cornish scenes with a feeling of pride and satisfaction."

"I felt that in *Full Circle*. Like a man coming home without losing one scrap of appreciation for the other places he had visited."

"Home," he said, savouring the word. "You're about right."

She glanced out of the windows.

"This is a beautiful place, Mr. Ashton."

"I like it," he said simply.

She wondered: was he married? Had he any children? Age occurred to her. It wasn't easy to assess. Thirty-five, she hazarded, or it might be a year or two more. On closer scrutiny it was borne home upon her that there were unmistakable signs of suffering behind his smile and that his quiet understanding emphasized this. No bombast, conceit or self-satisfaction tainted his attitude. It was as though he knew the emptiness of success when that success was not supplemented by happiness, and that the two were by no means concomitants.

He flicked the protective covering over her drawing.

"Shall I have this sent back to you? It is rather large and cumbersome to——"

Arden said breathlessly, "I will take it with me. I have my car and I live not so far away."

"Of course," he exclaimed. "I remember Miss Naunton telling me. I like Miss Naunton," he added sincerely. "Knows her job and has an extremely pleasant manner. Being an art editress must bring its headaches." He glanced at Arden inquiringly. "Are you in a hurry, or will you have a sherry with me?"

Arden assured him that she was by no means in a hurry. There was something fascinating about watching him and listening to his low, attractive voice which was, nevertheless, alert and purposeful. What were his hobbies? His plans? Had he expected the unprecedented success that had come to him in the past four or five years?

He sat down opposite her, having served their drinks. His clothes—which she noticed for the first time—had an unconventional appearance without being affected. His smile reached her rather like the sun touching the face after a bleak wind on a grey day.

"You do not confine your activities to this kind of work, do you?" He studied her intently and what might have sounded impertinent on other lips conveyed, by inflection, a compliment.

Arden answered swiftly, "No. Commercial art was not my original ambition. I like to believe that one day I may paint something worth while. Meanwhile one cannot live on dreams."

Instinctively, Lance Ashton glanced down at her left hand, noting the fact that it was ringless. The *Miss* Marchly told him nothing since women seldom, if ever, used their married name professionally.

"How right that is," he said with sympathy. "I tried it in the early days of my struggles."

Arden said naturally, "One can never imagine your being other than the Lance Ashton of to-day."

He smiled and sighed.

"I wrote unsuccessfully for several years. It was most uncomfortable. My family had no time for me whatsoever, considering me lazy and good-for-nothing." He stopped abruptly, and a note almost approaching stern authority crept into his voice. "That is in confidence, Miss Marchly. I really don't know why I am wearying you with all this. I deplore long biographical ditties about writers—gives them a false importance. You look surprised."

"I am," she said honestly, staggered by his modesty. Then "And your family now?"

His lips twisted in faint cynicism. "I believe my mother gives cocktail parties to celebrate the publication of any new book." He grinned broadly. "I visit her between publications."

"And between travelling, I presume?"

He astounded her by saying, "I haven't travelled for quite a few years. During the war I covered a pretty good area of the world. Research can often be more accurate than deceptive first-hand impressions. . . . No, for the time being, at least, I'm content to browse here—in peace."

That still did not tell her whether he was married, divorced or a bachelor. Her curiosity was aroused, but she could not satisfy it. She said slowly, "We learn a great deal in solitude."

"With time to think and allow past impressions to sink in, experiences to mellow. Life should be like a vintage wine—to be savoured."

Their eyes met and instantly Arden responded to the sensitive appreciation betrayed by his words.

"Ah," she said with a sigh. "Yet how often *is* it savoured?"

"How often do the right people meet to savour it?" he retorted almost curtly. "The whole conception of human relationships is a fantastic delusion, a distortion."

"And the remedy?"

"If I could answer that I should be the saviour of mankind instead of merely an entertainer."

"You hardly do yourself honour, Mr. Ashton."

He smiled wryly.

"I give myself the credit I deserve," he said un-selfconsciously. "As I see it, that credit is precious little."

"Then I'm glad the rest of the world disagrees with you."

He smiled, a smile that warmed and embraced her with a curiously tender, even indulgent, appreciation.

"You are a most heartening person, Miss Marchly, and, I feel, sincere," he added somewhat startlingly.

Arden said quietly, "I rate sincerity very highly, Mr. Ashton—if that doesn't sound priggish."

He finished his sherry.

"It is a commentary that we always have to apologize for a virtue, to-day!"

The clock struck twelve. Arden started. It seemed that she had been there a matter of minutes.

"Will you be at the cocktail party next Thursday?" he asked abruptly.

"In honour of your new book?"

"Yes . . . sheer courtesy and appreciation of my publisher's zeal demand my presence," he explained wryly.

Arden had received an invitation, for she was very friendly with the executive staff of the firm, and while she had accepted it, she had previously been doubtful of going.

"Yes," she said suddenly, "I shall be there."

"Then we must find a quiet corner and talk," he said naturally. "No one after they've had a few drinks will really be the slightest bit interested in me, thank heaven. Simple."

"That is absurd," she said flatly.

"On the contrary."

"You are incorrigible," she cried.

"Honest, I hope. . . . Have you time for a walk around the gardens? I'm rather proud of them. This was a wilderness when I bought the place two years ago. Reclaiming it was fun. I mow the lawns myself with a motor mower and the bits I cannot do I go over with a little hand fellow—much prefer him." A sudden boyish enthusiasm seeped through a former cynicism. "My secretary is rather inclined to frown on the activity."

32

"Brow-beaten?" Arden could imagine it.

"For my own good—yes. Authors have to discipline themselves—the hardest discipline of all—for there is no one to insist that they work to-day or to-morrow and their hours are their own. I'm very grateful to Miss Rivers for demanding to justify her existence." He added: "We are, in any case, excellent friends. She takes care of the staff for me, too, and everything runs very smoothly."

They went out on to a wide terrace, down a few steps and so to the gardens, and even as they did so Janet Rivers appeared from a nearby shrubbery. She approached them and spoke to Lance Ashton.

"Mr. Ashton, I'm sorry to interrupt, but you are due at the country club for luncheon."

"Good lord," he gasped. "Old Mortimer! Twelve-fifteen, wasn't it?"

"Twelve-thirty." She glanced at Arden without speaking and Lance Ashton said quickly:

"This is my jailor, Miss Rivers. . . ."

Janet Rivers said uncompromisingly:

"I am quite certain that Miss Marchly appreciates how very valuable your time is, Mr. Ashton."

He asked, "And what *is* the time?"

"Ten minutes past twelve. Do you want Baker to drive you?"

"No; I'll drive myself."

Arden edged towards the terrace steps.

"I must be going," she said swiftly. "I'm afraid I've already wasted far too much of your time."

Janet Rivers gave her a cold, calculating stare.

Lance Ashton smiled.

"On the contrary. You must come again, meanwhile I'll look out for you at the party." He spoke amiably and meant what he said. And he insisted on seeing her out to her car.

Janet Rivers rallied around him as he returned to the house. She had a grey flannel coat in her hand.

Lance glanced down at his comfortable old smoking jacket.

"Hell! Do I have to?"

"Of course! You can't go out looking like a tramp."

"Why not?" He felt suddenly irritated. "You know she's a very attractive girl," he exclaimed, thinking aloud. "Different from——"

"They are all 'different'," said Janet coolly, "until you get to know them. Really, Lance, after your experience I marvel that you are still so gullible. Oh, you appear to be the withdrawn, reserved cynic——" Her laugh was tinkling—like ice.

Lance stiffened.

"You, my dear, are jaundiced where your own sex is concerned . . . what did I do with my cigarette case? Yes, jaundiced. Time you found yourself a husband. How old are you? Thirty?"

Her face paled, her lips became a thin, bitter line in mask-like features.

"Perhaps if I wasted less time in pandering to your whims and looking after you," she rapped out, "I might have the opportunity to do as you suggest."

Lance threw aside his smoking jacket.

"My dear girl, if you find your job here a hindrance, for heaven's sake say so."

"Now you're being sarcastic."

"Nothing of the kind." He straightened himself and stood erect and a little commanding. "I regard you as a good friend, Janet; I value that friendship and appreciate to the full all you do here to enable my life and my work to run smoothly." He paused imperceptibly. "But I will not have my individuality threatened, or be dictated to as to my friends."

"Friends!" It was too much for her. "Just because I made a remark about a girl whom you've——"

He interrupted her.

"*That* is beside the point . . . your manner towards Miss Marchly was hostile to the point of rudeness; your remark about my time being valuable in the worst possible taste. Remember that when next she comes here, please. Now I suggest you get away from the typewriter and have a complete rest over the week-end."

"But—but I always look in on Sunday."

"Then make an exception to the rule. I'm not a slave-driver and at this rate you'll have a breakdown. I'm not blind and you've looked extremely tired lately. I think the best thing would be for you to have a fortnight's holiday."

"Holiday!" She made the word sound like an execution. "And what about your work?"

He said, with a maddening calm, beneath which was stern

authority: "I'm not satisfied with that last chapter. I shall leave it alone for a bit." He glanced up at her and then went back to filling his cigarette case. "You look amazed."

"I am."

"I may even stay in London, see a few shows, as I have to go up anyway next week."

"But—but," she stammered, "you never stay in London. I mean——"

His expression hardened.

"All the more reason to break that rule," he answered imperturbably. "If there is one advantage of my present position it is that it allows me to be my own master. I tell you what: you start your holiday while I'm away. Go gay. Forget The Manor House and its inmates."

She stood there burning with a resentment born of a deep-rooted frustration. This was Lance in a mood there was no challenging; Lance, stubborn, determined and aware of his own power. With a few well-chosen phrases he could detach himself completely from her just when it seemed she had insinuated herself into his life to a point where he must see her as a woman, instead of as a friendly employee to whom he allowed considerable latitude. The thought of Arden—wholly irrational—came bitterly. Had she been instrumental in this sudden and incredible change of plans?

She took a deep breath and said, "Very well. I'll do that." She glanced down at the desk and gave a sharp exclamation. Arden had forgotten the rough of the book jacket.

Lance laughed.

"You scared her away so quickly."

Instantly, Janet swished the drawing up.

"I will post it," she said hastily.

"Leave it. I can run it over."

She stared at him aghast.

"Lance, really! You're NOT a postman and in your position it——" She floundered.

"Let me worry about my position." He took it from her and strode out into the hall.

The telephone rang. Mr. Mortimer had been taken ill and would not be able to keep his appointment.

Lance looked suitably concerned. James Mortimer was a heart case.

Janet did not comment, but from the expression on Lance's face she knew that he intended to go to Arden's cottage. The idea outraged her. Lance Ashton running around after some little nobody. A chill sensation went over her body, sickening fear gripped her. Suppose he should fall in love with Arden Marchly? It was just the kind of thing that might happen. Yet, wasn't he completely uninterested in women, almost cynical about marriage? He'd seen the girl only that morning for the first time, after all. It wasn't reasonable to suppose . . . What had love to do with reason? Was there any reason in her overwhelming and all-consuming passion for Lance, since never for an instant had he shown her other than friendly courtesy and generous appreciation? Her steel-blue eyes narrowed. For all that, one day she would be his wife. It was a vow she had made to herself and she clung to the belief that if a woman intended to marry a man she would do so—by fair means or foul. Standing there, hands clenched, her body cold and shaking, she swore that if this Arden Marchly was likely to endanger her plans then it would have to be by foul means that she, herself, achieved her objective. It struck her that it might not be altogether a waste of time to find out more about Miss Marchly. Why did she live in such seclusion—and already Janet had ascertained that fact—and was she married? It might well be that her life was as innocent as she looked. But Janet Rivers doubted it. There was, she insisted, a skeleton in every cupboard—except her own. For although she was a smart, efficient and good-looking woman, she had never been physically attractive to men. There was a forbidding coldness about her personality, a reserve which struck at the very heart of feminine allure.

Of this she was unaware. She looked at Lance as he walked towards the door. He smiled at her.

"Will you be in for dinner to-night?" she asked, adding, "So that I can give instructions in the kitchen before I leave."

He hesitated, then, "No. I'll probably run into Wendover to see the Marshalls. Tell Masters and his wife they can have the evening off."

"These biographical notes for the *New World*? Have you forgotten that you were in the middle of them when Miss Marchly called?"

He said, with what was to her an infuriating calm, "I think

36

the *New World* will be happy to wait my time. Pack up, there's a good girl. I'll see you on Monday and we'll tidy up all the loose ends." His smile did nothing to comfort her. "Then you can go off on your holiday without a worry in the world."

He opened the front door, closed it and was gone.

Outside, he breathed deeply. No question about it, Janet could get on a man's nerves. So serious; so damned efficient. That was unreasonable. What possible good would an inefficient secretary be to any man? But she never relaxed. His house was run well and he appreciated it, but she was fast becoming a martinet in it. Funny, he'd never noticed that until the visit of Miss Marchly. He felt he owed the girl an apology. He slid into the driving seat of his Talbot. Attractive girl . . . unusual. Stimulating and yet, contradictorily, restful. He loathed the over-vivacious, too bright female who was perpetually laughing with little cause. Equally, he was bored by the too quiet, rice-pudding type, as he called them. An exciting happy medium was difficult to find. . . . Where had Miss Marchly said she lived? Damned if he could remember now, except that it was near Little Gaddesden. Better let Janet post the stuff. The thought disappointed him. He slowed the car down and stopped. An address might be on the back of the sketch. And it was: *Arden Marchly, Meadow View, Birch Lane, Little Gaddesden.* A smile hovered about his lips as he recalled Janet's almost scandalized expression when he suggested that he would deliver the rough himself. Poor old Janet! She had all the niceties tabulated to perfection and loathed any deviation from what she conceived to be the dignity and importance of his position—for which he, personally, had no time.

He put the car into gear and raced off.

CHAPTER IV

AT THE sound of the bell Arden rushed out into the hall, threw open the door, crying as she did so, "Darling, you're——" The word "early" died on her lips as she looked into Lance Ashton's amused eyes.

"Terribly sorry," he said with a chuckle. "I'm not 'darling'." He held out the drawing. "You forgot it."

She gave a horrified gasp, particularly as she had not noticed the omission.

"I'm most terribly sorry." She looked helpless.

"You left in such a hurry . . . my secretary is apt to be too pernickety about time. The appointment was cancelled, anyway."

Arden stared at him, aware that he was not making any movement which might suggest his leaving immediately and she spoke hastily, thinking of Derek, and rather unsure of herself.

"In that case may I now offer *you* a sherry?"

"If I shall not be making a thorough nuisance of myself, I'd love it." He glanced about him as he stepped into the small oak-panelled hall. "This is a charming hide-out you have here. Using the word advisedly, of course. I've been around in circles finding you."

Arden looked at him in bewilderment. Why couldn't he have sent the stuff over, or had it posted? Seemed odd to bring it himself.

"It was for me to fetch it," she apologized, leading the way into the lounge—a low-ceilinged, oak-beamed room with chintz, wood-block floor, well carpeted, and a large chimney corner.

"I was suddenly bored with myself," he said truthfully. "To be honest I wondered if you might be disposed to run out somewhere and have lunch with me." He held her gaze. "But I rather gather that you are already engaged."

"Yes, I'm afraid so; but thank you all the same." She opened the doors of a beautifully carved Jacobean chest which revealed a cocktail cabinet. "Would you prefer whiskey, or——"

"Frankly—yes. . . . You live here alone?" A swift apology escaped his lips. "Forgive me, the question was an impertinence, but I was thinking in terms of parents!"

"My parents are dead. Yes, I'm here alone."

He eyed her speculatively, aware of her sensitive, passionate beauty and, also, rather startlingly, of her curious aloofness which cautioned him that she had no intention of confiding in him further. He took the glass she offered and helped himself —at her request—to soda water.

To Arden there was something quite unreal about his being

there. Yet the magnetism of his personality held her, despite the fact that she hoped he would leave before Derek arrived.

"Strange," he said irrelevantly, "how suddenly one can feel bored and weary even of work. This is an oasis."

She stared at him incredulously. Was that the subtle flattery, by innuendo, of a calculated philanderer—a flirtatious Casanova? How could she tell what degree of sincerity lay behind that smooth façade? She said slowly, but with a compelling directness, "I find that rather difficult to believe, Mr. Ashton. Your life must, of necessity, be so full . . . boredom! No."

He breathed deeply as he thrust his hand in his pocket and drew out his cigarette case.

"The fact that, by some process—fluke if you like—a man's books become best sellers, does not automatically preclude him from all the irritations to which most humans are heir." He held her gaze masterfully. "You distrust any personal observation linked with a compliment. Why?"

Arden sat back in her chair and relaxed.

"Probably because I don't know you well enough to decide whether you——" She fumbled for the right words and he supplemented:

"To decide whether or not I habitually flatter women and am utterly insincere?"

"You put it succinctly."

"Meaning that I am right?"

"Meaning that I always give everyone the benefit of the doubt. You are a little surprising, shall we say."

"Too impulsive," he agreed honestly.

"I prefer that to calculation."

His gaze fell upon a small painting hanging on the wall beside him.

"I like that," he said abruptly. "The woman's face—the shadows and the space and light of the room." He glanced back at Arden. "That is your work," he added firmly.

"Yes. It was rejected."

He made a scoffing sound.

"Put a daub of red, blue and green squares on it and send it in next year," he said cynically. "It will be accepted and hung then."

She laughed.

"You do not care for the new art form?"

"I don't like having to stand on my head to look at a picture and, even then, not to have the faintest conception of what it is meant to represent. Perhaps I lack normal intelligence, but thank heaven I've enough to appreciate a Rembrandt or a Constable. And to-day, Sir Gerald Kelly, James Gunn and many others. The rest can keep their nursery daubs, for me! The decadence of intellectual snobbery."

He looked to Arden rather as though he were a fixture in his chair and in different circumstances she would have deemed his being there an event. Now as the clock ticked away she found herself tensing lest Derek should be early. The presence of Lance Ashton would be an anti-climax.

She said tentatively: "Can I offer you lunch, Mr. Ashton?"

He finished his drink.

"Thank you, no. I must go before your guest arrives and hates the sight of me."

Arden laughed.

Lance Ashton was curious. For years every vestige of emotion had gone into his work; it had been both expression and fulfilment. Now, suddenly and inexplicably, as he looked at Arden he was conscious of a quickening interest, a stirring of his senses. He was accustomed to the adulation of women who fawned sickeningly upon him; women who, without pride or dignity, flagrantly coveted his name and the position that went with it, and, therefore, Arden was a refreshing change since, while she appreciated his work, there was no trace of subservience, coyness, or flirtatiousness.

But in that moment the back door opened and Derek came through the cottage calling:

"Arden! I managed to get back early and——" He stopped abruptly at the open door of the lounge.

Arden had risen to her feet, Lance instantly getting up with her. She said, a trifle nervously, "May I introduce a friend of mine? Mr. Rayne ... Mr. Ashton." Her gaze travelled swiftly from Lance Ashton's face to Derek's. The former was smiling, the latter coldly uncompromising.

"I was just on the point of leaving," Lance said calmly.

Derek's first antagonism subsided. He felt Arden's gaze upon him—an apprehensive gaze—and said courteously, "I'm sorry. Your books have given me great pleasure."

"That's kind of you."

Lance Ashton studied Derek critically. He was not deceived by the flattery, or the swift change of attitude. Neither could he blame him for resenting the intrusion of a third party.

Arden hastened to say, "Could I persuade you to stay and have a drink with us?"

Lance laughed.

"Easily. For someone who never drinks before evening I seem to be doing very well!"

"Oh, good!" Derek had an air of a man in possession and having glanced at Arden, moved to the cocktail cabinet.

The drinks served, they sat and sipped them leisurely. Derek talked a great deal. Lance Ashton listened politely, then remarked, "High-powered advertising sounds a strain."

"Extremely competitive," Derek asserted. "One has to be on one's toes the entire time. I've always thought that publishers failed lamentably when it came to advertising. There's so much scope. They fall down badly on the job."

Lance's smile was quietly amused.

"I can't say that I, personally, have noticed it. And I believe that, in a great many cases, it has been proved that extensive advertising has had little effect upon sales."

Derek spluttered at what was to him pure heresy.

"I can't accept that for a moment," he exclaimed. "Advertising has——" he paused. He was going to say: "made you" and then substituted: "Advertising has certainly been your ally."

Lance never dismissed an argument out of hand, or adopted a superior or supercilious manner. He looked thoughtful as he commented: "And yet, you know, Mr. Rayne, I'd written three or four books each of which had received precisely the same amount of advertisement and then, for no known reason, that fourth became my first best seller. Doesn't that prove something?"

"Yes," said Derek, "that advertising can be a snowball and you reaped the harvest of previous advertisements—if I may mix my metaphors."

Lance smiled. The argument was fallacious. But he let it go and Derek was satisfied to imagine that he had scored a point.

Arden said quietly, "Advertising for commercial goods,

mass publicity, mass hysteria—yes! but when it comes to other things it seems that it is recommendation above all that paves the way *for* advertising, not the other way round. Then, admittedly, advertising keeps a name before the public, but it cannot *make* that name."

Derek frowned.

Lance said swiftly, "I think Miss Marchly has summed up very neatly." He glanced from face to face. And again he felt that strange, inexplicable attraction which gave Arden importance and awakened within him an urgent desire to see her in the future. "I should be awfully pleased if you would both have dinner with me one evening. We could then find something else to discuss and argue about," he added.

Derek was flattered, even though he secretly resented the fact that Lance Ashton's position was vastly superior to his own.

Arden said swiftly, "That would be lovely. I could then really see your gardens."

"Would next Wednesday evening suit you both?"

Arden glanced at Derek.

"Very well," Derek said smoothly. He looked at Arden for confirmation.

"I should have your work finished by then, Mr. Ashton. May I bring it with me?"

"Please do." He flashed her a vivid smile. "And leave it behind again!" He got to his feet as he spoke. "I parked my car in the lane," he explained as they walked to the front door. "I was by no means certain there *was* a cottage here."

"Ah," said Derek, "you had difficulty in finding it, too? This is certainly secluded."

Lance Ashton drew his brows together in a faintly bewildered expression. There was just something about the relationship of these two which intrigued him. He could not place them as an engaged couple and he hurried over the possibility that they might be lovers, telling himself that, in any case, it was none of his business. He'd probably been absurdly impulsive to invite them to dine with him and, if so, that was his second folly that day. On the other hand there were so few women in whom he had any interest. And Arden was a stimulating, inspiring person whom he knew he could not lightly dismiss. Without continuity he asked abruptly, "Are you fond of music, Miss Marchly?"

"Very. Gramophone records are my greatest extravagance. And the long recordings make such a vast difference when it comes to listening to symphonies and concertos."

"I didn't think," he said stoutly, "that you would favour crooners!" He added hastily: "Not that my taste isn't varied— it is. But the whining Willies I just cannot like!"

"Nor I," she confessed. "Music is a matter of mood."

"Then we'll have some records on Wednesday evening," he said eagerly. "Listening alone can be slightly depressing— makes one restless."

Their eyes met.

"I know," she said and her voice was suddenly tense.

He left and Derek said as they went back into the cottage: "Queer sort of chap."

"Why queer?"

"Head in the clouds. All that rot about advertising. And you rather let the side down, my sweet."

"I was perfectly sincere in what I said, Derek, but none of it is important. I'm so glad you're back early," she murmured.

"Are you? I wondered what on earth had happened when I saw him sitting there, and who the dickens he was."

"He brought over the sketch which, carelessly, I'd left behind."

Derek lit a cigarette.

"It all strikes me as being rather odd."

Arden felt irritated.

"What do you mean—odd?"

"His coming here at all. Or is he in the habit of running around like an errand boy?"

"Now you are being absurd."

"Am I? I certainly do not flatter myself that the great Mr. Ashton wishes for *my* company on Wednesday evening. . . . And isn't there a cocktail party on Thursday?"

She replied tersely, "You know there is." Her eyes were hard and questioning. "I fail to see the connection."

"No? Unless I am very much mistaken he will suggest that he drives you to it and brings you back." There was a sudden dramatic pause. "I don't want him involved in our private affairs, Arden."

She started and cried explosively, "I don't follow your——"

He cut in: "Very well, let me put it more plainly. I do not

43

wish him to know any of the details of our relationship—at this stage, or, for that matter, at any stage until we remarry."

"Am I likely to tell him?" Her voice rose in annoyance.

"You might—not unnaturally—in the course of any conversation that might take place at some future date. I should resent fiercely his misunderstanding my regard for you."

At that she softened.

"I think I know what you mean. . . . I shall not tell him, Derek."

"Promise?"

"I promise."

"After all, this situation is of your making. But I could not tolerate any man imagining that because you had allowed *me* to become your lover, you might well give him the same privilege. And I've summed Lance Ashton up pretty well. Over-sexed and convinced that he has only to look at a woman and she will fall in love with him."

Arden was trembling. She resented what she considered to be an unfair and presumptuous judgment. It seemed a little fantastic that in this short space of time Lance Ashton had become an issue. The magnetism of his personality lingered as though in some subtle fashion it had permeated the room. The power and strength of his character made it impossible to dismiss him and she was held by the belief that within him as a person was the same integrity which dominated his work as a writer. Derek's disparagement offended her and she said with spirit, "That is sheer prejudice, Derek, and it demeans you."

He stared at her, unprepared for the outburst.

"So! Already he has a champion in you."

"He has my respect until such time as I prove him unworthy of it. And isn't all this slightly ridiculous? A man whom I have met for the first time to-day and——" She paused and Derek leapt in:

"A man with whom you are tremendously impressed nevertheless."

"Is that so very strange?" she countered hotly. "When first his name was mentioned *you* were impressed and eulogized his work. I will not pretend—even to please you—that meeting him has not been interesting—it has. And if you are so small and petty that you cannot recognize——" She stopped, horrified, as she realized that they were on the brink of a quarrel.

Derek, no less shaken than she, stepped forward and drew her fiercely into his arms.

"I'm sorry," he said in a hushed, contrite voice. "I'm not being very adult. It isn't jealousy, Arden—I swear it. Just that I hated his being here when I wanted you to myself. Of course I know how you feel and I share your interest, really. In fact I liked the man!" His smile was broad and generous and Arden instantly responded, curving against him and surrendering to his kiss, argument, dissension, forgotten in the passion of the moment.

"I'm more in love with you than ever I was," he said thickly as he released her. "Perhaps being without you taught me far more than I ever realized. Oh, darling, we *must* make the future perfect. I want so *much* for you."

Arden looked up at him and surprise betrayed itself in her eyes.

"It doesn't seem quite possible that it is you who are talking," she exclaimed wonderingly. "Oh, *Derek*."

"Do you feel the same about me—honestly?" He held her again and looked deeply, penetratingly, into her eyes.

"Yes," she murmured breathlessly, caught up on a tide of passionate fervour. "And I want the future to make up for the past. I want *marriage*, Derek, not merely a legal formality. We've got to use these months, try to find out where we went wrong before." Her face, raised to his, was earnest, and beautiful in that earnestness.

Derek's voice was hushed as he answered, "I've got to get used to other men admiring you." He kissed the tip of her nose. "You're a tantalizing, exciting person, Arden, and the fact that you are, also, so completely natural makes your power twice as great."

She smiled at him indulgently.

"Darling! I'm not like that really—but so long as you think I am . . . beauty is in the eye of the beholder."

In that moment the telephone rang and Derek said: "Damn!"

Arden lifted the receiver.

"Martin!" Her voice was warm.

Derek looked at her. He had never really liked Martin Marchly, Arden's brother, and always felt that the reaction was mutual.

"This afternoon?" Arden's voice faltered, then: "Of course. I've a surprise for you. . . . Certain. Come for tea. Fourish? Splendid. Don't be curious: wait and see."

She replaced the receiver and turned back to Derek.

"So much for our outing," he said, faintly disgruntled.

"I couldn't avoid their coming," Arden replied. "And I see so little of Martin, anyway."

"Is Heather with him?"

"Yes. They've been to look at a school for Gail—at Amersham."

"I think she is about the dullest woman I've ever met," Derek exclaimed. "How on earth he ever came to marry her is quite beyond me."

Arden laughed.

"Everyone says that about everyone else. Nature always has the last laugh."

"Are they happy?" Derek lit a cigarette.

Arden sighed.

"They live together in peace. Heather is happy because she hasn't the faintest conception of the word. Martin lives for his work and the children."

"A pretty grim outlook."

Arden did not attempt to contradict the statement. But she said with great fervour, "Never let us drift into mediocrity, Derek. I couldn't bear it. I don't expect the heights all the time or any foolish romanticism, but neither could I endure the dreary, commonplace acceptance of each other which never allowed for any heights at all. We had almost reached that stage, you know. I can see it clearly now."

He grasped her hand and raised it to his lips.

"I know what you mean . . . and I'm with you."

"Then," she said simply, "we cannot fail."

CHAPTER V

MARTIN and Heather arrived promptly at four o'clock and at the sight of Derek they gasped in unison.

"This," said Arden, "is my surprise."

There was an awkward, shocked silence. Then Martin,

recovering, said, "I'm afraid that even my legal training doesn't teach me exactly how to greet an ex-brother-in-law in these circumstances." He added pointedly: "That is assuming I knew the circumstances."

Derek laughed.

"Suppose we say that Arden and I have settled our differences?"

Heather cried, "You mean you are going to remarry?"

"Later on—quite probably," Arden said.

Martin watched her closely. Between the two was a close friendship which since the death of their parents had deepened. Little was said, but great understanding prevailed and in that moment Martin experienced a sharp fear, an uneasiness difficult to define. On the face of it he had no reason whatsoever to distrust Derek or his motives, yet illogically—and he appreciated the fact—he did so. Then, swayed by the obvious happiness in Arden's eyes, he held out his hand and said, "Welcome back, Derek. You must excuse me if I'm a little startled."

"I should be the same in your place," Derek agreed.

Martin could not stay the utterance, "And I hope that in settling your differences you fully appreciate Arden's innocence in the case you brought against her?"

Derek stiffened, but replied smoothly, "I do; and I'm sorry. You've had justification for thinking harshly of me."

Martin relaxed. It wasn't outside the bounds of possibility, he argued, that Derek had been taught a lesson that might well improve him.

"Then we'll forget yesterday," he said generously.

Heather made a few inarticulate little noises which meant assent.

"I thought you had something like this in mind, Derek, when you were so anxious to find out where Arden lived." She made a twittering movement and pecked Arden's cheek in belated greeting.

"We've found such a lovely school for Gail," she said irrelevantly.

Arden could not resist a secret smile. That was so typical of Heather who was always completely wrapped up in her own problems and affairs and utterly uninterested in anything that concerned others. It struck her, then, that Heather was a strange woman, but, contradictorily, common among her sex.

Standing there in a nondescript, flowered silk dress and shapeless coat, hatless, she gave the impression that she had dressed in a hurry and forgotten her hair and make-up. A trace of powder lingered on her nose in a rather conspicuous blob and her florid, coarse skin looked like orange peel. Her hair was fair, but faded, wispy and seeming always to be in a state when it needed permanently waving. She had little interest in clothes, seldom wore stockings and disdained perfume. She was a mother first, a housekeeper second, and a wife through necessity.

She went upstairs with Arden, slid out of her coat and stood, a square, flat-chested figure, sturdy and unfeminine. For all that, no one disliked Heather: she was completely negative. Her interests were confined to domesticity in all its aspects, and even when there was nothing to do she was always busy because she prided herself on "never having a moment". She never thought of love, or sex. Martin was her husband and the word held no more significance than any other in her vocabulary. If she read the newspapers most of the subject matter failed to sink in and it was enough that she knew which party happened, politically, to be in power! She was a radio enthusiast and had her set blaring most hours of the day without listening to, or hearing, any of it and she could keep up a conversation with either music or a talk as a background noise without which she was lost. She loved the word "housewife" and bored Martin, on occasion, almost to the point of homicide, since he found it quite impossible to converse with her for any length of time. Once the triviality of the children's daily routine, the weather, the washing and what Mrs. So-and-So said, was exhausted . . . so was Martin. Heather, however, prattled gaily on. She had unending and avid interest in precisely nothing! Mention Plato and she would cherish the illusion that you were referring to a strip cartoon. Martin had met and married her on the rebound, but such was his loyalty and full appreciation of her many sterling qualities that he was doubly tied. Heather was not a smart, attractive woman who could build a new life. She was utterly and wholly dependent upon him in every sense of the word.

"Yes," she said brightly, and she seemed to talk twice as ast as was normal, "it is a lovely school, Arden. No *so* far from you, either . . . you know *your* garden is looking nice.

48

Ours is, too. You must come for a week-end. . . . So you and Derek——" She paused.

Arden could not dissemble, and she said fearlessly and honestly, "We are lovers, Heather. I cannot rush into marriage again. This way we shall have time to rectify our mistakes and make quite sure we want to spend the rest of our lives together."

Heather's eyes widened.

"Well, if that is how you feel——" She gave a little laugh. "Personally, it is the last thing I'd want. Such a *bother*. I never could get any interest in that sort of thing." There was nothing critical or condemnatory in her attitude.

Arden laughed.

"Strange how different we all are."

Heather peered at herself in the mirror.

"I suppose my face wants powdering. . . . Yes, we are all so different. I'd much rather do some ironing than go to bed with a man. That's the very worst feature of marriage. But Martin's wonderful really. He hardly ever bothers me now." She took out a powder puff as she spoke and went over her face like a motor mower over a lawn. "There! That will have to do!" She turned to Arden. "You look lovely. But then, you always do. That primrose and blue suits you. Nylon, isn't it? Mine's cotton. But with a couple of kids to look after a woman just can't expect to be smart. I haven't the time." She spoke without rancour and genuinely believed she was stating a fact.

Arden smiled. She liked Heather without having anything in common with her. At the same time she fully realized how sterile a thing Martin's life must be.

"So long," she said tritely, "as you are happy."

"Happy!" Heather laughed. "Too busy not to be. No use thinking about *happiness*. If the children are healthy and you've enough money to bring them up properly what more can one have? Or ask from life? That's what you need, Arden. Children."

"That is what I want to have when I am quite certain that Derek and I can give them a happy home."

That went a little over Heather's head. She glanced at the bed and the impact of Arden's words about her relationship with Derek sank in.

"Must feel funny to sleep with a husband after you've

divorced him," she said. "I wonder what Martin will think." A pause. "Are you fond of Derek?"

"Naturally. I'm in love with him."

Heather giggled.

"I don't believe in all that nonsense," she said imperturbably. "Novels! They give me shudders up and down my spine. All this thrill and romance business."

Arden stared at her.

"But surely when you and Martin were married——"

"No," came the forthright reply. "I was fond of him. I felt that I could live with him peaceably. I wanted children—above all. I'd have had more if I could. But this love stuff I never could understand. Oh, probably I'm to blame. But I'd far rather be a comfortable rice pudding. I just couldn't be doing with emotion." She added: "Such an awful waste of effort and for—what?"

Arden laughed.

"Heather, you're a delight," she said. "I've never talked to you like this before. Mostly women who feel as you are bitter and narrow—you're not."

"No time for that, either! Let everyone do as they please. It's a free world. My life wouldn't suit you and I'd loathe yours. Fair enough. . . . I must wash my hands, they're filthy. Can't stand gloves. I'll come downstairs to you."

She disappeared into the adjoining bathroom. Arden joined Derek and Martin. She was still thinking of Heather and once the novelty of her somewhat staggering revelations about herself had worn off, a curious, insistent fear penetrated her mind. Could any man be expected to be faithful to a woman in such circumstances?

Watching Derek during the next hour or so, Arden was impressed by his relaxed naturalness. During their married life he had shown a marked resentment towards Martin and treated Heather with a patronizing contempt. Now his attitude was that of a man accepting them as his own family—with familiarity, ease and, it appeared, a genuine regard. Almost as though aware of her reflections he said:

"You know, human nature is pretty queer. I've felt darned cut off—missed you both and, to be honest, I never quite felt that we hit it off before." His smile embraced them both. "It strikes me that it wouldn't be a bad idea for married people to quarrel and part sometimes—providing they came together in the end. We are so apt to take happiness for granted."

Martin lay back in his chair, his expression inscrutable. He was not a good-looking man, but he had an indefinable charm and friendliness of manner that endeared him to all those with whom he came in contact. Those for whom he worked held him in the highest esteem and even his opponents conceded him an indestructible integrity. Normally, his manner was gay, his smile frequent. To-day, however, it seemed to Arden that he was preoccupied and unusually thoughtful and she could not convince herself that her own problems entirely provided a reason.

It was not until after tea that she was able to talk to him alone. Heather wanted to see the garden and pick some fruit. Derek volunteered to accompany and help her. Martin and Arden sat further back in their respective chairs and, for a second, lapsed into a silence which illustrated their harmony.

Then Martin began:

"Are you quite sure about all this, Arden? Why didn't you get in touch with me?"

"I didn't want to be influenced even by the wisest of counsellors, Martin. And certainly I'd no idea that I'd ever see Derek again."

"You wanted to do so?"

She tried to be absolutely honest.

"I don't think I knew quite what I wanted—except that I knew I was lonely, restless and in limbo. Not a good state for my temperament."

Martin sighed, lit a cigarette and studied her intently.

"We sometimes clutch at illusion when we reach that stage. Escapism, if you like. Life means reality."

Arden countered:

"I hardly think that any association with a man who has been one's husband for a number of years could come into the category of escapism."

"Time isn't a factor. You can suddenly be attracted to a person you have accepted as a friend for twenty years or, alternatively, to one whom you have known for twenty minutes."

A tension crept into the atmosphere. The sudden silence was filled with drama and the impact of an emotion so real that it made itself felt as surely as though it were tangible.

51

"And," said Arden simply and quietly, "that has happened to you, Martin—hasn't it?"

He didn't protest; they were too close in their understanding.

"Yes."

She made a little, grieved sound.

"What are you going to do about it?"

"Nothing," he said with conviction. "There is nothing that could possibly be done in the circumstances."

"And—she?"

"It is mutual."

"Do I know her?"

"You met once." She could see that his hands were shaking, that his expression, despite his effort at control, was strained and tense.

"Catherine Newton." The name sprang to Arden's lips.

"Yes—Catherine," he replied and he invested the word with all the love that was in his heart.

Arden cried, "But . . . Oh, Martin, why does life have to be such an unholy muddle? Why can't love and emotion be controlled and fitted into some kind of pattern?"

He smiled wryly.

"It would cease to have any power, then."

She said shakenly, "Heather——"

"My dear, Heather hasn't the faintest idea how I feel about Catherine or anything else. She is perfectly happy in her world and I am essential to that happiness in a purely material sense. She is fond of me; she is an excellent mother, but she has never been in love in her life. That fact does not justify me in smashing my home. We're not at each other's throats; we never quarrel." A faintly cynical gleam came into his eyes. "There are no heights and no depths for Heather. She cannot be blamed for that."

"Do you see Catherine?"

"Only when we meet by accident, or at the houses of mutual friends. Her marriage, in reverse, is precisely the same as mine."

"But——" Arden spread her hands in an appealing gesture.

"I don't believe in beginning anything one cannot finish. And I loathe an anti-climax. She is *there*; we *know*. It is better than emptiness, Arden."

"Ah," Arden said with feeling.

"It isn't a question of being moral or lacking the courage to go blindly into an affair: it is a question of fighting to preserve what we already have. Love withers, dies through satiation far more than through denial," he added harshly.

"I'm so sorry."

"Don't be. I'd far rather have this than my life as it was before. I am at least alive. Feeling, emotion, makes us one with the world; it allows us to dream, to *think*. We cease being mechanical figures in a puppet world."

"And is she in agreement with you?"

"Perfectly—thank God."

"And her husband?"

"He is as happy as Heather—blissfully ignorant of everything beyond sport, his club and his business."

"How grim."

Martin nodded.

"It strikes me as being rather tragic the number of ill-assorted people there are in this world, carrying on in a vacuum, never at any time finding fulfilment in any sense of the word."

"And love is no guarantee of happiness," Arden said reflectively. "That is even more tragic."

"But it provides a foundation—if it is mutual. With love any two people have their future very much in their own hands and can come to terms. Without it, there is only an empty acceptance of duty and responsibility."

Arden leaned forward.

"That is how I feel about Derek. We love each other, therefore——"

"Are you quite sure? If so, why the caution in waiting to remarry?"

"Because we've proved love is not the open sesame."

Martin's lips curved into a half-smile.

"We are all so full of theories, Arden."

"But, Martin, you must see my point?"

"I do—perfectly. I just wish that you were so convinced about the rightness of re-joining your life with him that there would be no doubts anywhere."

"Isn't that rather foolishly romantic—the other extreme?"

"Quite probably. Perhaps I cannot help being a little subjective."

"There is only a matter of a legal ceremony involved," Arden said frankly. "In every other sense Derek is my—husband."

Martin got up slowly from his chair.

"I think you are making a mistake," he said forcefully. His gaze met hers. "You're the type to be drawn into conflict over such a relationship."

Arden gasped, "For heaven's sake—why? I'm not a child and Derek isn't a stranger."

"You misunderstand me. In these circumstances you would not lightly dismiss him, even should you ultimately discover you wish to do so. You'd begin arguing about duty; you'd have a conscience angle."

"But the physical tie——"

He interrupted her quietly. "The physical tie is nothing until it insinuates itself into a serious relationship. The lover taken impulsively and lightly can be discarded and forgotten. This is vastly different." He looked at her with an increasing concern. "May I ask if the idea was Derek's?"

"You may and the answer is: no. It was my idea."

"That consoles me a little," he answered. "Oh, Arden . . . I want the best for you. If you love Derek——"

"Why," she protested, "do you doubt the fact?"

"Possibly out of fear for you. There are so many loves, so many phases of emotional experience. And I cannot dissociate the idea that your loyalty to marriage, even to love itself, might well be a factor in all this."

"And is that such a bad thing?"

"No, my dear—only if it should conflict with the finding of a greater love."

She laughed.

"I've had plenty of time in which to find a substitute for Derek, you know." She added: "And aren't you being rather illogical? I thought you had such faith in the powers of love and its effect upon stabilizing relationships."

"I have. But I was not speaking of emotion which could spring from unhappiness and past suffering—to say nothing of an awareness of bitter injustice. There is more than love bound up in your reactions to Derek."

"Isn't that the case in every relationship?" she protested.

"Yes. . . . But self-deception can be a cruel enemy, Arden."

She said gently, "I know you have only my welfare at

54

heart, Martin, and that your concern is my happiness. Please believe me: I know what I am doing."

He turned to her.

"If he ever made you unhappy again——" he said with a sudden grim fierceness.

"He won't! Don't you see, Martin? His coming back—everything! No one can do more than admit they were wrong. Certainly he has no ulterior motive—even though I resent having to defend him because it seems an insult." Her gaze was a trifle stormy. "And that was in your mind—wasn't it?"

He stubbed out his cigarette.

"I suppose it was. But my memory is a little longer than yours, my dear. I know and recall the hell you went through when he refused to believe you about Brian. I feel you've been caught up by something stronger than your will to resist——" He put out his hands and clasped hers, his expression was earnest and appealing. "Make quite sure, Arden. Knowing what hell all this can be——"

She cried, swayed by his sincerity, "But Derek and I were happy before."

He eyed her slowly and contemplatively.

"Wasn't that because you subjugated your own desires? Was it ever fulfilment for you? And if not, why go *back*?" He made a desperate exclamation. "If only retrospect were not so kind. If only we could concentrate on the things we hated instead of being destined to recall only those we loved and to build up our past happiness out of all proportion."

Arden countered with spirit:

"Even if all that is true, Martin, there is the present to off-set it. The reality——"

"A passionate reunion between two, free people need not be reality—but, as I said before, a devastating illusion." He hastened: "I'm not saying it is, Arden. I am merely asking you to take a sober, dispassionate view—if that is possible. You admit that you do not want to make the same mistake twice."

"Naturally, and doesn't that show how very unlikely I am to do so?"

He turned away, helpless before the fervour and sincerity of her attitude. Then, "No, Arden. We invariably repeat our mistakes because we bring to each experience the same emotional weaknesses."

55

Arden smiled.

"Stop worrying, Martin. I know what I'm doing."

"Promise me one thing?"

"I don't make blind promises."

"Then, promise me to *think* rather than to feel, if ever the day comes when you prove that Derek is not the man with whom you genuinely want to spend the rest of your life."

Arden stared at him.

"Seeing that this is an experiment am I not already *thinking*? It would have been very easy to rush to a register office."

Martin nodded. He realized that his warnings were of no avail and took himself to task for worrying unduly.

He and Heather left soon after six. Derek's arms went around Arden and holding her closely, he said, "Welcome though they were, I've never liked them so much as at this moment, my sweet."

Arden felt a tremor of happiness surge upon her. Derek's arms brought a sensation of security which made Martin's fear for her almost ludicrous.

"I know," she whispered.

"Do you want to go out this evening?" His lips were against her cheek as he spoke.

"No," she answered and her voice was unsteady.

He looked deeply into her eyes.

"Let's be lovers like this—always, my dearest," he murmured earnestly. "I can see now how much we had lost."

Arden responded to his mood, thankful for his readiness to face facts, conscious of a swift merging of mental and physical desire and of an ever-increasing confidence.

Later, sitting together in the twilight, recalling Lance Ashton, she asked suddenly, "Will you really be able to come down on Wednesday?"

"For dinner at Ashton's?" Derek leaned back lazily in his chair. "Easily. I wouldn't miss it for anything. Why?" His eyes met hers in the soft, mellow light and they were teasing. "Did you want to go alone?"

Arden laughed spontaneously.

"Anything but that." She sighed—a luxurious, happy sigh. "This has been a marvellous day, somehow. And I've had my book jacket accepted. A modest enough ambition, I'll admit. But Lance Ashton is Lance Ashton."

"I've brought you luck, darling."

Arden reached out and clasped his hand. It seemed to her then that she was in tune with the universe and that nothing could ever dim her faith in to-morrow.

CHAPTER VI

JANET RIVERS looked acid and forbidding. Lance glanced at her as she walked briskly into his study and he asked sharply, "And just *what* is the matter with you?" He put down the proofs he was reading and stared at her critically. "You have the manner of a militant matron trying to find trouble."

Janet's heart was racing. She felt sick with emotion that was whipped to a frenzy of annoyance and frustration. Silence fell and throbbed between them like a pulse. Then, getting to his feet, Lance cried, "Of course! Miss Marchly and Mr. Rayne!"

Janet snapped, "It is nothing to do with me whom you have to the house."

Lance eyed her coolly. "Exactly, Janet. I'm glad you have the good sense to appreciate the fact. And now will you kindly change your mood? If not——" He paused. "I shall seriously have to consider making some radical changes."

"Meaning—what?" She could easily have burst into tears of mortification.

"Meaning that no writer can work in an atmosphere of hostility and rancour. I certainly cannot and have no intention of doing so."

Janet gave an imitation of a concertina as she sank into a chair. She felt rather like a possessive mother who, having managed to dominate and tie a child to her apron strings, realizes that her power has waned. For three years she had subtly influenced Lance, leading him, as she thought, gently towards a romantic attachment and the realization that he could not do without her. Now, in a matter of as many days, the whole pattern seemed to have changed.

She fell back on the trite phrase: "All I hope is that you know what you are doing, Lance."

Lance took up a position on the hearthrug and surveyed her blandly from there.

"If this is what having two dinner guests means . . . Listen, Janet, let's understand each other. Since I bought this house I've lived like a hermit——"

"From choice," she interposed sharply.

"Naturally," he said incisively. "Well, the time has come when I intend to change all that. I'm sick of the dreary routine of working, eating, and sleeping."

"You mean you're going abroad?" Her eyes lit up like a lamp in the darkness.

"No," he replied slowly, "merely that I need people around me again. It doesn't do for one to get bored. And that is precisely what is wrong with the book I'm on. It betrays my own apathy. You can," he added coolly, "scrap it."

The muscles in Janet's throat felt paralysed.

"But—but there's ten thousand words."

"I don't care if there are twenty. If it bores me to write it then I'm damned certain it will bore people to read it."

Janet stared at him in horror.

"But, Lance——"

He spoke quietly and reflectively as he said, "There comes a time when writing about the things you once felt deeply must give way to the things you feel at this moment." His gaze was level and his manner unyielding.

Janet found the words rushing indiscreetly from her lips: "Miss Marchly has certainly started something!"

Lance felt a burning annoyance; a resentment new to him.

"I suggest we leave Miss Marchly's name out of this, Janet. But at least you have given me your reason for this odd behaviour."

"*My* odd behaviour. Really, Lance, if someone did not point out to you——"

He cut in: "When I want your advice I will ask for it. And I suggest that if you feel such antagonism towards my guests you absent yourself to-night."

Janet paled. She was making herself unpopular and foolish and she knew it, but sheer emotion goaded her.

"Antagonism! Don't be ridiculous. That doesn't come into it. If you want friends around here there are dozens who would be honoured and thrilled. Take Lady Mooney and the Crichton-Doles."

Lance stubbed out his cigarette.

58

"You take them. I don't want museum pieces. I am quite capable of choosing my own friends."

"I doubt that, Lance. You hardly made a very good selection in your choice of a wife, after all."

Lance Ashton's face seemed suddenly to have been carved out of granite. His mouth tightened over clenched teeth. His eyes darkened with the pain of memory.

Instantly, Janet rushed to his side, abject, apologetic.

"I'm sorry," she cried desperately, "that was unpardonable of me. I don't know why I did it. . . . Oh, Lance—forgive me."

He relaxed and a faintly cynical smile twisted his lips.

"Forget it, Janet."

She went on urgently:

"I want so much for you, Lance." Her gaze rested upon him and the love she could not master was laid bare for him to see. "You're free from all that now and if and when you marry again——"

He said gently, "Let me worry about that. And as I haven't the faintest intention of marrying again——" He stopped abruptly, adding: "One divorce is quite enough. No one asks to be betrayed a second time." A flash of his former cynicism returned to harden his expression. "Now suppose you go and forget all this nonsense."

Janet regained her poise, critical of her own jealous folly.

"Very well . . . who is Mr. Rayne?" She added: "I mean is he Miss Marchly's fiancé?"

A withdrawn look came into Lance's eyes.

"I have no idea. Asking personal questions is not a hobby of mine. He just happened to be at the cottage."

Janet nodded. She was neither consoled nor satisfied.

. . . . .

Arden was conscious of an increasing excitement as she drove over to The Manor that evening. Derek had arranged to join her there, feeling that to do so would be in the interests of discretion.

Lance came forward to greet her as his manservant opened the front door, ignoring formality and saying with obvious pleasure, "Miss Marchly . . ." He paused. "And Mr. Rayne?"

"He is driving straight down from London," she explained. "He should be here at any moment."

Lance found himself wishing that Derek Rayne might never arrive, for looking at Arden he felt the sudden pull of attraction, a quickening of interest which, after numbness and apathy, brought him swiftly back to life.

Arden had never looked lovelier. Her dress was black with touches of white, slim and elegant but without hardness. An exquisite floral diamond spray was her only ornament and its brightness matched the sparkle of her eyes, the vitality of her personality. Looking at Lance Ashton she could not deny the thrill derived from the fact that *he* was her host. He whose work she had admired from afar and whose name had been inextricably bound up with her own ambitions. She walked with him into the large, sunlit drawing-room and there handed him the final sketch.

"I hope," she said anxiously, "that this is what you had in mind."

Lance took it and, studying it with expert eye, cried:

"It is better than I'd hoped it would be. Far better. You've managed to get just what I wanted." He smiled warmly. "Damn it, the jacket will be better than the book!"

"Just so long as it does not disgrace it," she said gaily.

Janet appeared on the threshold. Lance turned to her eagerly, holding out the drawing.

"Couldn't be better, could it?" he said with enthusiasm.

Janet nodded to Arden's acknowledgement of her and cast a critical glance at the sketch held out towards her. She knew that she could not find fault with it.

"It is excellent," she said and added subtly: "Personally, I can never see why anything more than a plain dust cover is necessary. All this is quite a waste of time, isn't it? I mean, the libraries strip them off and the bookstalls sell on the author's name." Her smile was vinegar in honey. "However, it would deprive many people of a living if the habit were discarded."

Lance felt the venom behind the words.

"And it would deprive the author of a great deal of satisfaction. A bad jacket, yes! It can be a thorn in the flesh. But one like this! This will stand out and be admired for itself on any bookstall. Thank you, Miss Marchly. I should be most grateful if, in future, you would take care of all my jackets. I shall certainly request it. Of course, that is if you wish."

Arden met his appreciative gaze and her own was filled with pleasurable gratitude.

"Nothing could please me more. It has always been a secret ambition of mine."

"Then having achieved it, don't allow your far more important ambition to fade," he said seriously. "Commercial work is by no means the limit of your ability."

Janet had insinuated herself into the conversation and as Arden made demur she said pointedly, "I was given to understand that artists"—she laid emphasis on the word—"seldom made a success of this type of work. Is that so, Miss Marchly?"

Arden turned a wide, honest gaze upon her.

"I would not know, Miss Rivers. I don't profess to *be* an artist. Aspiration is another matter."

Lance chuckled inwardly. Janet had asked for that. And, excusing herself, she left the room.

Cocktails were served and Arden relaxed in a chair opposite her host.

"This is the loveliest old house, Mr. Ashton."

"It could be," he said, surprising himself, "but it can, also, be lonely." His gaze held hers. "And could you make it Lance? I'm allergic to prefixes. If I could be honoured in any way it would not be a title I'd seek, but the right to be known and called simply by my christian name. Odd, I suppose, but——" He paused.

"Human," she supplemented, then: "You know my name, I think—Arden? I'd be happy for the Miss Marchly to be dispensed with. I share your aversion."

"Arden," he echoed. "An unusual name."

"It was my great-grandmother's. A very poor reason, I feel, for giving it to me! Particularly as I was not acquainted with her."

"Perhaps she had a history." Lance was watching her closely as he spoke.

"Or a past," Arden laughed.

"Isn't that the same thing?"

"Not exactly. A history implies achievement; a past can suggest failure."

"So you're a philosopher—eh?"

Her smile was slow.

"It was Bertrand Russell who said that philosophy was the

no-man's-land between Religion and Science. I must admit to a great liking for that no-man's-land."

The mood changed. Lance settled more deeply into his chair.

"And I. And, if I can quote correctly, Bertrand Russell also asked, in the introduction to his *History of Western Philosophy*, if there was such a thing as wisdom, or is what seems such merely the ultimate refinement of folly?"

Arden commented, "Being completely ignorant I'm in no position to comment, but I would arrogate to myself the right to suggest that in such a theory lies the negation of human progress through experience."

Lance tensed. Her words echoed strangely through the room, finding an answering chord within. He said slowly, "It is a great joy, Arden, to talk to a woman who thinks—if that isn't sheer presumption."

Arden countered with spirit: "On behalf of my sex, I protest. It *is* presumption. Thinking is not the prerogative of man."

He apologized, adding: "True; but it does not fall to the lot of each one of us to meet many women who are not absorbed in purely feminine pursuits and interests."

Arden sighed.

"Is that so very surprising? Why should it be belittling to a women to behave like one, while for a man to be other than masculine is an insult! We are supposed to be the illogical creatures, but how fallacious that is!"

Lance laughed.

"You are deliberately and provocatively misunderstanding me!"

"Perhaps." Arden was enjoying herself. "Quite frankly, as a woman I cannot stand too much woman's talk, either! I love clothes and all the normal feminine things, but I hate an undiluted diet of them!"

He made a gesture of assent.

"There we are—in complete agreement!"

"You are not," she said naturally, "a bit as I imagined you might be before I met you."

He inclined his head, his expression questioning.

"And just how did *you* imagine me?"

"Eccentric or horribly conceited—or both." She stopped, appalled by her own frankness.

He laughed heartily.

"Don't look so horrified. I love your frankness. It is a welcome change."

Arden felt the force of his personality reaching out and drawing her into its spell. His ease of manner, his ability to inspire confidence and invite truth, awakened within her an appreciation deep and a trifle disconcerting. Again she was aware that although they were still strangers they were yet closer than many friends. Closer. She rejected the word as foolish, even deceptive. It was, after all, comparatively simple for a man in his position to be charming. His life was a pleasant oasis from which he could survey the rest of mankind indulgently—herself included. She said hurriedly, "I'm afraid it is one of my many failings—for all that."

She glanced out at the gardens.

His gaze followed hers.

"Would you care for a walk before dinner? It will be almost dark afterwards."

Instantly she responded. Her lungs felt denuded of air and a tension had crept into the atmosphere.

The long, tapering shadows of the August evening fell upon the grounds protectingly as they stepped outside on to the terrace. The sun, holding the mellow light of approaching autumn, splashed liquid gold upon the tree tops and spilled little pools of amber over the vivid, green lawns. There had been rain earlier in the day and the earth had darkened and freshened. A heady fragrance rose from it and the smell of damp bracken sharpened in the cool, clean air. Views sweeping across ridges of the Chiltern Hills in the direction of Bledlow concentrated on the glory of beechwoods typical of the county. They lay in the stillness and splendour of evening, rifted with gold as if a giant brush had tinted them.

Arden felt emotion surge within her. Here was beauty that seemed absolute and touched the heart like music.

Lance said quietly, "This is a favourite hour of mine, particularly at this season of the year. The light appears to change and soften. It may be purely my imagination."

"I don't think so. Buckinghamshire is a curious and beautiful county." She gave a little laugh. "Certainly nearly all the races which successfully invaded England swept across it!"

"True—Celts, Britons, Romans, Saxons, Danes! Sometimes in the northern parts you can distinguish dark Celtic types. . . . You are interested in the history of places?"

"Tremendously; appreciation can be built only on some knowledge of a subject, surely." Arden paused. "Yet I could contradict myself, for thousands of people enjoy good music who haven't any idea of its technique."

Lance drew her gaze to his.

"Shall we say that the connoisseur's palate in everything is perhaps sharper and more selective!"

In that second Derek's car swung into the drive and flashed at great speed towards the house, coming to an abrupt stop.

Hearing it, Lance smiled.

"Your friend has arrived and you are destined not to see the gardens!"

They walked around the side of the house and reached Derek as he was about to mount the steps.

Arden was trembling with faint excitement, and as her glance met Derek's there passed between them that swift, passionate recognition, itself a caress.

"I'm terribly sorry I'm late. It took me longer to get out of London than all the rest. The traffic is a nightmare."

Lance told himself that he was going to make every endeavour to like this Derek Rayne and to meet him half-way, yet the sight of him started a fantastic irritation. He replied, with understanding, "I had rather overlooked the fact that you would be coming from London. It's good of you to make the journey and time is unimportant. I'm sure a cocktail will be welcome."

"It will." Derek greeted Arden with suitable reserve.

They walked into the drawing-room and Derek said gratefully, "This is heaven. London was an oven to-day." He looked at Arden. "Be thankful you haven't to work up there every day."

"I am," she admitted.

Again Lance conjectured about their relationship. He asked with solicitude, "I hope you haven't to make the journey back there to-night, Mr. Rayne?"

Derek flashed Arden a meaning glance as he replied, "I'm afraid so. I have an early appointment or I would certainly have put up at the hotel." He paused deliberately. "I was very comfortable at Little Gaddesden."

Lance felt that his unasked question had, subtly, been answered. And again he reminded himself that their affairs had nothing whatsoever to do with him.

"I've heard that it is very good there. . . . Why don't you get a cottage down here? There are quite a few about."

"It had," said Derek, "been in my mind. . . . Thanks." He took the drink.

Janet Rivers made an entrance at that moment and Lance introduced Derek to her. Her acid, disapproving manner vanished and she beamed upon him. Within ten minutes she was discoursing intelligently upon the technique of advertising until Derek exclaimed, "You are remarkably well versed in the subject, Miss Rivers."

She smiled a slow, confident smile.

"I used to be personal secretary to the head of one of the big agencies. Then I met Mr. Ashton——" She paused significantly.

Lance laughed.

"And from then she was doomed!"

Arden watched Janet River's gaze as it embraced Lance in a look of passionate, yet almost resentful, adoration that was unmistakable and Arden's heart curiously missed a beat. It was obvious that she was in love with him, but not so easy to determine his reactions to her which, on the face of it, appeared consistent with friendship and appreciation.

"On the contrary," she corrected him, "then I fulfilled my ambition." She looked at Derek. "Are you going to the party to-morrow night, Mr. Rayne?"

Derek laughed.

"Nothing like that. I'm not in the literary world."

Lance looked at Arden.

"It occurred to me that you might be going up from here, Arden." His use of her christian name had an impact upon the atmosphere, and was followed by a small silence. He added confidently: "Arden and I apparently share an equal dislike of prefixes. I never bother very much with people whom I *wish* to call Mr., Mrs. or Miss."

Derek's expression was inscrutable as he said, "I've never thought of it. But, then, I *have* to observe the conventions. I

am not in the happy position where I can make my own terms."
He looked hard at Lance as he spoke and although his tone was
light and in no way offensive, it held an underlying note of
sarcasm which Lance did not miss.

Lance sipped his drink and smiled. Then imperturbably:

"I was saying, Arden . . . should you be going up from here
may I not give you a lift? It seems rather foolish for us to be
driving in the same direction in our respective cars."

Derek shot Arden a glance as if to say: "What did I tell
you?"

Arden struggled to keep the colour from her cheeks. No
excuse came readily to her mind, but she said, "That is very
kind of you, but I shall be staying the night and——"

"I, also, had intended doing that. I could drive you back
the following morning, or afternoon, as you please."

Derek took command.

"Arden is dining with me that evening . . . but it would be
helpful and kind if you would see her to the party."

Arden felt a tremor of excitement. Derek had subtly intruded without giving offence and she thrilled to the note of
authority in his voice.

Lance inclined his head.

"I should be delighted. If we leave here about five?"

Janet said, the words wrested from her in a fever of
jealousy, "I must not forget to tell Baker——"

Lance said calmly, "I shall drive myself as I am remaining
in London. I don't want any encumbrances."

"On holiday?" Arden spoke lightly.

"Yes; on holiday. Janet is going off, too. We both need a
break."

"I was in Capri some two months ago," Derek said casually.

"How wonderful." Janet looked from his face to Arden
before asking suddenly, and with what Arden felt to be a
simulated calm: "By the way, Miss Marchly, do you happen to
know a Brian Newton? He's manager of one of the subsidiary
companies of the firm." Her pause was timed and held significance. "Although I suppose it is rather ridiculous to assume
that you know a fraction of the members of the firm."

Arden panicked without knowing why and then regained
her composure.

"I know a very great number. Yes, I've met Mr. Newton

and know him well, although I've not seen him for some time. . . . Is he a friend of yours?"

"My sister-in-law knows him," said Janet coolly. "Her husband was in the army with him at the latter part of the war." A Mona Lisa smile creased her eyes. "It is a *very* small world and one is always meeting people who know one's own friends."

Derek spoke and his voice was slightly unsteady.

"And is Mr. Newton a friend of yours, also, Miss Rivers?"

Janet leaned forward and put her glass down on the small table beside her.

"No; I've never met him. He is sure to be at the party to-morrow—at least, I imagine so."

Arden chilled; a sense of foreboding possessed her. Yet suppose this embittered—and she sensed that bitterness—woman should know the truth? What did it matter? In a few months she and Derek would be married again. . . . Yet, for all that, there was just something from which she shrank, and the presentiment gripped her lest Janet Rivers might be out to cause trouble. Yet, she reasoned, wasn't that ridiculous since there was nothing that could possibly happen to jeopardize her life with Derek? Lance did not come into it. Her gaze went swiftly to Derek who exclaimed carelessly:

"I didn't know that Newton was with the firm, Arden. I suppose I must have confused him with someone else, but I understood he was with Willers."

Janet, rather rudely, interposed, "He was. There was some trouble—something to do with his private life, I believe—and I think he found it more comfortable to change jobs." She looked at Arden. "You may know the details, Miss Marchly."

The silence was electric, as though all the warring elements had converged ready to explode. Arden took a deep breath, steadied her nerves and said smoothly, "No, Miss Rivers. There is so much gossip, and so many rumours, that I never believe anything about anyone without the proof of personal knowledge." She smiled: "And even then I doubt half of it!"

Lance gave an exclamation of hearty assent.

"If there is anything I loathe, too, it is scandalmongering. In any case, I maintain that people have a perfect right to do as they please with their own life."

"The generous judge," Arden hastened.

"Definitely not even the judge," he corrected. "It is always easy to condemn the other person for something of which we, ourselves, might well be guilty—in a particular set of circumstances."

Arden felt heartened.

"Indifference can masquerade as virtue. It is easy to reject a thing you do not desire."

"Ah!" Lance smiled—a quiet smile of reflection. "How true."

Derek asked rather sharply, "Isn't that an extremely cynical attitude? There is such a thing as control, or"—he paused significantly—"or do you subscribe to the philosophy that moral standards are merely hypocritical and obstructive?"

Lance was aware of the challenge and of an underlying note of hostility in Derek's voice.

"On the contrary."

Arden said tensely, "I think it is very much a matter of personal codes."

Derek looked at her.

"That can be a most convenient viewpoint."

It was an evening of strange conflicts. After dinner they sat and listened to Beethoven's *Pastoral Symphony* which Arden had selected from Lance's extensive library. Derek lay back in his chair. He did not enjoy it, for music was not a love of his.

To Arden it was a feast and she was lost completely to her surroundings with the exception of one or two occasions when, raising her eyes, she met Lance's intent, almost inquiring gaze and felt a curious sympathy stealing between them. But each time Janet intercepted their glances and the tension mounted. Her vigilance and jealousy were disturbing and distasteful and Arden could not rid herself of the feeling that in some inexplicable, even fantastic, fashion Janet was destined to play a part in her own affairs. It was a relief when, soon after ten o'clock, Janet left, saying sweetly to Derek:

"I hope we shall meet again one of these days, Mr. Rayne. I am sure we must know many mutual friends."

By eleven o'clock Arden was becoming increasingly absorbed in listening to Lance Ashton's accounts of his travels—accounts for which she had pressed and not which he had voluntarily inflicted—but Derek, bored and faintly annoyed by the familiarity with which Lance addressed Arden, said firmly, "We must be going, Mr. Ashton." A pause. "It has been a most enjoyable evening and I hope that sometime you will have dinner with us. Either in London at my club or at some hotel of your own choosing in this district."

"That would be enjoyable; thank you." Lance made no attempt to press them to stay. But he was mindful of the fact that the following evening he would again have the pleasure of Arden's company. He saw them to their respective cars and stood between the two vehicles, talking to Arden while Derek stood watchfully by.

"I will call for you at five," he said quietly.

Their gaze met in the moonlight; hers a little afraid, his dogged.

"Thank you," she murmured; "and for to-night."

Derek shook hands with Lance and then, before getting into his car, said to Arden, "I'll follow you as far as Birch Lane and then strike off from there."

"Very well."

Arden drove mechanically. At the lane leading to the cottage she slowed down. Derek swung past her and turned, giving a faint toot on the hooter. She followed. Their respective cars came to a stop within a few feet of each other. He moved swiftly from his and helped her out.

"You didn't imagine that story about returning to London was true, did you?" he said softly.

A pang shot through her. Even though her affairs were no concern of Lance she detested anything in the nature of subterfuge.

"I wondered why you troubled to explain." She slipped her key into the lock of the door and they went into the hall. Derek switched the light on.

Arden felt desperately tired, as if drained of vitality. Derek said abruptly when they reached the lounge, "You didn't tell me that Brian was with the firm."

She stared at him.

"It didn't occur to me. I never come in contact with him." She met Derek's gaze very levelly. "And I don't particularly like your tone, darling."

"I don't like the prospect of your seeing him," came the gruff retort.

She turned on him. "*Derek!* Not again! I couldn't bear any

69

further nonsense about Brian. It is so futile, so adolescent. We've had an enjoyable evening and——"

"You may have enjoyed it. I haven't. I don't like that man after all. And what did I tell you about his inviting you to drive up with him?"

Arden gave Derek stare for stare.

"If Mr. Ashton has any ulterior motives for what is a perfectly ordinary courtesy, then I shall soon discover the fact. Until then, *please* let's not jump to conclusions. What *is* all this, Derek?"

He looked awkward.

"Just Janet Rivers mentioning Brian." He changed his mood. "I'm sorry, darling, but I'm only human, after all."

She said gravely, "I don't agree that being human comes into this. If you trust me and accept my word about the past, this would never occur to you." She paused, adding significantly: "And if you don't trust me then all this—our present relationship—is so much waste of time and an insult to me." She was heated and desperately sincere.

Derek flung away a half-smoked cigarette and moved to her side.

"You are quite right, my darling. I'm an idiot. Only now I'm scared of losing you for the second time."

Faint colour flooded her cheeks.

"What *do* you mean?"

"That Ashton has a pull and I can well imagine his particular brand of charm being effective with women. As a man I reckon he has brought it to a fine art . . . you don't agree?"

"I am not in a position to agree or disagree. I speak as I find."

"But you like him?"

"Very much." She was defiant and her eyes flashed. "And if you continue to talk in this strain I shall probably fall in love with him," she finished breathlessly. "Oh, Derek, don't you see how ridiculous all this is?"

"Yes." He sobered. "Look, Arden, how about marrying me again—immediately? This is rather like living on a volcano."

She hesitated, swayed by his persuasiveness. Then:

"No, Derek. When I feel I have your absolute trust and that we are really two people unable to live without each other——"

"I am that already," he insisted. He looked at her very steadily and unnervingly. "Does that mean——"

70

"It means merely caution." She added: "I don't want to hear anything more about Brian or Lance Ashton. If there is anything to tell you *I* will soon do so."

"I know, my darling." He gave a short laugh. "Funny how the fact that you are free of me awakens all manner of fears and jealousies that, normally, are foreign to me."

She studied him uneasily. The words sounded glib and, in any case, they were not true. His jealousy of Brian had precipitated them into the divorce court. But, generously, she let the mis-statement pass. Everything would work out if she were patient, she told herself.

"Let's forget it all," she said softly. Her eyes met his intent, reflective gaze. "Have you to leave very early in the morning? Is there an appointment?"

His arms tightened around her.

"What do you think, my sweet? Early, for us, is midday. I must leave then and curse an appointment that prevents *my* taking you up to the party . . . but we'll have the following day in London together?"

"I'd love that," she agreed, passion rising as his lips came within an inch or two of her own.

CHAPTER VII

LANCE arrived at the cottage precisely at five o'clock the following evening. Arden was ready and she said with a smile: "Just to prove that a woman can be punctual."

They went out to the car. Arden stood for a second breathing deeply of the cool, fragrant air that was heavy with the perfume of newly-mown hay. Lance appraised her as she stood there in a dress of powder blue, exquisitely fitted to her slender body. A minute sparkling cap fitted her small head and formed a perfect contrast against the burnished gold of her hair. Happiness bubbled about her heart; the world seemed hers for the taking. She and Derek had parted in a mood of ecstasy and understanding and now here she was setting out with Lance Ashton to a party. Nothing marred the thrill of that fact.

He assisted her into the car and then slid into the driving seat, smiling at her as he did so.

"I'm in luck. I'd dreaded this chore and suddenly it has become an adventure. You work miracles, Arden."

"I wish I did."

"What miracles *would* you work were the power really yours?" he asked lightly as the car purred down the lane.

"Happiness," she said without hesitation. "A simple, obvious acquisition, I know."

"Implying that you are not happy now," he suggested.

"Not necessarily, but making certain that I should be happy—to-morrow."

He gave her a swift glance.

"And are you quite sure you know just what represents happiness to you?"

"Quite sure."

He asked abruptly, "What *is* happiness? I've never found the answer to that question."

She stared at him.

"But of all people you, surely, must know it."

He gave a low laugh.

"If I may say so in all modesty, success can be as far removed from happiness as the earth from the heavens. Success is, at best, the fulfilment of ambition. But one's personal happiness—that deep-rooted, fundamental need. No."

He reached the main road and Arden waited until he had moved into the stream of traffic before she said: "Do you mean—marriage?"

He hesitated.

"I suppose I do. But when you've had one failure you get rather a jaundiced view and are reluctant to try again." He added: "I doubt if you knew I'd been married, and please respect my confidence."

"Of course."

"We're divorced." He gave Arden a meaning glance. "She preferred a secretary of mine. Fair enough; but it was the deception and lies which shattered me. I could have forgiven the infidelity."

Arden shivered without quite knowing why.

"I'm sorry." She studied him intently, and dared to ask, "You still care?"

"No," he said honestly. "Once, yes—I cared deeply. Now that is utterly finished, thank heaven. For all that I'm not

72

sure I didn't prefer the suffering to the numbness, the emptiness—emotionally."

She said swiftly, "I wondered; but, being you, I felt certain the newspapers would have all the details."

"I've been adamant on that point and, in any case, Lance Ashton is a nom-de-plume, Ashton being my mother's maiden name. My former wife has remarried and has a boy of six. No reason why, because I happen to have become a writer, they should be subjected to the publicity hounds."

"You will marry again one of these days."

He glanced at her and back at the road ahead.

"I'd have to trust the woman implicitly. I don't think I could stand disillusionment for the second time."

Arden countered, "And don't you consider women on the whole worthy of trust?"

"That is too general. . . . I would qualify it by saying that I rate loyalty and faith rather highly in human relationships. God forbid that I should ever judge, or condemn, anyone, but when you are deliberately deceived . . . what possible stability can there be, what hope of building a future?"

"I agree," she said earnestly.

"And I hate failure."

Arden's heart quickened its beat. There was so much she wanted to say. The impulse to confide in him was great, but set against it was her promise to Derek to do nothing of the kind.

"Failure always leaves a rankling sense of guilt, doesn't it?" she exclaimed. "A queer, dissatisfied and depressing reaction."

His voice was suddenly alert.

"You said that with a wealth of meaning, Arden. And your life? Has that been happy?"

"In patches," she admitted, adding swiftly: "I had a very happy childhood and I adored my father. His death was a great blow and then my mother was killed suddenly in a street accident."

He murmured a few sympathetic words. Then:

"And—love?" A pause. "Don't tell me that hasn't entered into the scheme of things. . . ."

"Naturally it has entered into it."

"And Mr. Rayne? Will you marry him, Arden?"

She hated the subterfuge, but she replied as honestly as was possible, "I think so; but I must be sure. Like you I'm sceptical and human emotions can be treacherous and misleading."

"But there's no engagement?" he persisted and gave the question a seriousness.

Arden's voice was not very steady as she answered, "No; no engagement."

"Splendid. They do put a damper on things." He spoke with banter, but a curious relief surged upon him. "In that case, will you have dinner with me after all this is over?"

Arden hesitated, thinking of Derek. Then:

"I'd love to," she agreed.

"We'll find somewhere quiet and it might be as well if we made all the arrangements now."

She said swiftly, "But you will probably be drawn into all manner of things and you certainly cannot get away early."

"Exactly . . . provided I do my job, greet all the right people and don't drop any bricks that the Press can lap up . . . a dinner engagement is going to be my salvation. How well do you know your London?"

"Pretty well."

"There's a restaurant tucked away off Wigmore Street. Fleur d'Argent. I know the proprietor."

Arden's thoughts raced ahead.

"Surely if I met you *there*? We'll get separated in the crush and I certainly cannot monopolize your time. Should you not be able to join me I shall understand perfectly. That way, you will not be restricted." She smiled warmly. "Or concerned because I'm starving!"

"I'll meet you there at nine. We haven't discovered if you know the place yet."

"Yes, I know it." By a strange coincidence she had dined there with Brian some years previously.

"Oh, splendid. Incidentally, where do you live in London?"

"My flat is very near Cavendish Square. In a block. I can leave it for weeks on end without having to bother."

"The independent young woman?"

"If you like."

"May I ask if you've been there long?"

"Just over a year. I managed to get it through a friend who

74

was leaving it—and at a controlled rent. My aunt left me Meadow View, so I am very fortunate."

"You are indeed." He was not wholly satisfied with the explanation because he still knew nothing of her life and, while he argued that she had freely answered his questions, she had certainly not volunteered any information.

They drove to the Savoy in what seemed to Arden record time. There she said briskly:

"This is where we go our separate ways, Lance." As he was about to protest, she added hastily, "The directors and chairman will be awaiting you and you'll have your time fully occupied. Let us keep to our arrangement. I will be at the Fleur d'Argent at nine. And should you not be able to join me please do not worry. I've a home to go to and can get to it in a matter of minutes from there."

He allowed her to talk, then added coolly, "You can't escape me as easily as that. Nine o'clock. And I shall look for you in the crush."

And crush was the right word, for despite the vastness of the River Room, it was crowded. Every celebrity in the world of art was present and the noise was like the thundering of a weir in silence. It came in a deafening wave, its impact shattering.

Arden knew a very great number of the guests and more than a few of the firm's authors, managers, and general staff and she felt a sudden gaiety as she stepped among them. And although the view and the general scene were not new to her, there was something about it all on that occasion which tugged at her heart. The river flowing by, tranquil in the midst of turmoil, serene against the cacophony of a City . . . a tapestry hung to enhance the elegance of the room accustomed to receptions, to the splendour and the glamour of famous personalities.

A faint fragrance of perfumes intermingling hung in the air, the sudden flash of a diamond spray, the swish of taffeta as pin-pointed in a mass of dresses of all kinds and descriptions—some appallingly bad, some exquisite in their simplicity.

Lance was now surrounded—but discreetly—by the directors who introduced to him just those people whom they felt he should and would care to know. Once, and almost with a sense of shock, his gaze met and held Arden's and the next second he was beside her.

"Now I can evaporate for a bit," he said boyishly. "You *have* a drink. . . ." He raised his glass. "Here's to us, Arden. You'll never know what a difference you've made to all this."

She smiled a wise little smile, and inclined her head to acknowledge the compliment without giving it undue importance.

"You don't believe me—do you?" His voice dropped.

"Wouldn't you find it rather difficult—in my place?"

It was then that a man reached Arden's side, and hesitated as he saw Lance.

She said swiftly, "Brian!" Then, hastily: "May I introduce Brian Newton . . . Lance Ashton."

Brian said courteously, "I have had the pleasure of meeting Mr. Ashton before."

Lance looked puzzled and then:

"Of *course*! Sunningdale. The Taylors' party. You were the chap they flung in the swimming pool with all your clothes on!"

Brian laughed.

"I was."

Arden smiled.

The editor of a Sunday newspaper came up and spoke to Lance. Arden and Brian moved away.

Arden's heart was racing, but not through emotion, as it affected Brian. All the grimness of the past, its suffering, rushed back at her like a snarling animal intent upon her destruction.

"I've wanted to see you," he murmured tensely. "I kept away because I felt you would prefer it."

Brian Newton was a man of medium height, slight of build, whose manner was pleasing and friendly. He was the type whom most women regarded with great and brotherly affection; the man who made the perfect friend. He had dark, sympathetic eyes, full of consideration and a gentleness which was often taken for weakness—erroneously. His face was tanned and had an out-door glow about it, testimony of his love of sport of all kind.

"It was the only way, Brian—in the circumstances." She felt awkward and uneasy. Derek would, she felt, hate this meeting.

"I'm still in love with you, Arden," he said sombrely. "I've done every damn thing to cure the malady, but it is as stubborn as I suppose I am." His smile was appealing and without self-pity. "I'd be lost without it now, I guess."

"Oh, Brian!" There was consternation and concern in her voice. "Surely——" She stopped. How futile and adolescent to give advice beyond one's own power to take.

"Surely—what?"

"Nothing. Emotion is about the most cussed thing on earth."

"And—you?" He eyed her carefully. "You've never looked more beautiful, younger or more radiant." His voice cracked as he spoke and she noticed that the hand which held his glass shook. He hurried on: "Have dinner with me. . . . Listen, my dear——"

"I can't." She gave a little half-regretful sound. "I've already arranged to have it with Mr. Ashton."

"You know him well? Of *course*! You're almost neighbours."

"That is true, but I got to know him simply through doing a sketch for the book jacket of his next novel. Very menial and prosaic."

"Not when it involved his meeting you," came the swift retort. Then: "Do you ever hear anything of Derek?"

Arden knew that she could not dissemble. This man who had been dragged through the divorce court for her sake, deserved the truth. She said, quietly, "Yes, Brian. As a matter of fact he came back into my life a little while ago."

"*What!*" Disbelief and horror showed in his expression. "But—why? It doesn't make sense. After all that happened."

Arden explained Derek's attitude, ending with, "We all make mistakes and jealousy can——"

"Jealousy! It didn't stop there. . . . So now he believes we were innocent. That's very decent of him." There was bitterness and cynicism in his tone.

"You have every right to feel like that," she conceded. "But since you find emotion so difficult to overcome, why should it be so strange that Derek, also—to say nothing of me—shares the folly, if you like to call it that?"

Brian looked at her very levelly.

"If I believed that he loved you as deeply as I, you wouldn't find me arguing with you over that statement, my dear."

"He's changed, Brian. Things will be quite different."

He shook his head.

"That means you are thinking of remarrying him."

"Yes," said Arden sombrely.

Brian looked distraught.

"I just cannot grasp it," he said. "After all you went through." He made a helpless gesture. "I just don't understand women," he finished almost savagely.

"I doubt if we understand ourselves," she admitted. "Oh, I appreciate how it must look to you, but if you care for someone you are ready to forgive them. It is as simple as that, really."

A dogged look came into Brian's face.

"But if you're wise you don't stick your neck out to be hurt again," he said fiercely.

"I've never had cause to doubt Derek," she countered, a trifle hotly.

"Perhaps not. But he's no good, Arden. Sorry; nothing will ever change my opinion of him."

Arden paled.

"You have justification for prejudice," she said with dignity, "but no right to go beyond the matter of the divorce. You don't know Derek and——"

"I know him far, far better than you, my dear. Mine is a man's judgment."

"Coloured entirely by the fact that he wronged us both in his accusations. I do not minimize that."

Brian gulped his drink.

"It all goes much deeper," he said hoarsely. He looked at her closely. "And if, as you say, Derek believes in our innocence, I suggest you tell him of this meeting and say that I'd like very much to take up the threads of our old friendship." He looked at her very steadily. "If he *is* going to make you happy then I'd be more than ready to revise my opinion."

Arden's heart was thumping, her body shaking. She tried to find the right words and failed.

Brian challenged her, "You're afraid. He wouldn't stand the test—would he? He deals in words—not actions."

Instantly, she countered: "On the contrary. I will most certainly tell him what you say. And if he is ready to shut the door on yesterday—as you are—will *that* convince you?"

Brian said with reserve: "It would go a long way." He

78

paused before adding: "And if he refuses, Arden, for pity's sake think twice before you remarry him."

Arden's head went up a trifle proudly.

"I'm not afraid he will refuse—not in the least afraid."

He said gently, "Your loyalty does you credit . . . he's a lucky man. By heaven he is."

Arden relaxed.

"Oh, Brian!"

"I know, my dear. You're so *fond* of me. I'm the brother you would have liked." His smile was wry.

She didn't laugh and they lapsed into silence which he broke by saying jerkily, "Does he know how I feel about you?"

"Yes; when he came back and I explained the facts——"

"As you'd explained them so many times before," Brian put in harshly.

"True. . . . But he challenged me about your feelings."

"I'm glad you told him the truth."

At that point a woman looking very much like a grasshopper alighted at Arden's side.

"Miss Marchly! You know me: I'm Theo Martin . . . you did a simply wonderful jacket for my last book. I'm simply thrilled with it. . . . Ah, Mr. Newton. . . . A wonderful party. Wonderful party. Who is that glamorous woman over there? I've been watching her. I know her face from the newspapers. . . . Oh, Rita Morton. She's *clever*, too. Wish I were. Mine's drivel, of course. Absolute drivel, but if people like it . . . well, I say, give it them. Have to live. You're looking very charming as usual. You've not been to see me yet. Naughty of you. My cottage is looking beautiful just now. Even allowing for this perfectly filthy weather. Filthy. Ah . . . Miss Gordon——" She whisked herself away, beaming as she went.

Arden smiled, without ridicule.

"She's really a dear."

"I hope she doesn't write as she talks."

"She does—mostly."

Brian sighed.

"This gathering is certainly a matter of infinite variety. How do you get on with Ashton?"

"Very well." She glanced across to where Lance was surrounded with women. "He's certainly popular."

"And certainly our most tractable author. And if he hasn't

79

a swollen head now the chances are he never will have. That in itself is refreshing. He's made a packet."

"Even allowing for the Inland Revenue. I like the book I've just read better than his others," Arden said honestly.

Brian nodded.

"His stuff will live," he said. "That's the test."

An elongated young man, immaculate and soulful, saun-tered up to them, his legs moving as though they were hanging from his hip sockets by means of string. His accent was nauseatingly exaggerated Oxford.

"Gorton Main," Brian whispered and groaned. "He's angling for Ashton for Television. Very precious type."

"Hello there," said Gorton Main and looked at Arden. "We've met before. . . . At another crush somewhere. . . . Newton, old man, I want to get in touch with Lance Ashton and persuade him to give a talk . . . he isn't keen." There was a pained note in the voice.

Brian laughed.

"I think Ashton can get along very nicely even without Television," he said lightly.

"I know . . . bit of a bind, that. Well, do what you can." He grinned at Arden, grabbed a drink from a tray at his elbow, and made his way through to a famous actress who was giving a most excellent performance in the art of being natural without even knowing the meaning of the word.

Arden smiled at Brian. Words were unnecessary. They both knew that where celebrities were concerned ignorance was bliss.

"I must go over and have a word with old Nutford," Brian said regretfully. "He's the up-and-coming columnist on the *Century*." His gaze met Arden's pleadingly. "Get in touch with me."

"I will. Derek will," she added with defiance.

Brian didn't smile as he said, "He owes me an apology, anyway."

Arden hardly saw Lance again and just before eight-thirty she slipped out into the forecourt of the hotel, breathing deeply and grateful for the sudden comparative silence and fresh air. A feeling of expectancy and anticipation possessed her. She was prepared to dine alone at Fleur d'Argent for, although she gave Lance credit for being sincere when he extended the invitation, she was aware of the many demands he would have upon his time. It seemed suddenly rather ridiculous that he should bother with her.

The restaurant was exclusive and had a continental air. Candles flickered invitingly on tables gleaming white and gay with flowers. It was small and intimate and tiny alcoves concealed many diners from prying eyes should they wish for particular privacy. A beaming proprietor bustled to greet her and when she explained that she was meeting a friend who might be late, showed her to a corner which gave a view of the entrance, while explaining that when her friend arrived she could move.

Lance joined her exactly fifteen minutes later, very apologetic.

Arden stared at him.

"But I didn't expect you for at least half-an-hour."

His gaze held hers in the candlelight.

"And you had resigned yourself to the possibility of my not appearing at all."

She laughed.

"Well, you might so easily have been caught up in some invitation or other."

"I might; but I am not in the habit of asking a woman to dine with me and then not turning up. Or is that kind of behaviour consistent with your views of writers?"

"No; not at all." She looked at him. "I'm sorry. Perhaps I find it surprising that you want to escape from all the admirers."

He sat down opposite her.

"Meaning that you are not one of them evidently," he mocked.

"You make me say all the wrong things," she apologized, confused.

"I don't mind what you say. I like listening to you," he exclaimed stoutly. "It was a good party, wasn't it? Everything went off well, I thought. This is the best part of it. To relax!"

In that moment the proprietor recognized him and came forward, his voice raised and excited. "But M'sieur Ashton . . . I not know you come . . . Madam she not say. . . . Now what I get you?"

Lance looked inquiringly at Arden who said, "I leave it to

81

you. The luxury of having a meal chosen for one can be a delight."

"Very well then. . . . *Foie gras* . . . pheasant . . . and a bottle of my special Burgundy. . . ."

"This," said Arden, when Lance and the waiter had finished their discussion of the wine, "is an intriguing place. I love it, although it is a long while since I was here."

"You look bewitching," he said as though he had not heard her.

"Candlelight is very deceptive," she warned him. "And very kind."

Just then she felt completely detached from her normal life, almost as though she had been wafted into some unreal but enchanting world where personalities ceased to be important.

"I have also seen you in the cruel light of day," he murmured. "You are not in a hurry? I hate having to watch a clock and I'd like to monopolize you for the rest of the evening."

Arden responded to his mood.

"No; my time is my own."

"You're an enigma, Arden." His words startled her.

"I?" She ridiculed the idea.

"You tell me everything and nothing."

She forced a little laugh.

"Is that so surprising since this is only our third meeting?"

"Do you measure relationships in time?" he asked significantly.

"No, but——"

He said softly, "Don't worry; I won't probe. I've no right, of course, and it isn't mere curiosity. Just interest."

"Copy?" Her voice was low and teasing.

"No," he retorted sharply. "I do not use my friends."

The reflection of the candles flickered over their faces; and a sudden silence fell, in which there was a mounting tension, a sharp, inescapable surging of emotion as though they and their surroundings had become one.

She managed to say, "You make friends rather easily?"

"On the contrary. I never use the word without permanence. . . . Or is that presumptuous in your case?"

She was trembling with a suppressed excitement, aware of the magnetism of his presence and ready to admit that it was an occasion of fantasy rather than sober reality. Also that the intoxication of it had little to do with alcohol.

"Anything but that," she whispered. "I'm going to be naïve and say frankly that you are still rather on a pedestal. The celebrity I've honoured from afar. I can't be *blasé*. Perhaps having loved your books so much; found them such feasts, Lance——" She stopped. "Yes, even using your christian name has a significance."

He looked at her lingeringly and with tenderness.

"You make success very rewarding. It hasn't been before." He added, rather bitterly, "Everything must be shared to be appreciated. No one is wholly self-contained."

"But," she protested, "all your friends—they must have been thrilled and——"

"True," he interrupted swiftly; "but even that can be impersonal. This isn't."

She lowered her gaze.

"It isn't real, either, you know. . . . A moment held in the glow of a rather enchanted evening. Transient."

"That has to be proved," he said quietly. "Even what seems to be truth can, on occasion, be false."

"We are," she reminded him, "always earnest and sincere at the time, so ready to plunge into new dangers, so convinced that the last experience—should it have been disastrous—will not be repeated."

"That sounds as though you understood disastrous experiences," he prompted gravely.

"Has anyone escaped them—when it comes to it?"

"The skeleton in every cupboard." He looked at her unsmilingly. "Janet delights in clinging to that belief."

Arden trembled.

"And in dragging those skeletons from their cupboards?"

"Quite possibly." He added loyally, "I should have been lost without her."

"I'm sure she revels in her job. What could be nicer?"

"Thank you, although I'm quite certain you were unconscious of paying me a compliment."

"I refuse to pander to your vanity by enlarging on the remark," she countered banteringly.

They laughed together with a light-hearted and almost absurd abandon, enjoying every moment and savouring it as

83

they savoured the mellow wine that was like velvet to the palate.

When the meal was almost over and the restaurant in process of shutting, Lance said regretfully, "Now I must see you home."

Impulsively, without conscious thought, she cried, "I make excellent coffee."

He held her gaze.

"I hoped you might," he commented smoothly.

Once in his car Arden was swirled back to reality. She ought not to have invited him back to the flat. It was quite unnecessary and might easily be misconstrued. In addition, Derek might not like it. Yet, was there any reason why she should not obey a whim? The night was young and anything less would have seemed an anti-climax.

"You're very earnest about something, Arden. It couldn't be that you'd prefer I didn't have that coffee, could it?" He flashed her a swift glance. "You can retract the invitation without any hard feelings."

Arden laughed.

"It wouldn't be very easy to hide one's feelings from you. The author's uncanny k: : of reading thoughts."

He braked to avoid a bus as he said, "If so, such a knack is very elementary. Yours were noisy!" He glanced at the road ahead.

"Turn left," she prompted. "And it is the block on the right." A pause. "You can run the car into the square by the main entrance."

He smiled and did as he was told.

Arden's flat was small but attractive, with a circular entrance hall from which three rooms radiated. It was both light and lacking in any suggestion of stuffiness, with large windows giving an extensive view of London which included a great deal of green for which Arden had been thankful. She had come to it after her divorce, in a state of bewildered misery and loneliness, uncertain of the future and completely indifferent to her fate. And out of that wreckage she had made a home that had given her sanctuary so that her love for it—despite her preference for Meadow View—was deep-rooted and satisfying.

"You," she said as they stepped into the hall, "will hate flats."

"Wrong again." He took in his surroundings, liking the white walls and apple-green decorations with here and there a touch of petunia, by way of lamp-shades, cushions and the little ornaments that seemed to blend into the general scheme. "And this is charming. No, I like to be right in London or right in the country. Never did care for compromises or half-measures." He nodded approvingly at the pictures. A few good prints adorned the walls and over the mantelpiece an oil painting—a Dutch Interior—gave sudden life and artistry to the scene.

"Nicholas Maas," he said, studying the picture with interest.

"My most treasured possession," she admitted. "I adore paintings, but they have to be good. If it is snobbism to like the best in everything then I'm an unadulterated snob!"

"Which makes two of us."

She looked at him, suddenly moved by the realization of just who he was, not because he was a celebrity, but because he was a man capable of writing magnificent books. A man whose simplicity and unaffected charm had already made an indelible impression upon her. His presence brought some strange impressive note into the flat and she knew that his personality would linger long after he had gone.

"And now that coffee," she said, wanting to avoid a too personal note being introduced.

"Ah! Am I allowed in the kitchen?"

"If you wish. I can't imagine it can hold any great attraction," she added blithely as she preceded him into the hall and so to the kitchen.

"Then you must be singularly blind," he remarked. "But you are not looking through my glasses—are you. . . . This is a perfect modern paradise for a woman!"

"Everything to hand," she said. "Plenty of cupboards, all built in. I can stand in one spot and reach for most things I need and be at the sink and gas stove at the same time!"

"The woman is practical, too!"

"Not by nature—only through necessity. I loathe domesticity, but I loathe the woman who makes a song and dance about it even more."

"Splendid. So do I and I've always noticed that the ones who moan the most actually do the least. They only *think* they get away with it!"

In a short while they sat together drinking the coffee which Arden had made. The London traffic had died down and a silence settled over the flat. Softly shaded lights from artistically placed desk lamps illuminated the room, creating an atmosphere that inspired confidences. They were two people who had shared an experience, joying in the relaxation that followed it.

Arden lay back against the cushions, her slim legs stretched on a footstool. Lance took up most of the settee, looking completely at home. The clock struck midnight, but neither noticed it.

"May I ask if you're writing a new book now?" Arden set down her cup and waited.

"I'd begun one; but I've scrapped it." He looked at her intently. "It was empty—quite empty."

"Can you be absolutely certain of that?"

"Meaning that the writer is seldom the best judge of his or her own work?"

"It has been proved many times, hasn't it?"

"Yes. This is different. I've written and drawn on what I've felt. . . . The past tense is not good enough and stale to me. The writer mustn't be bored—that's fatal."

Arden appreciated that and said so.

"You weren't in *Full Circle*. It breathed life and colour and the richness of all you'd seen. Your characters; they're so perfect, drawn with almost a Dickensian perception. I know them, love and remember them. How do you feel when you're writing?"

He grinned, almost shyly.

"I disappear," he said honestly, "one is not really conscious of writing, only of thinking and feeling. Words tumble out. At least I find it works that way. And when they cease to do so . . . I stop. I can't labour it. I can polish, but no more than that. But what of you, Arden? Haven't you anything—any of your work—here to show me?"

"I wouldn't bore you," she said stoutly.

"I shouldn't ask if I thought you would," he retorted. "I'm serious. Wasted talent is a crime."

"I've never seen myself as having any talent. I think I told you that before. So many people want to paint, think they can and cannot. And I fall so far below any standard I can set myself. Therefore, like you, I don't compromise: I go in for the commercial stuff. It pays," she added with a touch of cynicism.

"You think beyond that," he murmured, his gaze deepening.

She capitulated.

"Yes; but it doesn't do to dream, or to live in one's imagination, Lance."

"One might ask where reality ends and dreams begin. You cannot imprison the soul of man and curiously enough very little has ever come out of a mind crammed only with facts."

His words died away into silence and Arden knew that she could have gone on listening to him for hours. His voice was deep and yet vital; a voice one could hear distinctly in the imagination, long after he had stopped speaking. His manner was easy and devoid of all arrogant assertiveness while ringing with the strength of his convictions. Arden asked herself just what kind of a woman his wife could have been to prefer another man in his place and came back to the incredible and unpredictable qualities dominating human emotions. What was that spark which suddenly leapt between two people? Was it of heart, mind or body, or all three? She thought of Derek. After all the past misery she had gone back. . . .

Lance's words were not lost on her and she said quietly, "A spiritual force against a material one, perhaps." Her expression hardened almost without her realizing it. "I detest a mind absorbed entirely by money—there's something utterly sordid about it and the meanness it inevitably breeds. I prefer improvidence to that," she added fiercely.

Lance watched her closely. Her face was vital and expressive. Her eyes flashed as she spoke, mirroring her thoughts and, at times, defiantly challenging, rather as though she were waging a private war.

"Against what—or whom—are you fighting, Arden?"

His words came slowly and deliberately; they fell between them like threads tightening to bind them together.

"I don't know what you mean," she replied feebly.

"You do." He got to his feet and looked down at her. "But I won't pursue the subject. . . . Now I must be going," he said reluctantly. "Thank you for all this."

"I've enjoyed it enormously."

"We must see a show," he said easily and as though their

relationship were already accepted. "That is," he hastened, "if you wish."

She didn't know just what to say. From his point of view she was neither married nor engaged, therefore he was not prepared to give Derek undue priority or consideration.

"It would be nice," she murmured, hating the banality.

He held her gaze masterfully. "I did not mean some vague appointment in the far distant future. I'll 'phone you."

They walked out into the hall side by side and in silence. At the door he turned. Eyes met eyes in strange emotional betrayal. Arden struggled against the sensation that crept upon her almost as though, for a second, he had mesmerized her. Slowly he lowered his lips to hers, at first touching her gently, lightly and then as passion mounted, kissing her with a violent hunger, and feeling her response. She backed away, startled and shocked at her vulnerability. Words failed her. The impulse had been mutual and she could not hide behind outraged dignity.

"Good-night, Arden," he said softly and before she had time to speak, had opened the door and disappeared down the long corridor to the lifts.

She stood, shaking, where he had left her. The scene had been out of character and she drew on cynicism to still the heavy beating of her heart. Obviously, Lance thought no more of kissing a woman than of talking to her. It was part of his technique and a fitting end to a somewhat fantastic evening.

The thought of Derek came back soberingly and reassuringly. And she decided that while it had been exciting and even a novelty to meet Lance Ashton, she would avoid him in future. Nothing must be allowed to cut across the deep satisfaction of her reunion with Derek. And the Lance Ashtons of the world were dangerous, without being in the least rewarding.

Thus having explained him away to her own satisfaction she hummed blithely to herself as she prepared for bed.

CHAPTER VIII

AUGUST slid in an unseasonal cold and rainy spell into September. Autumn crept stealthily upon the countryside, mists gathered in the valleys and frosts painted hedges and trees in premature mosaics. Heavy dew glistened like powdered diamonds upon sodden lawns.

Arden stayed more often at the flat, for it was easier for Derek to visit her there than to make the journey to Meadow View.

It was one Saturday morning when they were sitting lazily together over breakfast that she glanced up from the newspaper she was reading and said: "So Rachel and her mother are on their way home from Barbados. It recalls the tragic death of her husband." She handed Derek the newspaper which he scanned idly.

"I understood they were to be away until the spring."

Arden looked reflective.

"There was just something *about* Rachel."

"What do you mean?"

"I never knew whether she liked me or not. She professed to be a friend, but that friendship didn't stand the test very well. I wonder what her attitude will be when she discovers we're together again."

Derek put aside the paper and lit a cigarette.

"I don't see that there is a question of any attitude."

Arden smiled.

"You remained friends—didn't you? Fair enough; she was on your side—if one can use the objectionable term." Her gaze was steady. "In fact, quite honestly, I thought that you and she might have married."

Derek laughed.

"My dear woman, Rachel wouldn't have looked at me. I'd no money—in the sense that she desired it when she married."

"That need not answer my question. Suppose you had been very wealthy?"

Derek leaned forward and took Arden's hand.

"Doesn't my being here answer your question? And the fact that Rachel was widowed before I returned?"

"Of course." Arden's smile was warm and confident.

He asked abruptly, "Is Brian coming down to the cottage over the week-end?"

Arden looked surprised.

"No—why?"

"I just wondered." He spoke reflectively. "Queer chap. If

anyone had told me I'd have accepted him back into the circle! Amazing how the whole picture of life can change."

Derek had been honest and generous towards Brian. Honest in his apology for the past; generous when he was prepared to take him on trust knowing that he was in love with Arden.

"These have been wonderful months," she said softly.

He looked at her earnestly. "I wonder just how real they have been, my darling."

Her heart missed a beat.

"What do you mean? Real?"

"Perhaps I'm afraid of romantic illusion. We've escaped the routine of marriage after all. This is an easy pattern for living."

"No pattern is easy unless two people are in harmony," she replied sagely.

"True . . . by the way, darling, I've to go to Rome in a few days' time."

"Another account?" Arden smiled. "Want me to come with you?"

He didn't hesitate.

"No, my sweet. I've Italy lined up when I've a right to travel with you—as your husband."

Something in his tone arrested her attention; something in no way linked with the substance of his words. She said urgently, "Is anything—wrong, Derek?"

He struck his lighter to a second cigarette, having stubbed the previous one out before it was half smoked.

"Nothing. Why should there be?"

Arden hesitated.

"I don't really know."

"Fanciful darling. . . . How about getting ready, or we shan't get to the cottage until it is time to come back."

"Derek?"

"Yes."

"What have you in mind for the future? I mean——"

"You mean when you decide to marry me?" His tone had an edge to it. "This hasn't been easy for me, Arden. Suppose you make up your mind while I'm away."

Arden started.

"It hasn't been just a question of making up my mind," she insisted. "Oh, *Derek*, it was being sure—for both our sakes."

Her gaze was pleading and anxious. "I felt that you understood."

"I have done . . . perhaps I love you more deeply than you love me. I don't like this no-man's-land relationship."

She asked without knowing why, "Has Rachel's return anything to do with it?"

His smile was slow and significant.

"Is it your turn to be jealous now? What on earth put such an idea into your head?"

Arden shrugged her shoulders.

"I don't honestly know." She looked at him steadily, but it was as though a blind had suddenly been drawn between them.

He moved to the door. She followed him, her eyes wide and faintly troubled. He reached out and drew her close to him.

"On second thoughts I believe you do love me," he said teasingly and held her with a sudden rough passion. Then, "Damn," he said explosively, as the telephone rang.

Arden answered it.

"Lance . . ."

Derek sauntered back and stood beside her.

"Thursday evening?" A pause. "The Haymarket." Her eyes flashed Derek a rather appealing glance. He nodded and whispered: "I'll be in Rome."

She accepted the invitation and agreed that he should 'phone here on Wednesday evening for the final arrangements. The call seemed an anti-climax as she turned back to Derek.

"He's certainly persistent," came the laconic retort. "Is he in love with you?"

Arden laughed in ridicule.

"Lance! That's the last thing."

"Why? He's done nothing but invite you out ever since you met him."

"And I've mostly refused to go—which could be why he is persistent." She sighed and then remembered. It wasn't easy to dismiss Lance and pretend utter indifference.

"True. I must say you've handled him very well, my sweet. I'm just waiting for my turn. He'll be surprised."

Arden's face clouded.

Derek said meaningly, "There is a price for everything—even freedom. Ah well, I must find myself a glamorous Italian."

Arden said solemnly, "Don't forget that you have imposed

the secrecy about our relationship, Derek. It isn't easy to snub people without giving a reason."

He nodded in understanding.

"I know, darling. I was only joking. Besides, I've had to prove to you that the old tyrant jealousy has gone. And that I trust you implicitly. I'll envy him on Thursday, but you'll go with my blessing."

She said with sudden fierceness: "Why not let me come with you?"

"Only because it wouldn't do—not on a business trip of this kind. And I was serious in what I said just now."

She reached out and their hands met. She knew that her final decision would have to be made long before the stipulated six months were up, just as she knew, in all fairness to Derek, that she approved of his impatience.

The week-end took to itself an importance which highlighted every simple pleasure. Never had Derek been more attentive, more lover-like or more tender. It was as though, wordlessly, he were pleading his cause, leaving no possible doubt in her mind of the passionate intensity of his love for her and his need of her, while making it abundantly clear that for her finally to reject him would deal him a mortal blow.

And it was in this mood they parted on that following Wednesday morning before he left for Rome. A morning which Arden was destined never to forget.

CHAPTER IX

THE calm detachment in which there was, nevertheless, a degree of pleasurable anticipation, deserted Arden the moment he stepped into the hall of her flat on that Thursday evening. It was impossible to eliminate the emotional impact of his presence, or to deaden the feelings awakened the moment she heard his voice. Every meeting was an adventure, enriched by his knowledge and ability to impart it with a casual charm in conversation. It wasn't a question of comparing him with Derek—such comparisons always being highly dangerous—but of accepting the fact that, mentally, he was the type of man able to hold her interest. It had nothing to do with love in the accepted sense, but everything to do with a curious mental affinity.

In turn Lance studied Arden after having adm᷑ her exquisite gown of delphinium blue ninon that swat her figure, and left one shoulder bare to gleam under the light like alabaster, and all his good intentions, his philosophical arguments upon the folly of emotion, vanished before one glance from her dark, passionate eyes. He retreated from the banality that she was different from any other woman he had ever met while yet knowing it to be so. And .at difference had its inception in her interest in life generally, her catholic tastes, her fundamental naturalness and her ability wholly to reject any coy femininity without loss of charm.

She said in greeting, "I wondered if it was your intention to get a taxi. If so, I can ring down to the porter."

They looked at each other, and, for a reason neither could have explained, refrained from shaking hands. A swift tide of understanding removed the necessity for conventional observations.

"I had thought of that," he admitted. "I didn't want Baker with me and I detest having to park the car and walk miles to the theatre. If you could ring down."

Arden did so. They looked at each other as she replaced the receiver and he said with directness, "This is an achievement on my part. I wondered if you were ever coming out with me again."

Arden averted her gaze.

"I've been rather busy."

They had met twice since the night of the cocktail party and each time in Derek's company.

"Is that meant to be an explanation?"

"Naturally." She flashed him a smile. "Don't you believe me?"

"I believe in the statement of fact, but not in relation to the excuse."

"Then it would be foolish of me to argue," she retorted gaily.

The spark of a mutual interest sharpened on the edge of friendship.

"And I am no nearer the truth," he suggested quietly.

She flashed him a swift smile.

93

"But you are here, which should prove something. . . . We'd better go down; by the time we get there, a taxi will be waiting."

He helped her into her shimmering brocaded coat and she felt acutely conscious of his nearness without in any way being able to interpret the emotion into desire or physical contact. The same strange excitement possessed her as she began to walk beside him, as had characterized her reactions from the moment of their first meeting. Thoughts tumbled in conflict through her mind. Derek, the future . . .

The taxi awaited them at the entrance and in a short while, by virtue of a labyrinth of side streets, they reached the theatre. It was already dusk and lights danced against the smoky autumnal background which nevertheless held an enchantment of a gaiety beginning a trifle breathlessly after the prosaic routine of the day. Streets were thronged as an audience milled around the foyer, the buzz of voices came at them as they stepped inside and then went into the stalls to their seats.

A critic hailed Lance as he stood, a distinguished figure in the aisle. He chatted for a moment and then escaped. Arden had completely forgotten the writer in her concentration on the man.

"I believe this is pretty realistic and sordid in parts," he commented as he handed her a programme.

"Which is far better than being wholly untrue to life," she said briskly. "I do like to be given credit for a little intelligence."

It was, however, a gripping, dramatic play, exquisitely acted, and they sat through it enthralled, tension mounting as it swept to its tragic climax, leaving the house hushed for that breathless second before applause broke like thunder.

Arden dashed a hand across her eyes and felt Lance's gaze upon her without being embarrassed for she knew that, in his turn, he was no less moved than she.

They left the theatre in silence, almost as though comment at that point would be sacrilege. Lance had already made arrangements with the commissionaire for a taxi and in a matter of seconds they were on their way to the Savoy where he was staying.

"I felt," Lance explained, "we might renew memories of a previous occasion."

Arden flashed him a gay smile.

"Never go back—one can seldom, if ever, recapture yesterday . . . the play was magnificent, wasn't it? The tension at the end almost unbearable."

"Yes," he agreed, "a fine piece of work on the part of both author and actress—for it was certainly Morna Gray's play. She dominated it."

"An enchanting personality," Arden said warmly.

He looked at her.

"She reminded me of you." As he spoke there was a note in his voice that warned her not to ridicule the remark even though she might not agree with him.

To his surprise, Arden commented reflectively, "It is strange how individuals remind us of each other and how varied our respective ideas are of the same person. Attraction, liking, are the most fascinating mysteries."

The street lights, the neon signs, the floodlit buildings which turned night into day, poured their reflection into the taxi so that, for a second, Arden's face was illuminated. And in that second Lance knew that he was in love with her, and that she represented everything he had ever hoped to find in a woman. The realization was without shock, for it was rather an acceptance of a truth instead of a discovery. From the moment of their first meeting, he had *known*, while flatly refusing to acknowledge the swift and shattering impact of her personality upon him.

Their eyes met and her gaze fell abruptly and he said almost tersely, "Would you mind if we changed our plans and went to the Fleur d'Argent? It would be quieter and I don't want to run into people I know, or be dragged into some party or other."

She smiled.

"By all means. I love that cosy, intimate little place."

"Have you," he asked, "been there lately?"

"Not since I was with you," she answered and the words seemed to have an undue significance. Faint uneasiness stirred within her which touched the fringe of nervousness. The thought of Derek obtruded, reminding her of problems that no longer could be avoided. She knew that the time of freedom without decision was over, just as she accepted the truth that she was loth to take any final, or irrevocable, step.

95

Conversation was fitful during supper. A barrier seemed to have sprung up between her and Lance which she was at a loss to understand and it disturbed her. Above all she prized the harmony and companionship of what had come to be friendship. She remembered suddenly his kiss and swiftly dismissed the recollection. He said abruptly, "I want to talk to you, Arden."

"Talk to me!" Her eyes widened and she made a little, wry face. "Are we not——"

"No," he said firmly, "this exchange of pleasantries isn't what I mean." His gaze held hers. "Are you in a mood to make coffee?" he asked, forcing a lighter note.

She hesitated, then influenced by the seriousness of his expression, she said, "Of course. Come back to the flat with me. We can talk there." She looked anxious. "Is anything wrong, Lance?"

"That," he answered enigmatically, "rather depends."

He paid the bill, guided her out of the restaurant and hailed a taxi. In a matter of minutes they were at the flat and as they went into the lounge and Arden slipped out of her evening coat, an almost unbearable tension mounted between them. Their eyes met, the distance between them suddenly annihilated by a look which set Arden's heart thumping madly and started within her a sharp, inexplicable fear.

Lance's voice was low, and throbbed into the electric silence.

"I'm in love with you, Arden."

She stared at him, speechless and bewildered, emotion impossible to describe washing over her.

"But, Lance . . . I——"

"Is it so difficult for you to believe?" he asked hoarsely. "Surely you must have sensed my feelings."

"No." It was as though she were fighting through a dozen conflicting possibilities. "I appreciated your—your friendship——"

"Friendship." He smiled wryly. "There isn't such a thing between a man and a woman. In the end one, or both, desire more." He went on urgently: "I'm asking you to marry me and——" he added deprecatingly, "making an extremely poor job of it." He moved to her side, looking down into her troubled eyes, whispering her name as a caress.

Instinctively, she backed away. This was the last complication she had envisaged, or wanted. What, she asked herself then, were her feelings for this man? At first she had been flattered, then interested and out of that had grown something approximating an exciting regard. It was impossible to bring any prosaic element into a relationship with a personality as vital and arresting as his. So she had accepted, without self-deception, the fact that their friendship was lifted out of the normal rut by an incomprehensible affinity having nothing whatsoever, she argued, to do with being in love. The thought of Derek came swiftly and relentlessly. This was not the time for new loves, but for the consolidation of an old one. It was with Derek her future lay. . . . She could not accept failure for the second time and dismiss him from her life. They loved each other and anything, any emotion, that cut across that love could be merely transient and deceptive. She met Lance's dark, appealing gaze and a tremor went over her, because she was not indifferent to his proposal and she accepted it as wholly sincere.

"I'm so *sorry*, Lance . . . I can't marry you."

Instantly he was alert.

"And—love?"

"I am not in love with you," she said quietly.

A longing came to her to tell him all the facts, to explain in detail her position, but her promise to Derek held.

His hands gripped her shoulders, his gaze seemed to draw her magnetically to him.

"Are you sure?" he demanded masterfully.

She stood there in the calm of a decision which brought freedom from swift, inexplicable desires.

"Yes," she answered firmly. "Quite sure."

His hands dropped from her.

"Derek Rayne," he said thickly. Then: "Are you going to marry him?"

She hated the deception more than ever as she said, "Yes, Lance; I'm going to marry him."

He studied her intently.

"There's just something about it all that I cannot quite grasp. You and he——" He sighed. "I'm probably being fanciful, indulging in wishful thinking. You're so entirely different in every way from him."

She challenged him.

"In that case it is a question of opposites harmonizing."

"And if he were not in the picture?" Lance watched her carefully.

She smiled faintly.

"I'm sure you know that is an impossible question. He is in the picture," she insisted. She added: "I promised to give him my answer on his return from Rome next week." That, she thought with a little, depressing distaste for her position, was true.

Lance startled her by saying, "Are you being absolutely honest with me, Arden?"

She paled.

"Why do you ask? What is there to be—be dishonest about? You——"

He interrupted her.

"Something in your manner. It has always been there. I cannot quite describe it except by the word guarded. . . . Listen, if there is anything—anything at *all*——"

"There isn't anything that could possibly have any bearing upon my decision so far as you are concerned, Lance."

"Will you marry him—soon?"

"At once," she said, a little amazed by her own resolution. It was as if, as she stood there, she were a married woman rejecting a would-be lover; a woman bound by ties and obligations she could never ignore. She had been Derek's wife and, in her heart, was still his wife. Her loyalty was absolute, to a marriage in which she had believed and to which she had given everything that lay within her power to give. She saw the future as a vindication and a triumph; herself and Derek walking towards it in the fullness of understanding, their love strengthened by the suffering and separation. That there would be pitfalls, adjustments, she could accept with an adult sense of responsibility. Derek's honesty in returning to her, his steadfast devotion even in the face of what he had believed to be her infidelity, entitled him to her life-long devotion. It struck her, then, that even had she been in love with Lance, she doubted if she would have been able to discard Derek and thus smash all his hopes and dreams for the future. In that Martin had been right, and she was thankful that such a crisis, a choice, had not to be made.

98

Lance stood sideways, one elbow resting on the mantelpiece, hand supporting his chin, and looked at her very steadily and with passionate, seeking eyes.

"There is a part of you that no other man will ever possess, Arden. A part that belongs to me," he said with telling emphasis. "Some spark of affinity, some mental fusion."

She avoided his gaze and managed to say shakenly: "I should hate to lose your friendship. There are so many kinds of regard, Lance. You know that. Attraction, fondness, desire . . . but marriage is so different."

"Is it? Doesn't it demand all those emotions? Or are you trying to make it fit a conventional pattern?"

She didn't retreat as she said, "No; but a realistic one. There must be romance, but there must, also, be a solid foundation. Not merely a transient infatuation."

He countered, his voice compelling, "And has your regard for me been that?"

She sighed.

"I could not begin to analyse my regard for you," she answered honestly. "It has been based so much on my admiration of your ability, the way you think and write."

"Lance Ashton and not the man?"

"That could be very near the truth," she admitted frankly.

"I wonder."

"Please, Lance——"

He stepped away from the hearth and reached her side.

"I wish I could convince myself that I was hearing all the truth, Arden."

She spread her hands in a gesture of appeal.

"There is nothing more I can say."

His gaze held hers with a burning intensity and his passionate earnestness communicated itself to her in a sudden, overwhelming appeal. His power was great: she knew that, but rejected it with a fierce control.

"Then further words are useless," he said dully.

A sense of loss made her feel suddenly bereaved. She had valued his friendship and the possibility of being denied it in future seemed unendurable.

"Please——"

"I know," he said cynically, "you still want us to be friends. To continue a relationship in which neither of us could believe. And to which I am perfectly certain Derek Rayne would object." He added fairly: "Not without cause, since I feel as I do."

Arden became the escapist for one panic-striken moment. "Why—*why* has it to be like this?" She was like a child lamenting the loss of a favourite toy.

He gave her a swift, almost indulgent glance.

"Life makes its own terms, Arden. We accept them."

She looked at him, seeing him again as on the moment of their first meeting, trying to get accustomed to the somewhat fantastic idea that he was in love with her and had asked her to marry him.

"We have free will," she protested, and drawing a hand across her forehead, added: "I never dreamed of anything like this."

"Not when I kissed you?" His gaze was steady and disarming.

She didn't smile.

"No; I regarded that as a purely flirtatious technique."

"Not distasteful to you at least."

She was utterly honest as she replied: "I do not profess to be other than human."

"And—Derek?"

She knew what he meant and answered fearlessly, "I doubt very much if there is anyone in this world who, being in love with one person, cannot, on occasion, be a little stirred by another—even though he or she might never admit it." She added: "The tragedy, or folly, lies in building *up* a purely momentary emotion."

Her words died away into the silence. They were to be recalled by her in near anguish.

"I agree . . . I give in, Arden. Something tells me that this leaves me nothing I can fight. If you are in love with Derek and are going to marry him then, heaven knows, I do not want to complicate things."

She lowered her gaze.

"Oh, Lance," she said brokenly. "If you knew how it hurts me to hurt you." Her sigh was deep and regretful. "I like you so *much*."

"But not enough," he said briefly. "And I cannot be content with less than all, Arden, the way I'm made." He shrugged his shoulders. "I suppose one cannot expect to be lucky in everything. Evidently love is not for me."

She gazed at him wide-eyed.

"But that is absurd."

"Don't," he said sharply, "reduce this to banality by telling me that I shall soon forget, or find someone to replace you. I'm aware that there are thousands of women in the world and that among them I might find one who would possibly fall in love with me. God knows there are many loves—all different. And that one can give to each a great and deep emotion. For all that, there is in every life one outstanding person with whom one has so much more in common—mentally, spiritually, and physically—than the rest. You are that one so far as I am concerned. It is bad enough to *be* deceived: I never deceive myself."

She said unevenly, "I know."

"And Derek is that to you." He sighed. "So be it." His eyes were filled with a sudden tenderness. "You know that I want the very best for you, Arden, and that I wish you all the happiness in the world." He added fiercely: "And how I detest those trite words!"

The room became silent, the atmosphere changed. Gone was the excitement of glances provocative and challenging; of gaiety and pleasure. Now there was the deflated and depressing mood of love defeated, attraction cut off, friendship broken. Arden could not find sanctuary in her own happiness because she found herself within the shadow of his defeat. And while she had, before her marriage to Derek and afterwards, rejected several proposals, never had the task been so painful as now. For a few, brief months, she had basked in the delight of a companionship and friendship different from anything she had ever before known and infinitely more enriching than she had ever dreamed possible. Now she was faced with the knowledge that, in future, all that would be denied her. Realistically, she did not deceive herself that the mere fact of her love for Derek and her happiness in promise of their future together would, automatically, dismiss Lance from her mind. Equally, she accepted the truth that it would not be fair to Derek to continue the association even were Lance the type disposed to do so.

She said gently, "Words are always trite and inadequate

when one wants to say so much that is sincere." She looked at him fearlessly. "Even though our meetings have been few, I shall never forget them." Restraint and control vanished as she cried: "Oh, why did you have to fall in love with me?"

"Few women deplore being loved," he suggested.

"I do," she insisted earnestly. "I wanted your affection, your approval of me," she admitted. "That sounds childish, I suppose. If it does then I must *be* childish."

"Unrealistic, my darling. And I don't honestly think you imagined we could take this friendship much further."

She looked at him.

"No," she said, "I suppose that is right. But I didn't want to see, or to think. Just to be happy—as I was."

"And have you been so unhappy in the past?"

"At times—yes." She changed the trend of conversation to avoid any questioning on his part.

He lit a cigarette, trying to maintain some semblance of calm. He felt that he was battling against some wild, tempestuous sea, struggling to reach a shore which would prove a mirage.

And he burst out fiercely, "For all this I cannot convince myself that you are in love with Rayne."

She started nervously, the colour rising to her cheeks.

"Whatever makes you say that?"

"I couldn't explain if I tried," he admitted desperately. "You won't be happy with him: you just do not speak the same language."

It was dangerous ground for Arden could not reinforce her confession of love for Derek by a statement of the facts. She said quietly, "Isn't that simply wishful thinking? I assure you that you are wrong—absolutely wrong." Her voice rang with a conviction which was like a knife plunged in his heart.

He seemed to square his shoulders in that second like a man resolute in the acceptance of defeat. Only the burning intensity of his dark eyes, the grim set of his jaw, betrayed the emotion that was seething within him as he looked at Arden standing there, unutterably lovely in her solemn appeal.

"I suppose," he said hoarsely, "that is about the truth." He glanced at his watch. "Now I must go."

His words fell with a curious significance on the sudden deathly silence. She knew that he would not come back.

102

They went out into the hall and there he turned, saying tensely, "If anything should happen . . . if ever you should need me, I'm there, Arden. I shall not change."

She said, her voice cracked and unsteady, "You speak as though we were never going to meet again."

There was a purposeful expression in his eyes as he answered, "I should complicate your life and be at war with Rayne. We have not been in harmony in any case and I've a shrewd idea that he thinks as little of me as I of him. . . ."

Arden could not protest. For a second every instinct cried out for her to tell Lance of the divorce; she hated his going in ignorance of the facts; loathed the idea that he might hear some garbled version at a later date. But it was too late to begin explanations. Once she and Derek were remarried the past would have no meaning, in any case. The knowledge consoled her.

The door opened. The corridor yawned like a dark, ugly chasm. She cried, "I hate all this."

"I've been blind," he said almost curtly. "But I was foolish enough to hope—subconsciously—that your guarded attitude, your discretion in seeing me, might mean more than mere friendship. I refused even to admit that I was in love with you until to-night. Don't worry, or look so anxious. I value your concern for me, but it isn't concern I want," he finished roughly. "I shall hear about you," he hurried on with what might have seemed almost casualness, but which was a control designed to overcome the fierce desire that shook him, "and if you still feel inclined to——" He stopped helplessly. Then: "Will you go on with your work after you are married?"

Arden's voice was unsteady as she answered, "Not in the commercial sense. I want a real home and——" She floundered. Somehow she could not bring herself to say: "and children."

Lance said it for her.

"You want children?"

"Yes."

Lance's sigh was deep and envious.

"I hope he realizes how fortunate he is. My God, I do," he added almost savagely.

Arden was trembling.

"That cuts both ways," she said loyally.

Again their eyes met.

"Good-bye, Arden."

He stood there, the pain within him like a wound which could never be healed.

"Good-bye," she whispered.

He walked away and did not look back. A current of cool air came up at her like a wall as she stood there watching him, A second later his tall figure disappeared.

Slowly and quietly she shut the door and wandered into the lounge. The whole scene took to itself the unreality of fantasy. Could anyone have told her six months before that Lance Ashton would have asked her to marry him she would have considered them mad. Thoughts piled turbulently upon thoughts. Their friendship had been high-lighted by an excitement, a vitality which she had never before known in any other relationship. Yet, taking a completely subjective and selfish viewpoint, had it not enabled her swiftly and irrevocably to make up her mind about remarrying Derek, or had not that intention been a foregone conclusion? She was not quite sure. If only Derek were in England; if only she could rush to him at that moment and tell him how she felt.

A calm took the place of a former conflict. She and Derek would rebuild their marriage. These months had served a good purpose, warning her that there was no Elysium to be reached without effort and compromise. . . . Lance Ashton's wife. . . . Suppose Derek had not been in the picture. . . . Her heart quickened its beat, but she knew that, without loving him, she would still not have consented to be his wife, no matter how great her admiration and affection were for him.

Lance picked up his car and, completely forgetting his hotel booking, automatically turned it in the direction of The Manor. A hunter's moon turned night into day, lighting up the countryside so that it lay glistening like a diamond-dusted carpet in the distance as frost touched it with magic. The roads were glassy and two or three times he skidded, reacting automatically and bringing the four wheels back on an even keel. Arden and Derek Rayne. . . . An agony of hope defeated lay upon him like a sickness. Sentimentality, mawkishness, were abhorrent to him. The rejected lover nauseating. Life was, he told himself, damned queer. Of all the women he had met he had to fall in love with someone whose affections were elsewhere. Derek Rayne. He disliked the fellow intensely. Something sly and secretive about him. Attractive to women, no doubt. Was that sheer prejudice based on jealousy? He knew it wasn't. Rather was it a man's judgment. Wouldn't trust Rayne any further than he could see him. And unless he were very much mistaken he'd make Arden unhappy.

He reached The Manor and swung into its drive. It stood in a wide beam of moonlight, glistening, bluish-white. A world apart, inanimate, serene. Loneliness pierced him, sharp as a dagger; a sense of isolation, of complete and utter purpose-lessness. Writing, making money, achieving success. For what?

He ran the car into the garage, banged the doors and went around to the front of the house. His feet felt the crunchiness of frost on gravel—like icing sugar.

Opening the front door the warmth of the hall came at him in a wave, and in the silence he heard the tapping of the type-writer. It was almost as though some supernatural power had taken possession of his study. Half alarmed, he flung the door open. Then:

"Good Lord, Janet!"

She started.

"What on earth are you doing here at this unearthly hour?" he demanded. "Do you realize the time?"

She glanced at the clock. It was one-thirty.

"I'd forgotten time. I wanted to get all these notes typed for the new series." She stared at him. "I thought you were staying in London to-night."

"I had intended to do so." He flung himself down in an armchair.

Instantly, she was filled with solicitude and in that moment he was grateful for her company.

"Would you like some coffee?" she asked swiftly.

Coffee and Arden. . . . He said abruptly, "Tea."

Janet suppressed a little exclamation of amazement. He never drank tea except in the afternoon! If he had said poison she could hardly have been more surprised.

"Of course," she hastened, aware of his strained, rather tense expression and the unutterable weariness that character-ized his every movement.

He stopped her with a gesture.

"Pour me out a whiskey," he said.

Janet did as she was told. Excitement possessed her. He had taken Arden Marchly to the theatre . . . what, then, had happened between them to bring about this demeanour—foreign to him? Her heart thudded so violently that she felt physically sick. It had been useless deceiving herself: he was infatuated with the girl. The word love she had flatly refused to use. Had she rejected him? The very idea seemed ludicrous. Questions raced through her mind, but she dare not ask them. She handed him his drink. There was nothing for her to do but to listen and appear suitably sympathetic no matter what he might have to say, or even to confide.

"Thanks." He took the glass and gulped. "Damn cold outside." His expression changed. "Hell! I left my case at the hotel. They'll think I've absconded without paying the bill." Despite himself he grinned. It was not the first time he had absent-mindedly failed to return to the right address. In fact there was an occasion when he had booked at one hotel and checked in at another.

Janet was instantly businesslike. She picked up the receiver, gave a number and explained that Mr. Ashton would not be returning that night, but would be there the following morning.

"I'll send Baker up, then," she said coolly.

He nodded; he was preoccupied and distraught.

"Was the play good?" she asked tentatively.

"Very."

Janet trod carefully.

"You're upset, Lance. Can I help? I don't want to pry, but . . . well, we've been good friends."

He relaxed. Poor Janet! If she were in love with him then she must know something of what he was going through then. He looked at her with gentleness.

"There's nothing, my dear. One of those things. . . . I think it's about time I took another trip. Been hibernating too long. I told you I'd got in a rut. . . ." He sighed ruefully.

Janet made a few calculations and decided that she had nothing to lose by mentioning Arden. He could only jump down her throat, but in his present mood she doubted it.

She began carefully, "There's a rumour that Miss Marchly and Mr. Rayne are to be married. I thought it only fair to tell you." There wasn't one word of truth in the statement but it was, she felt, an excellent starting point.

To her relief and amazement he said tersely, "For once rumour is correct. Trust a village to be ahead with the news."

Janet gave him a steady stare.

"Surely it was always obvious." She paused effectively. "Everyone around here thinks they are lovers anyway."

Lance cut in, "By heaven, why can't people mind their own damn business!"

She gave a little laugh.

"My dear Lance, there's nothing in *that*! Just a little romantic morsel. But no man can visit a woman and stay in the cottage from time to time without someone talking." She added with a deceptive, generous air: "I'm not *criticizing*, or being stuffy in the least. It is entirely their business anyway."

Lance paled.

"I don't believe it for a moment." He stopped. Wasn't he being slightly ridiculous? What difference did it make? Arden was lost to him and was, in any case, going to marry Derek Rayne. He, Lance, was not her judge or a court of morals. But the jagged edge of a knife seemed to be prodding at his heart, nevertheless. Why the deception, the secrecy, the pretence that Rayne was always returning to London? The sickness of disillusionment swept over him. Couldn't she, at least, have been honest with *him*—particularly that evening? There was the rub, the hurt, and he could not deny it. She had talked so convincingly of friendship. Did she rate it so low, after all?

Janet, having sown the seed of doubt, was satisfied. She said, "Neither do I. I may not have any great regard for Miss Marchly, but I'm quite sure she would have the courage of her convictions and be prepared to be honest with her friends. Apart from that, as I said before: it is her affair entirely."

Lance brightened.

"I agree. Incredible how rumour starts."

Janet said casually, "I believe this originated through the daily woman at Meadow View. She, apparently, disapproved of the 'goings on'." Janet laughed and, realizing she had gone far enough, added swiftly, "Another drink?"

"No thanks." He got to his feet. "I'm going to run you home or else"—he paused before continuing cynically—"or else the gossips will have it that we, also, are lovers and that there are 'goings on' at The Manor."

Janet smiled. A little of the dull ache which had weighed on her heart lifted. So Arden Marchly was out of the picture. She had not hoped for so swift or so satisfactory a solution. And she was grateful that she had not been drawn into any scheming to achieve her ends.

"While they are talking about us they will not be pulling anyone else to pieces."

Lance's brows were puckered.

"I'd always thought that Meadow View was so off the beaten track as to be immune."

Janet scoffed:

"No one is immune in the country—it's like suburbia. Perhaps, fundamentally, it's boredom."

"Quite likely." His mind was absorbed with Arden. Janet had been right: Arden was far too courageous a person not to be honest with her friends. She would have told *him*—of that he was certain. Yet hadn't he always been struck by her evasiveness, her reluctance to talk about herself or her personal affairs? Rebelliously, he dismissed the idea. He realized, then, that quite apart from his love for her, he had valued her friendship immeasurably and believed that she had given to it an integrity he could not, would not, accept as sham.

CHAPTER X

ARDEN received Derek's telegram announcing his return with a swift, overwhelming excitement. He would be with her for dinner. Throughout the afternoon she arranged flowers in the flat, prepared a meal which could be eaten cold and at any hour and got out a bottle of champagne ready for the ice bucket. By five-thirty she was bathed and dressed in Derek's favourite shade of blue, restless with anticipation as she watched the cars streaming into the forecourt of the flats. Derek would come by taxi from the coach station at Victoria. And every time the tinkling flag bell went on a taxi meter, she felt her heart miss a beat as she watched the occupant of the vehicle get out. And at last, after an hour of waiting, she saw him. . . .

Just then, for an instant, emotion was stilled. She was going to remarry Derek and the occasion became suddenly solemn. Gone was the torment and conflict of the past, healed were the wounds of injustice and bad faith. He had redeemed himself, and now they had both wrested success from failure. *Marriage.* The word held for her an all-sufficing importance, just as divorce had been an anathema. There would be no more loneliness, no more uncertainty. This was security and fulfilment. For a second she thought of Lance and hurriedly dismissed him. He had no part in the present or the future, but that did not lessen her admiration and respect for him.

She went to the front door and opened it the instant that Derek reached it. She felt almost nervous, even shy, as she met his gaze.

"Hello, my sweet," he said lightly. "Missed me?"

His kiss was swift and they laughed together as, his arm about her, they walked into the lounge. There he looked about him and said approvingly, "Festive."

Their eyes met; hers bright; his inquiring.

"This," she said shakenly, "is a very special occasion."

He studied her contemplatively. "When I get my answer?" His voice held a note of interrogation.

"Yes . . . although you know it—don't you?"

He smiled slowly.

"I'm far too wise a man ever to assume that I know anything about a woman's feelings," he retorted.

For a second she felt abashed; it was almost as though, in an otherwise perfect sympathy, a note of discord had been struck. It wasn't quite as she had envisaged the scene. But she rushed on, chiding herself for her romanticism, "Then I shall have to tell you in plain words!"

"You do that," he answered slowly.

"Then I'll remarry you to-morrow, darling—or just as soon as ever it can be arranged."

Silence, deep, heavy, greeted the statement. It lay between them like a wide, impassable river and she felt the muscles around her heart tightening, her breath caught chokingly in her throat as she looked at him, waiting, tensed, for his comment.

It came shatteringly, unbelievably.

"So! You'll remarry me, eh?" He gave a little harsh, ridiculing laugh. "The trouble is that I have no intention whatsoever of remarrying you."

His expression in that split second changed. His eyes were glinting slits of steel in a face mask-like and satanic.

Arden stared at him, a little gasp of horror escaping her lips.

"Derek! What do you mean? What is it?"

He lit a cigarette with slow, deliberate movements, eyeing her between movements, enjoying to the full what he conceived to be the triumph of his position.

"I've fooled you completely—haven't I?"

Still she could not grasp the situation. She was shaking, feeling sick with apprehension.

"Fooled me?" she echoed. "But——" Helplessness overcame her.

"Yes, my dear—fooled you." His voice hardened, his eyes met hers in fierce and bitter condemnation. "Did you think for one moment that I was sincere?"

She cried, "Are you trying to tell me that——"

"That I'm not in the least in love with you—yes. That I haven't been and have never had the slightest intention of marrying you again."

She heard his words almost as though they had been shouted at her down a long corridor.

"It isn't possible," she whispered. Then: "But why—why?"

"Revenge," he said simply. "I wanted you to know the humiliation and defeat that I knew when you betrayed me with that little rat Newton." He added fiercely: "Do you seriously imagine that I believed your wishy-washy story of your innocence? Never for a second. No, my dear. You had it coming to you. I don't like being fooled—never did. And I detest failure. Now I'm satisfied. *You* would remarry *me* again. That is really funny."

"I think," said Arden, "you must be mad."

"No; just one step ahead of you." He looked at her through the faint smoke haze of his cigarette. "You couldn't be faithful to any man."

"How dare you!" The words rapped out.

"I like the truth. This time it would have been Lance Ashton—if it isn't already. *Friendship*," he scoffed. "Did you expect me to swallow that one, also? And the idea of your continued *friendship* with Brian. I was never fooled for a moment!"

She sat down, denuded of strength, unbelieving and yet appalled.

"It doesn't seem possible that any man could *think* of all this."

He smirked.

"I thought of nothing else from the moment I divorced you. I was still in love with you, then. I suffered tortures." His eyes gleamed in sudden hatred. "Well, now I'm free of you, my dear. Free, thank God."

She looked at him.

"What a mean, *little* soul you must have, Derek."

"Insults won't help you. . . ." He sighed. "I must say that you played a pretty clever hand. But, then, I expected you to do so and was quite prepared to be kept—waiting." He gave her a hateful look. "Although not on such, shall we say, advantageous, intimate terms." His mouth twisted into a sneer. "But, then, what is one more lover to you? *I've* proved that."

Arden's voice rang through the silence.

"Will you please go?"

"In my own time," he said coolly. "I congratulate Brian on not marrying you. You'd have let him down just as you did me."

Arden tried to fathom his mind, to understand, and at last she said slowly, "I can see now. All this is your inordinate vanity. Vanity. It was never love or jealousy. You must be supreme—in everything. You resent men who are more success-ful than you; you loathed the idea that I might prefer someone else *to* you . . . and when, in your distorted, abnormal brain, you had decided I'd been unfaithful . . . again, it was your vanity that was wounded. You, Derek Rayne . . ." She shook her head. "If you knew how tawdry and pathetic you seem, you would never have gone to these lengths."

He paled; his lips tightened. She had struck at a truth.

"You would have remarried me," he said, a note of triumph in his voice. "Nothing you can say now has the slightest value. That was all I wanted . . . to have the inordinate pleasure of rejecting you and of telling you that it so happens that I am going to marry Rachel."

At that she started.

"Ah! Now we have some interest," he said sibilantly.

"And are these past months the measure of your loyalty and fidelity to *her*?"

A dull flush spread over his face.

"That is my business," he rapped out.

Arden's gaze was merciless in its perception.

"I understand. With Rachael out of the country, I offered diversion; an opportunity of settling an old score."

"Put it that way if you wish."

"I congratulate you on having given an excellent performance. You were most convincing."

He eyed her with insolent familiarity.

"I am a man and you are physically attractive. That part of it was not difficult."

Arden's hands clenched.

"How I despise you," she said shakenly. "It doesn't seem possible that anyone—anyone could——"

"You placed me in an invidious position. A man whose wife prefers someone else. . . . Divorcing you gave me nothing and robbed me of much. On the other hand this has been vastly different. You're in love with me . . . and when I walk through that door you'll never see me again. This is a humiliation *you* are not likely to forget in a hurry, whereas mine—mine is over! It's your turn!"

That, she thought, in an agony of defeat, was true. Would she ever be able to erase the loathsome, degrading memory of it from her mind? She looked at the flowers massed in their pottery vase. How lovingly she had arranged them. Now, even their beauty mocked her.

He followed her gaze and sneered.

"Rather a waste—what. And the new dress. I suggest you get in touch with Ashton!"

At the mention of Lance's name some fierce strength came to life within her and she said, her words sharp as machine-gun fire, "Mr. Ashton asked me to marry him—just in case your mind persists in wallowing in mud."

Derek looked startled and angry. Jealousy and resentment burned like a flame within him.

"And that no doubt appealed to your vanity . . . yet you preferred me. . . . Too bad, Arden. The great Mr. Ashton," he mused.

"Yes; and for that very reason you could not endure him,

could you, Derek? You cannot stand anything, or anyone, who reveals you to yourself as the mediocre adolescent I now realize you are."

He laughed to hide his fury.

"And just what do you think Ashton will say when he knows the truth about you?"

Arden shivered.

"Men are funny like that. They hate being *deceived*. I'm not the only one. . . ." He looked suddenly nervous and suspicious. "Or did you go back on your promise and tell him the truth?"

Arden sat sick with disillusionment that surged over her like a sea, buffeting and destructive. Now she understood just why Derek had insisted on secrecy. She said scathingly, "You haven't even the manliness to see the irony of that question. Don't judge my standards by your own. I told Mr. Ashton that I was going to marry you."

Derek gloated.

"That could hardly have pleased him."

"We will not discuss the matter."

Derek frowned. His mean spirit could not endure the possibility that Arden might, after all, find happiness with Lance Ashton. He was the dog-in-the-manger over everything. The thought of Janet Rivers came insidiously. It might not be a bad idea to contact her.

"I wish you happiness," he said cynically. "But don't count on his shoulder to cry on."

Arden stared at him. The words "But she must have known what type of man he was" came, rather absurdly, to her mind. Yet, despite the past and his unreasonable attitude at the time of the divorce, never for a moment had she suspected that Derek would be capable of *this*. She had not been blind to his faults—even during the past months—but she had always argued that since, in his turn, there was no reason why he should be blind to hers either, living together was a matter for adjustment and compromise. Those defects must not be allowed to loom too large on the horizon. No one was perfect. But, where Derek was concerned, all the time beneath the surface had been the man she now saw standing before her: an arrogant, vain and vindictive man, puffed up by his own conceit, capable of stooping to the depths for what he conceived to be revenge. How true it was that character emerged

113

only according to circumstances—circumstances to which people either rose nobly or sank ignominiously. The terrifying thought gripped her: after this could she ever trust anyone again? She said, with a quiet dignity, "We have nothing further to say to each other, Derek." She paused, then, suddenly, "As I look at you I can't help wondering what devilish plan you have in your mind for Rachel. Certainly you are not in love with her or you could never have spent this time with me."

"Love!" He echoed the word scornfully. "You cured me of *that*, my dear. This time I am interested in money."

"And should Rachel find out about all this?"

"Since no one knows, that is unlikely." His eyes blazed with anger. "Or is it in your mind to tell her?" Fear and consternation betrayed itself. It was, he told himself, one possibility he had overlooked.

"It would be beneath me even to answer that question." As she spoke she got up and moved to the door and opened it. "Now, will you please go?"

He looked at her with insolent gaze.

"I'm afraid this has been a shock to you. . . . I can well imagine the type of reunion you had planned."

The colour mounted her cheeks. She felt physically sick.

"I can see I was not wrong," he said with hateful innuendo. "You will not easily forget me, my dear. I'm more than satisfied."

She flashed at him:

"Since you rate my fidelity so low in other respects why assume I shall change? Or is that further proof of your colossal vanity?"

"No; merely a psychological angle. You're in love with me and you thought I was utterly devoted to you. Which is precisely how I intended it. The situation is exactly reversed. Once I did the suffering. It has been amusing to stand back, as it were, and watch you. For a woman of experience I must say you were very gullible. I expected you to doubt me long ago, but as I had nothing to lose I didn't precipitate matters." He paused, then: "Good-bye, Arden. By the way: Rachel and I are being married next month and I'm starting on my own. Her financial backing is indispensable. Worth far more than the allure of your sexual charms," he added brutally.

Arden was shaking. Her face was deathly, her eyes dark in their anguish. It was like some nightmare from which she must,

114

she told herself, awaken. It couldn't be Derek—Derek standing there talking in such a manner.

She didn't speak, but her gaze met his in withering contempt. For a second he hesitated, then abruptly turned and left the flat.

Arden stood, her hands pressed against the pit of her stomach to stay the heaving sobs that shook her. She could see into the dining-room where the meal she had so specially prepared was laid. The cut glass sent off prisms of light to reflect in the silver. The tall, Georgian candle-sticks that had been intended to flicker over the scene would now never be lighted. . . . She uttered a sharp, heart-rending cry. Derek. . . . And in that second it seemed that she had lost hope, faith and even the will to live. This was to have been an evening of reunion, of rededication. Almost blindly she groped her way to the telephone and gave Martin's number and when eventually she heard his voice she gasped, "Oh, Martin . . . could you come to see me? *Could* you?" A pause. "No, I'm not ill. . . . Thank you."

Martin took no longer than it was possible for him to drive from Clement's Inn. He reached the flat anxious and breathless, and, taking one look at Arden's stricken face, he said grimly, "Derek." His voice dropped. "I've been waiting for this."

They went into the room together and without comment he poured two cocktails.

"Drink this. . . ." It was an order. "And there's plenty of time. They're 'phoning Heather. She'll expect me when she sees me."

Arden's eyes betrayed her gratitude and then, stumblingly, almost incredulously, she told her story, omitting nothing and giving him Derek's words almost verbatim—so branded were they on her mind.

Martin did not interrupt beyond a few violent exclamations, but when she had finished, he said grimly, "Now it makes sense. Now I know just why I've been so worried about you, so terrified lest he intended to go as far as remarriage. Oh, Arden, if only I could have spared you this."

She smiled in an effort at control.

"You warned me in every way possible. If only love weren't so *blind*. I trusted him so implicitly. Why should I doubt him? He didn't have to come back to me. Everything he said made sense."

Martin made a little sound of disagreement.

"Everything made too *much* sense." He looked at her with great earnestness. "It was all a little too perfect. His attitude —everything. And that isn't, as you know, being wise after the event. Derek is just the type to find satisfaction in a cheap, disgusting revenge. He wasn't big enough either to accept your word at the time of the divorce, or, had you been guilty, to forgive you. What he has done now follows through—hideous though it is."

"It's like being smeared, tainted," she said with a shudder of distaste.

"I know." His voice was gentle. "But I still thank God for it. He was never the man for you, Arden. Even without all this to-day, even had you remarried and had he been moderately sincere, it still wouldn't have worked for long." He paused. "And you would have been tied to a man whom you realized you did not love."

"I find that difficult to believe," she said honestly.

"You were caught up in the emotional instability of the past," Martin insisted. "You were carried along on a wave of your own passionate enthusiasm for a cause—the cause of marriage. You hated failure; you hated divorce. And suddenly it was made possible—as you thought—to wipe all that out. You were in love with the idea, in love with love, with marriage, but I swear, Arden, never with the *man*—with Derek himself."

She said brokenly, "I know only that I thought—less than two hours ago—that I was the happiest woman alive."

"One day," Martin said with conviction, "you will be that woman. Oh, you can't possibly believe me *now*, but this will pass, my dear. Before, you were chained to Derek through the power of his injustice. Not to be believed when you knew you were innocent . . . don't you see? Sub-consciously, that in itself created an emotion that masqueraded as love. Then, when he *did* accept your word, you built up the illusion of love for him in a false gratitude. Oh, you weren't aware of that. But it was there. Arden, you've got to believe me and while, heaven knows, I would have spared you this to-day, nevertheless you will live to thank God it happened."

She looked down at her hands and back to meet Martin's intent, anxious gaze.

"I want to believe you; but it isn't easy."

"That I appreciate. It is always so simple to sit back and analyse the other person's emotions, bear their pain. Don't think I'm insensible to that. But I know *you*. The very fact that you refused to remarry Derek immediately, proved conclusively to me your own uncertainty. Had your divorce happened out of the blue on an act of infidelity for which you were wrongfully accused and then Derek came forward vindicating you . . . what *reason* was there for any testing time? No, Arden, your own self-preservation imposed that. You weren't certain of him. Somewhere, somewhere deep down within you, doubt festered. My *dear*, love is the greatest folly known to mankind and its greatest weakness is the one you, oddly enough, rejected! The belief that no matter how great the odds it will triumph! Alas, love does not so wisely and conveniently allow us to stop to think with such sober judgement."

"I had to be sure," she protested. "Surely, you, a levelheaded person, can see that."

"Of course I can see it . . . but I maintain that it was *your own feelings* you had to be sure about, Arden."

"Was that so strange after all that had happened?"

"Not in the least, but you cannot have it both ways: the very indecision proves my point. You merely told yourself that you were behaving in that manner because of the past—it was a case of sheer self-deception."

She sighed.

"I cannot concede that." She stopped, Lance's words tearing down the corridors of her mind, echoing mockingly: "*I cannot convince myself that you are in love with Rayne.*" Faint colour stole into her pale cheeks.

"But you will," Martin said quietly.

Arden thrust the thought of Lance from her. To seek sanctuary in his love now would be dishonest and dangerous and grossly unfair to him.

"Pray God you are right," she murmured. "At the moment I cannot think beyond the hideousness, the degradation of all this."

Martin, grave of face, his manner infinitely gentle and solicitous, studied her intently before asking, "Have you any ideas in mind for the immediate future?"

Rather to her own surprise, she said, "I think I'd like to get away—right away. Take the car and wander for a bit."

"Alone?"

A look of defiance came into her eyes.

"Yes. I'm not in the mood for company, Martin. Oh, I shall get over it." Bitterness lashed her words. "I've been a fool and that's that." She looked at him with a great earnestness. "There are very few men about like you," she said gently.

"Rot!" The exclamation was explosive.

She shook her head.

"It isn't rot. Oh, why can't we fall in love to order? Why has there always to be this misery, this ghastly disillusionment?"

"If I could answer either of those questions I'd be a genius," he retorted. "To get back to you . . . I cannot say I'm particularly keen on your going off alone. Just the wrong thing. Brooding won't help."

She said with sudden spirit, "I shan't brood, Martin. I hope I have some courage. If anything in the world could kill love all I've been through this evening should accomplish that miracle. But it doesn't solve the problem of living. I'd suddenly come to belong again; to plan and dream and hope. To think in terms of security and children. Now I'm back in the wilderness and it isn't any use deceiving myself."

Silence fell; a tense, dramatic silence. Martin's hands closed around his glass; he looked down at it almost as intently as though it had the power to foretell the future. Then, his voice low and throbbing, he said, "Security can be a wilderness, darling. Don't forget that. You've escaped it. I thank God for that."

Arden looked at him and her heart contracted. She said suddenly, her own heart-ache forgotten in her overwhelming concern for him, "How are things, Martin?"

He put down his glass and traced his fingers around the cord of the chair upholstery. His gaze was lowered.

"Much the same."

"And—Catherine?"

"She's away. Europe. A tour for three weeks." His voice was almost harsh as he endeavoured to hide his emotion.

"You miss her."

He raised his gaze.

"Damnably. Even though I rarely see her . . . there is always the chance that I might run into her somewhere. One is so cut off."

Arden's sigh was almost a groan.

"Is there *nothing*?"

"Nothing," he echoed tersely. "If we did other than we are doing now we'd be the most miserable people on earth. . . ."

Arden nodded.

"I think I understand."

He leaned forward.

"How about coming to stay with us for a while? Heather would be only too pleased." He stopped abruptly. Heather, good though she was, would drive Arden crazy.

"Thanks—no, Martin. There are some things that one has to fight through alone. I shall be perfectly all right. Talking to you has helped; given me back a sense of proportion which we lose in those first moments of panic." She finished practically: "And now it's time for you to eat. There is a meal all prepared." She added cynically: "It was to be quite an occasion."

He said in a strangled, hushed voice, "Don't get bitter, my dear. He wasn't worth it. Bitterness is a blight."

"I know." She clenched her hands and drew in her breath sharply. "But control can be easier in cynicism. One dare not think, dare not *feel*, Martin."

He got to his feet. His arms went around her sobbing, heaving figure. No word was spoken.

CHAPTER XI

ARDEN set about clearing up all unfinished work in order to get away with an easy mind and the knowledge that no promises had been left unfulfilled. She took the last rough of a book jacket to the offices of the publishers and saw the Art Editress, Miss Naunton, who greeted her with friendliness and not a little thankfulness. Arden was the one artist who could turn in the kind of art work they needed and they were hard to come by. She looked swiftly at the drawing Arden handed to her.

"Excellent. . . . And that was a darn good job you made of the Lance Ashton jacket. Feather in your cap. He was in here only a matter of minutes ago."

Arden heard the words without feeling any emotion. She

seemed to be floating in a strange, unreal world unable really to interest herself in anything. She felt Miss Naunton's gaze intently upon her and made an effort to respond. After a few commonplace remarks, she said, "I'm going for a holiday . . . this clears up everything on hand at the moment, doesn't it?"

Miss Naunton smiled. She had a pleasant, charming manner and was friendly without effusiveness; direct without bluntness and helpful at all times. In appearance she was slim, blonde and as attractive as she was efficient. Her shrewd eye observed the pallor of Arden's cheeks and the blue shadows beneath her eyes. The contrast—remembering their last meeting—was so great that she was shocked.

But she asked no questions and spared Arden banalities as she said briskly, "I think so. There will be the new Rita Paul and Margaret Vain books. You can have the MSS. when you get back. No hurry. Good time of year to go for a holiday. I like early autumn. No crowds and often far better weather than the summer we never have."

Arden smiled.

And in that second Brian Newton swung into the room.

"I say——" At the sight of Arden he stopped, his gaze leaping to hers. Then: "Good-morning," he said, the tone of his voice belying the formality of the greeting. "Or is it good-afternoon?"

Arden murmured something inarticulate.

"It's almost lunch-time," said Miss Naunton.

Brian handed her a file and said with an understanding nod: "It's all yours."

Arden drew on her gloves and prepared to leave. Brian followed her out into the corridor.

"Will you have lunch with me?" he asked abruptly, but without hope.

Arden was thankful for his company and to his delighted surprise she assented.

He shot her a curious, inquiring look. The last time he had seen her at Meadow View she had been radiant and gay. Now there was a stillness about her that struck a note of poignancy.

"Is there anywhere you would particularly like to go?"

"I'd like most just to be relieved of making a choice," she admitted.

They went out of the massive building, into the rather

chilly October day that was nevertheless lit by a pale, unpredictable sun. A taxi took them to Fleur d'Argent.

Once seated at the table, their meal chosen, Brian said quietly, "Something's wrong, Arden. When last I saw you——"

"That," she hastened, "might have been in another life, Brian."

"Just two weeks ago," he reminded her.

"Did you have a good holiday?" Her voice was unsteady.

"I hated every minute of it," he said honestly. "I was going to telephone you to-day in any case to see if you and Derek would care to join me at a film *première* next week."

Arden didn't lower her gaze. But very briefly she outlined the facts, watching Brian's face pale, his eyes darken with an anger that almost frightened her.

"So," he said heavily, "my instincts were right about him. By heaven, Arden, that he should *dare* . . . Oh, my dear, I'm so sorry."

"One pays for folly and blindness," she said harshly. "I suppose I ought to have known it was all too good to be true."

"We believe what we most want to believe," he said with a sigh. "You know, although he was so pleasant to me, seemed genuinely to have regretted the past . . . I *couldn't* believe him. I always felt I was looking at a film with a scene missing." He made an exclamation of disgust. His gaze deepened. "What now, Arden?"

"Pick up the pieces," she said with a trace of cynicism.

He reached across the table, his hand closed over hers.

"Can't I help to do that?" he asked earnestly.

And just as his last word died away, Lance Ashton's tall figure stopped at their table.

Brian instantly released Arden's hand and got to his feet.

Lance glanced at Arden. The little scene had not escaped him and there was a sudden, baffled expression in his eyes as they met hers.

"This is very unexpected," he said with significance.

"It is unexpected for me, too," she murmured, suddenly ill at ease and conscious of him and of a magnetism that still held, despite her wretchedness.

"Won't you," said Brian courteously, "join us?"

Lance hesitated and then, "With pleasure," he agreed, almost doggedly.

A chair was instantly placed in position for him and when the menu had been discussed, he looked deliberately at Arden and inquired politely, "And how is Mr. Rayne?"

Although Arden had expected the question, its utterance reduced her to a state of shaking nervousness. There was so much she now wanted Lance to know and had already decided to tell him—but in her own time. But she said, trying to keep her voice as steady as was possible and to meet his gaze levelly, "I imagine he is well. Our relationship is over."

Lance felt that his pulse rate had suddenly doubled. Elation surged upon him. He could not conceal the emotion he felt, for his expression betrayed him. And into the sudden, dazzling brightness of his reflections the shadow of Brian Newton obtruded. Just where did *he* fit into the picture? Memory sharpened. They were old friends, yet the scene upon which he had intruded hardly maintained any platonic standard. Jealousy, new and shattering and which he heartily despised, consumed him. But he managed to say soberly, "I'm sorry."

A tense, awkward silence fell. For Arden it was an untenable position. Nervously she resorted to flippancy.

"There is nothing certain in life—least of all human emotions."

She loathed the words the moment they were uttered and grew hot and ashamed of them.

"That," Lance suggested, "surely depends on the reliability of the people concerned." His gaze held hers and the memory of their last meeting flowed between them inescapably. And Janet's story of life at Meadow View suddenly echoed in his mind and stung. He became aware that Arden had used the word "relationship" a moment before. Not *engagement*.

Brian, sensitive to the undercurrent, plunged into what he knew to be blatant "shop" talk, steering the conversation away from the personal and gradually drawing Lance Ashton out until, despite the circumstances, he and Arden listened enthralled by what was said, aware of the brilliance and perception of that lucid brain and appreciative of the utter lack of vanity or self-importance. Abruptly, however, he stopped. "I seem to be doing all the talking."

Arden looked at him.

"That is extremely easy to bear," she said with a generous smile.

Brian persisted, "I understand that you are off again on your travels, Mr. Ashton."

Instantly Arden became alert.

Lance held her gaze.

"I have that in mind, but nothing is definitely fixed." He sipped his liqueur. "Is the rumour true that you are letting Meadow View furnished, Arden?"

Arden gasped.

"But I put it in the agent's hands only yesterday."

He laughed.

"The country Tom Toms." He added deliberately: "Never delude yourself that your affairs are your own."

Something in his tone brought the colour to her cheeks.

"For all that, no one even knew of Meadow View's existence —or even my name."

He looked at her through the faint cigarette-smoke haze.

"I shouldn't count on that." A pause. "So you *are* letting?"

"Yes. Although it is rather a forlorn hope at this time of year." She added swiftly: "I'm going on holiday at the end of this week."

Her gaze was curiously appealing and he sensed the terrific strain under which she was labouring.

Brian by this time was watching the clock a trifle uneasily. He had an appointment with one of his own authors at two-thirty and was forced to break in, having settled the bill with unobtrusive swiftness, "I'm most awfully sorry——" He shot Arden a worried glance. "But being a working man——"

Lance caught sight of the time.

"Good lord, I've to be at Lenare's in two minutes. I'd forgotten."

Arden collected her bag and gloves and got to her feet. They went out into the street. It was obvious that she must share Brian's taxi and remain with him, but a desperate urge overwhelmed her: she must talk to Lance before she went away. It suddenly seemed vital and urgent, where, before, it had merely been a future intention.

"Can we go your way—drop you anywhere?" Brian asked.

Lance replied, "I parked my car in Wimpole Street, thanks all the same." He looked from face to face.

Brian was searching for a taxi. He moved away a pace or two and Lance, drawing Arden's gaze to his, asked tensely,

"Will you have dinner with me to-morrow night?" He added half-cynically: "Or am I intruding for the second time?"

Arden followed his glance in Brian's direction.

"No," she said almost sharply.

"Then, will you dine with me?"

"I'd like to."

"I'll call for you at your flat at six-thirty," he said firmly.

Brian rejoined them. A taxi moved in to the kerb.

Lance said good-bye to Arden and held out his hand to Brian.

"Thanks for a most enjoyable lunch," he said warmly.

They went their separate ways. Brian said as he and Arden were settled in the taxi, "Much as I wanted you to myself, I must say I appreciated his company."

Arden nodded assent. She felt suddenly restless and anxious without quite knowing why. She wished that she had asked to see Lance that evening. Both their meeting and their parting had been a painful anti-climax so far as she was concerned.

Lance, meanwhile, did what was to him a chore: Press photographs. Then, with relief, he turned the car for home. He felt ten years younger than when he left The Manor that morning. The prospect of seeing Arden the following evening filled him with a hope so exquisite as to resemble pain. A frown puckered his forehead. What on earth could have happened between her and Rayne in that short while? Where was the mystery? For mystery—he insisted to himself—there must be.

Reaching home, Janet met him, her expression suggesting suppressed excitement which he was quick to see. She said breathlessly, "I've heard the most extraordinary story to-day. It would honestly make a good novel."

He stared at her in no mood to listen and yet arrested by a certain inflection in her voice which suggested that he, also, would be interested.

"Really! This district appears to be coming famous for them. Who is it about this time?"

She shook her head.

"No, Lance. It isn't gossip. I had coffee with Derek Rayne this morning. We met by chance in the village," she lied.

"I see." He felt irritated. Obviously Janet knew that the marriage would not take place. "What was he doing down here?" There was an aggressive note in the question.

She replied pointedly, "Collecting a few of his personal things from Meadow View. He told me the whole story. At first I could hardly believe it: Arden Marchly was once his wife. He divorced her."

Her words fell upon the silence with all the explosiveness of thunder that reverberated ominously. Lance stared at her in speechless disbelief, his voice almost unnatural as he cried, "*What?*"

She basked in the triumph of her own success. She knew just how to build the story up without appearing critical, and how to use the truth to suit her own purpose until it became near-lies.

"I was absolutely staggered. At first I just couldn't believe it. Then he showed me the cuttings. Brian Newton was the co-respondent."

Lance felt that his heart was trying to thrust itself through his ribs. Arden and Brian Newton. *Newton!* He felt sick. But he countered, "That being so, wasn't it a queer set-up afterwards? Newton remaining in the picture. And what was Rayne doing, having divorced——"

Janet did not let him finish as she said with a sigh, "Sometimes men can be as foolish over women as women over men. He still loved her. And he wanted her back. He was ready to wipe out the past and, seeing that she and Brian had not married, it was easy to convince himself that the whole thing came under the heading of infatuation."

It made sense which Lance could not deny.

Janet went on smoothly:

"But she refused to remarry him, preferring that they should become lovers. Quite an intriguing situation when you come to think of it. He was, of course, a weak fool. She even persuaded him to accept Brian again as a friend." Janet gave a little, significant laugh.

Lance felt that every drop of blood in his body had turned to ice that sent a shudder over him. He moved to the fire instinctively. Suspense beat about him like imaginary wings. He hardly dared to ask the question that burned on his lips. Then, avoiding Janet's gaze, he managed to say:

"Well? And what is the end of all this?"

She simulated regret.

"He had deluded himself that she would remarry him. In

fact she had promised to give him a definite answer when he returned from Rome. He'd been there on business. Instead of which he discovered that she had gone back to Brian. She told him quite frankly that, when it came to it, she didn't want to be tied and that so far as she was concerned *their* association was ended. There are women like that. They can't be faithful to any man for long and they enjoy their conquests." She shook her head. "You should have seen him to-day. He looked a dejected mess. Not that I have a scrap of pity for him. He asked for what he got."

Lance didn't speak. He could not. The memory of the scene he had witnessed only that lunch-time between Arden and Newton seemed to leap out to mock and torment him. There was no argument about *that*. A sudden cold fury gripped him. So! For the second time in his life he'd been the victim of lies, deceits, bad faith. First his wife, now Arden. How easy it was to see the whole picture. There's no engagement, she had insisted in the beginning. No engagement when all the time she was with her ex-husband! How sincere she had been when she had talked of emotion being transient! Her words when he had referred to kissing her, echoed to sear him: "*I do not profess to be other than human.*"

"He has my sympathy," said Lance grimly.

"And apparently Brian Newton is just as mesmerized. Ready to accept any conditions she cares to make." Janet added swiftly, and with what she considered tact: "One has to admit that women like that certainly have a tremendous power and influence over men. Derek said she was the type who loved to collect scalps. Ah well. . . . Did you have a good day? By the way, there are several invitations in by the afternoon post." Her laugh was light. "I don't think you'll be impressed by them."

Lance didn't hear her. He was wrestling with demoniac thoughts that tore through his mind wildly. *Arden.* Derek's wife and his mistress as she was now Newton's. It was an unbearable realization. And greater than his moral condemnation of her was his disillusionment at her deceit. The words he had used about his former wife came back tormentingly: "*It was the deception and lies which shattered me: I could have forgiven the infidelity.*"

It was, he argued desperately, true that Arden owed him

no allegiance, but she had listened to his sentiments, expressed agreement with them and pretended to value his friendship. She had lied to him, by implication, from the very beginning about Derek Rayne. Why the secrecy? The pitiful lack of courage? And even when she knew that he, Lance, was in love with her and wanted to marry her—*still* she withheld the truth. And what now? Now that Rayne was out of the picture? Would she feel it worth her while to entice him, Lance, back? *Scalps*. He remembered grimly how she had responded to his kiss. It was true what Janet had said: such women could not be faithful to any man and it was nature's cruel joke that they always seemed to be above reproach—the last type in the world to be credited with immorality. And in their sordid, miserable little lives, wasn't there always one man to whom they returned? One man capable of holding their interest when all other loves waned? Evidently Brian Newton was that man in her case.

Janet watched Lance with stealthy gaze. She did not make the mistake of overstatement. And she had left nothing to be disputed. It would hardly matter what protest, what vigorous denial Arden Marchly might indulge in, the truth condemned her. Lance was a man who loathed being fooled or deceived. It was for him the unforgivable sin.

"Pour me out a whiskey," he said resignedly.

Janet obeyed and handed it to him. He said, shaken and depressed, "Your woman's intuition was evidently right."

She pretended not to understand, then in surprise, "Oh, you mean—Miss Marchly? Or should I say Mrs. Rayne? Yes. It wasn't dislike, but distrust. I felt, somehow, that you, as Lance Ashton, were destined to *be* a scalp. And that she was sufficiently clever to run in the opposite direction for a while."

Lance gulped half the drink.

How true that was. But suddenly all the love, the passionate desire that had become a part of his life, surged upon him and he said sharply, "We've had only Rayne's version of all this."

She did not make the mistake of leaping to contradict him.

"Well, it isn't really a question of any version," she said conversationally. "Mr. Rayne wasn't even condemning her. He just blurted out the story like someone demented! He didn't fool me, either. Given half a chance, he'd still go back. Of course, he is hardly an inspiring specimen. Weak as water.

When you think that he divorced her, went back to her and forgave her, accepted her terms and even tolerated Brian Newton!"

Lance interjected, "I suppose he's asked for all he's got." He spoke almost as though trying to impress the fact upon himself.

Janet bustled about the study.

"I must be going."

Lance shunned the thought of his own company.

"I was wondering if you'd nothing better to do whether you'd have dinner with me."

She looked up from the desk.

"I'd love to." Her smile was warm and friendly. Inwardly she purred and congratulated herself on her achievement. Arden *Marchly* would never live *this* down.

CHAPTER XII

ARDEN awakened the following morning, conscious of the pleasure of anticipation as she faced the prospect of Lance's visit that evening. Once he knew the truth, she told herself, she would be able to wipe out the hideousness, the folly and her own sense of guilt for ever having accepted Derek as her lover. Emotion had, in any case, died down. The first, sharp agony of disillusionment and humiliation had gone and she was surprised to find a sudden uplifting of spirit, a renewal of hope as she realized her miraculous escape. From the moment of her divorce Derek had been an issue. Circumstances had given him an importance he in no way merited. His condemnation of her had, even as Martin pointed out, constituted within her a stubborn affection. Gradually, in the light of sanity, the picture came into focus. And in that light, cruel and perceptive, she faced the truth: Martin had been right. She had loved an image, love itself, marriage—but not the man. Her heart was still at the thought of him. Only contempt and a withering scorn remained and even that would fade on the altar of her indifference. With a tenacity inseparable from a woman's affections, she had clung to her faith in her love for Derek. That faith had sustained her during their reunion. . . . Yet, after all, had not her hesitation in remarrying him been the greatest betrayal? In that hesitation had been the uncertainty of loving which she had brushed aside as representing caution, wisdom and a desire not to repeat a former mistake. She felt suddenly like a prisoner let out of prison while yet aware that freedom could be exceedingly strange.

She went about her shopping with zest that morning, replenished her store-cupboard and experienced a sensation very much like returning home after an illness. By five o'clock she had completed all the tasks she had assigned herself.

She tried to sit nonchalantly as the hands of the clock crept to six-thirty and was irritated by her own sudden restlessness and inability to concentrate on the papers or to remember a word she had studiously read. She got up, glanced at herself in the mirror, pushed back a recalcitrant curl from her forehead, and wished she had worn a different dress, although the pencil-slim cocktail suit of black, exquisitely embroidered and tucked at the bodice, could not have been faulted. Her body felt hollow and filled with butterflies. Suppose Lance shouldn't understand? It wouldn't be easy to explain all the facts and she shrank from the ordeal of explaining to him that last sordid scene with Derek.

A strange faintness descended upon her. The room swirled and then, suddenly, her heart thudded. Tears gushed to her eyes and dropped slowly down each cheek, although no sobs rent her body, for in those tears were exultation as she knew, suddenly and with a staggering revelation, that she was in love with Lance and that there she had her answer to the conflict and indecisions of the past months.

She sat down weakly on the arm of a chair, almost blinded by the emotions tearing through her heart, and yet afraid. Life could never be quite so simple, or so wonderful. . . . Suppose he had already changed . . . suppose, even if he hadn't, all she must tell him would achieve that tragedy?

In love with Lance. There was a glorious intimacy, a familiarity and yet a fascinating strangeness in the knowledge, that made her feel curiously shy.

Six-thirty. . . .

She went to the window and looked down on the square courtyard, her heartbeats choking her. One car out of all the dozens milling around that area. . . . There was something fantastic in the changing pattern of life, the incredible and inexplicable awakening of emotion. Yet hadn't such love been inevitable? Hadn't it crept into her heart, body and mind from that very first meeting? Arrested only by a loyalty and blindness as she clung to her faith in her devotion to Derek and all he stood for?

The doorbell rang suddenly and she jumped violently, took a deep breath and went to answer it, praying that she might achieve some semblance of composure.

Lance stood there, smiling with his lips but not his eyes as he greeted her, aware anew of her charm, her loveliness and the fragrance that always surrounded her. It wasn't *possible* that all he had heard could be true. Yet it was fact with which he was dealing and he refused to be diverted from his grim purpose.

Arden's gaze rested upon him with the sudden intensity of a love that seemed to rise within her in a wave of sharp overwhelming adoration. All the deep regard, admiration, awareness of him and his magnetism, crystallized into an emotion that made control almost impossible. She said stiffly, because her lips felt incapable of movement, "A most punctual person."

Inane words serving to conceal her nervousness.

Lance followed her into the familiar room.

"I always believe in keeping my word . . . six-thirty." He watched her with stoat-like gaze, aware that she was not at ease and that she avoided meeting his eyes, also that she was breathing swiftly. "You look very attractive. But, then, you always do."

Something in his voice made her start. Was she dreaming or was that a note of cynicism?

In that second he reached out and his arms closed around her as, without a word, his lips found hers.

To Arden that moment was an ecstasy such as she had never before experienced, for to it she gave heart, soul and body in a love all-embracing; a love that had been born out of misery and disillusionment. She clung to him hardly daring to believe in the passion sweeping between them, lest she might awaken to find it a dream. His kiss was fierce and she responded with an equal fervour, her arms reaching up to encircle his neck, her lips hot and seeking until it seemed that all breath, all strength had left her body.

130

And even though, at her touch, at her unmistakable abandon, Lance knew the sharp stab of desire, the hunger of his need for her, so, inwardly, did his anger mount and his disgust and scorn grow. This was the proof he needed of her absolute wantonness, her lack of moral scruple; proof that, in addition, she was a consummate actress who could easily have convinced *him* of her absolute sincerity.

She drew back, his name escaping her lips, her eyes meeting his in all the tenderness of adoration, and then her expression changing almost to horror as she saw the hostility and condemnation with which he gazed upon her.

"So," he said icily, "I'm next on your list, after all. Derek Rayne, your lover and ex-husband; Brian Newton, the co-respondent reinstated. Just *what* rôle had you in mind for me? Or perhaps, as you have appeared to set so much store by my name, the prospect of becoming my wife might have overcome your prejudice against the conventional tie."

The words hurt him and they fell upon the silence as a requiem.

Arden stood there, her body seeming to be no more than a giant pulse, sickness overwhelming her.

"You *know*," she said shakenly, without even the ability to think of any defence.

He said curtly, "Obviously. Thank you for sparing me denial or explanation."

She said frantically, "But you don't *understand*."

He looked at her very levelly. "I'm not setting myself up as your judge. I've no right in any case. Just tell me this: Derek Rayne *was* your husband; he *did* divorce you; and, recently, he has been your lover?"

Arden's face was so pale, so stricken that, for a moment, Lance was afraid. She said, her voice low and anguished:

"Yes, but——"

"Spare me details, Arden. I'm not concerned beyond the facts which are indisputable." His eyes burned down into hers. "Couldn't you have trusted me with the truth?" he cried bitterly. "Was it your idea of friendship to pretend and lie, to behave without either courage or conviction? And when I asked you to marry me . . . even *then* you kept up the pretence about your relationship with Rayne." Scorn filled his voice, springing from the searing pain and frustration within him.

Arden groped amid the shadows of defeat for words that should plead her cause, and could find none that did not sound feeble, or a greater untruth. Already the poison of distortion had seeped into Lance's mind, where, had she been allowed to explain the facts, the whole picture would have been seen in a different light. An agony of regret surged over her. If only she had told him. Now it was too late. Once before in his life he had been betrayed; it was only natural and inevitable that he should now class her with his former wife.

She said, breathing with difficulty, "I was going to tell you. It wasn't *deceit*——"

He interrupted her and now his voice was emotionless and deadly in its resignation.

"Let's not add insult to injury. Your affairs are your own. You can have a succession of lovers and it is no business of mine. But I believed in your honesty, Arden, the sincerity of your friendship. Now I can see that you were truthful only when you spoke glibly about emotion being transient. Oh, you were consistent, I'll give you that. You could lie in Rayne's arms and Newton's and still find satisfaction in my kisses—that more or less on your own admission." He paused, his expression stern. "And just now, that charming little love scene of ours . . ."

"No! *No!*" She cried out in anguish. "Oh, Lance, if only I could make you understand."

"I do understand," he said bitterly. "You collect *scalps*. Lovers. I don't ask for perfection and heaven knows had you loved me, the mere fact of the divorce would not have made any difference . . . but the bad faith, the assumption that I could be fooled! That's another matter. I told you once that I should have to trust a woman implicitly. . . . I trusted you, although I always *felt*—and you know it—that there **was** a mystery somewhere." He added cynically, "But even I was not prepared for all this."

Arden's brain was numb. She could find no words that would absolve her. Her story was one that needed time in which to be told, not to be jerked out in a few disjointed sentences against a wealth of evidence based on truth. But one fact leapt out to be refuted and she cried, "You mentioned Brian Newton just now. He has never been my lover."

Lance's expression hardened.

"Is that why he was co-respondent in your divorce case? For God's sake, Arden, I can't stand any more lies." He added swiftly: "And the touching little scene I interrupted yesterday. Was that platonic, too?" He made a sound which betrayed his impatience and disgust.

To Arden the agony of her position was intensified by the fact that for the second time in her life she was the victim of injustice. First Derek and now Lance. . . . She stopped, struck by the irony of Fate. Was it not the same with Lance? His faith had been shattered before and was now being shattered again. She looked at him with great earnestness in which conflict was at an end. She could not argue or protest without incurring his further scorn. She said quietly, "I have a story to tell, Lance. A story I was going to tell you to-night. In the face of all this . . . you would not listen to it, or believe it. So be it. There's nothing more I have to say except that I am not guilty of the things you so despise me for."

He said hoarsely, "I wish with all my heart I had faith enough to listen to you." His gaze travelled over her face. "But even faith cannot ignore truth," he finished curtly.

"But," she said, and her voice held a stillness that was to haunt him, "love can inspire faith."

"Love!" His voice rose. "What do you know of love?"

"You wouldn't believe me if I told you," she answered shakenly.

For a second they looked at each other, emotion holding them in its vice; for a second the overwhelming desire surged upon him to reach out and draw her into his arms, ignoring everything but his own passionate need of her. Then, in disgust, he turned away.

"No," he answered, "I'm afraid not. I believed a woman once before." His voice cracked in ridicule. "Never again."

He knew, then, that the anger raging within him had become a blind jealousy. That the thought of her belonging to any other man was a torment. Useless to deceive himself that only her disregard for the obligations of friendship was at stake. It went far deeper, blinding him to reason and even to justice. The pain and disillusionment ate into him, rendering him powerless against its slow and insidious blight. He walked to the door, control and endurance at an end as he said, "This is good-bye, Arden."

She felt that she was dying as she stood there, helpless, vulnerable, desperate because she had managed to say so little in her own defence and yet shrinking from his further contumely should she enumerate facts that were utterly distasteful to her. And which he could not be expected to believe. She stood condemned by a situation more damnable in its injustice than that which had earlier wrecked her happiness. How feeble, how futile to begin to explain Derek's elaborate revenge upon her, or to plead that *Derek* had requested her silence. . . . It would savour of pettiness that would invite only contempt. Far better that she should be damned on the facts as they stood, than demeaned by those unrevealed.

Good-bye. . . .

Was it less than an hour or a century ago that she had stood in that very room glorying in the discovery of her love for him? A love she had meant to declare in the breathless hush of that reunion. A love which she knew nothing could destroy or minimize. She clenched her hands, fighting for courage, for that fast-dying control. This was the end where she had thought of it being the beginning. The wilderness of life stretched before her, more barren, more lonely than anything she had ever been called upon to face. She looked at him as though she would imprint every feature upon her memory; conscious of his power over her, his vital, unforgettable charm. Now he despised her . . . even if the ghost of his love remained. Inwardly she groaned as a sob started in the pit of her stomach and made her body feel paralysed, her mouth parched.

"Good-bye, Lance," she whispered. "I shall remember," she added, "remember a friendship I valued beyond words."

He stared at her, shattered by what seemed to him to be her ability to ignore the truth of the situation.

"You are incapable of knowing the meaning of the word," he answered heavily, drawing upon anger and bitterness as his only ally.

And with that he strode from the room and from the flat.

Arden slid on to the floor in a dead faint and when, after some minutes, she came back through the nauseating worlds of giddiness, a cry escaped her; a cry in which there was an agony of longing for death. Consciousness was a knife cutting into her heart and brain. Frenzy gripped her and died in the wake of her own helplessness.

And only as she groped her way back to the edge of normality did the thought occur to her: from whom had he obtained such information? In that second she saw the jealous face of Janet. . . .

A rush of desperate regret surged upon her because she had managed to say so little in her own defence. Defence. She had not stressed the fact that the divorce case had been defended and doubtless it would be the one fact which Janet would have withheld. Even so, she argued, in face of all that had happened, was it likely that Lance would have been prepared to give her the benefit of the doubt? It was her relationship with Derek recently that had been the blow . . . savouring of deceit, mocking a professed friendship. Again, Lance had seen her with Brian. . . . How could she have entered into long explanations when no such opportunity had been possible? . . . Useless to torment herself on that account. She had been discredited beforehand by what were, on the surface, indisputable facts. And her attitude, her innocent remarks to Lance during the period of their friendship, had strengthened the case against her.

No blame stirred in her heart towards him. He'd been hurt before by lies and disloyalty, therefore he was the more vulnerable and sensitive to those vices now. She appreciated that with the severing of her relationship with Derek, Lance—and hadn't it been obvious?—had found renewed hope in the belief that she might reconsider marrying him . . . and then . . . Doubtless, Janet had struck. And Arden in no way overlooked the possibility that Derek had been behind it. He would have hated the idea that she, Arden, might find happiness with a man like Lance Ashton.

She looked around the room helplessly. It had lost all personality and become a room without a soul. The telephone mocked her, for this time she could not confide in Martin . . . no one must know how she felt.

Mechanically, she put a coat on over her suit. She could not remain there . . . a walk . . . anything. She went out into the square and wandered without being conscious of direction. The theatre crowds jostled her on the pavements, but she was not aware of them. Within her was the burning, smarting pain of a suffering not only concerned with the loss of hope, of love itself, but the deadly hurt of knowing Lance condemned and despised her. Had she been mad not to tell him how she felt? Her lips twisted wryly. He could not, in all fairness, be expected to have believed her. At its best such a betrayal could but have seemed a convenient exploitation.

How far she walked she never quite knew. But the streets were quieter, the rush had died down and dusk had given place to a hazy darkness, herald of later fog. Exhaustion crept upon her; her feet became leaden. She hailed a taxi and gave her address, but it no longer seemed home . . . only an empty shell—as she had become.

CHAPTER XIII

IT WAS a fortnight later when Arden—having lived through those weeks in a trance while on holiday in Worcestershire—returned to London and realized that removing her body from one place to another would not solve any of her problems or fortify her against unhappiness. She despised weakness or self-pity and a stubborn, almost cynical resistance took the place of a deadly depression.

She had not even thought about unpacking her suit-cases when the bell rang and set her nerves tingling, for, although she knew it could not be Lance, nevertheless his was the name that rushed to her lips and set her heart thudding wildly.

But, as she opened the door, to her amazement and disgust, Derek stood there.

"You!" Her voice rang with the revulsion that engulfed her.

"Yes," he said quietly. "I must talk to you, Arden."

She withered him with a look.

"We have nothing further to say to each other," she rapped out.

He looked subdued as he said, "There is something I *must* say to you."

Arden sighed and let him in. It was a matter of indifference to her what he had to discuss, but co-operation was easier than argument.

"Well?" she demanded, when they reached the lounge.

He looked at her very steadily. "I'm here to apologize, to grovel if needs be."

"What!" She was taken off her guard in sheer amazement.

"I behaved despicably," he said with sudden fervour. "No matter what you had done, what I thought or felt, my attitude was damnable. I've not had a moment's peace since I was here last."

She stared at him, her brows puckered, her eyes narrowing in suspicion. This was, surely, out of character; and yet was she, too, going to join in the hideous pastime of misjudging every action?

"I cannot say I'm sorry about that, Derek. The whole thing was beneath contempt. I want only to forget it."

"And—me?"

She thought, then, how strange and how terrible it was, that love, once dead, left nothing in its wake except sheer indifference. She could look at him now without emotional reaction of any kind, cured of him to an extent which made even anger futile. And while she appreciated the logic of every word Martin had said to her—and which she had since proved to be true—nevertheless, while she believed *in* her love for Derek—no matter what its source might be—then, to her, it was absolutely real. Now, he was just a man who wanted to talk to her; a man whom she saw critically and whose features had become sharp and mean. She looked at him very steadily.

"I have already forgotten you. You held my affections because of the injustice I'd suffered. You were almost like a disease. Your return created an altogether false emotionalism. It was not *love*. I only deluded myself it was."

She saw the surprise and the disappointment that leapt into his eyes as he said, "I've deserved that."

She picked up a cigarette box and handed him a cigarette, taking one herself which he lit and then his own. She blew a little cloud of smoke into the air as she said, "Are you trying to tell me that now—through some miracle—you believe my word?"

For a second he hesitated, then, "Yes," he said firmly. "I've been wrong all along, Arden." His sigh was deep and effective. "Well, I've suffered for it."

"Not very greatly, Derek."

"You could hardly be expected to believe other than that. It isn't pleasant to see oneself as a heel—particularly to anyone of my temperament."

Arden gave him no quarter.

"And just what has brought about this amazing change of heart?"

He moved awkwardly, but refused to sit down. Arden settled herself in an armchair and studied him as she might have studied an exhibit.

"Rachel," he said startlingly.

Arden countered, "Because you have an idea that, after all, you are in love with her?"

"Because I know I am," he replied.

It was, Arden told herself, feasible. Love had been known to bring about some fantastic changes.

"I wonder," she said reflectively.

"Can't you give me credit for sincerity?" he asked almost humbly. "Oh, I know my coming here must seem almost an imposition—even my talking like this. But I had to make peace with you. I had to," he repeated fervently.

Arden said coolly, "And Rachel? Have you told her how you feel about me and the past?"

Silence followed her words; an uncanny, revealing silence which he broke by saying, "Not exactly."

Arden didn't help him out.

"Why?"

"She's rather jealous of you." His words were jerky. "It isn't easy."

Arden said deliberately, "As the story stands and from her point of view, she has just cause."

"I know . . . the trouble is that she'd never forgive me if she found out the truth, and there's so much at stake——" He stopped. "It isn't easy to make you understand. I've an idea that, before long, she'll come to see you—trying to find out how you feel."

Arden was watching him carefully.

"My telling her will not present any difficulties." Her voice was coolly practical.

Derek tried to assemble the right phrases, unnerved by Arden's scrutiny just when he had begun to feel that he was making solid progress.

"The point is——"

Arden leaned forward.

"The point is you want me to set her mind at rest—should she come here?"

He brightened.

"I knew you'd see things my way."

"Perfectly." Arden got to her feet. "Just a question of convincing her that, although I've seen you from time to time during these past months, there was nothing between us?"

Derek smiled and sighed with relief.

"Exactly."

"Do you think she would be inclined to take *my* word?"

"In this instance—yes. Mind you, this is purely guesswork on my part. But I'm certain she has her suspicions and now that I feel as I do about her——" He broke off to give his words greater significance.

Arden continued for him, "You, naturally, want to convince her of your fidelity during her absence."

He looked a little sheepish.

"I know it is deception, but I'd go to any lengths rather than lose her."

"I'm sure you would."

Derek sat down, his relief immeasurably great.

"I must say I don't deserve your generous understanding, Arden."

Her smile was slow and enigmatical.

"We don't always get what we deserve." She studied him intently and he moved nervously beneath her gaze.

"What is it?" he asked apprehensively.

"That you should dare to imagine for one moment I'd be fooled by all this, Derek. That I'd be a party to your loathsome scheming; that I'd support you in your lies. And for no better reason than that you come here and talk glibly of being sorry for all that has happened between us."

A dull flush mounted his cheeks which died to leave him pale with anger.

"You mean to tell me that you've listened and *pretended*——" He stopped.

She said curtly, "I think even you will see the humour of that. I just wanted to find out how far you would go."

Words failed him for a second, but then he burst out, "Very clever. I might have known. I came here——"

"You came here wanting something from me, Derek, and not because of any change of heart. Do you seriously think I'm so lacking in common sense? You would have made a better impression, believe me, if you'd left out your protestations of regret. They did not ring true—not for a second."

"Damn you," he said fiercely. "So you'll tell Rachel?"

Arden's voice was hard and determined.

"I shall answer any questions that may be asked me; answer them truthfully, Derek. But, just because of all that has happened, I shall not go out of my way to blacken you. I've nothing but pity for Rachel. You've no more love for her than you have for me. You want her money—that and nothing else. I don't think I've ever despised anyone so much in my life. You're mean and despicable. There isn't a single, redeeming feature about you anywhere. If you'd been sincere in your regard for Rachel, but you're not. I've nothing more to say to you, now, or at any other time."

He looked desperate. The prospect of marrying Rachel had never appealed to him more than in that moment. His avarice and greed fed on the possibility of her financial help which should enhance his prestige and enable him to achieve his lofty ambitions. He wanted power to dominate and money *was* power. Rachel was in love with him, of that there was no question, but if Arden told her the truth—should she seek that truth—then all his future plans might be ruined. At the thought of it his hatred mounted almost to homicidal intent.

The doorbell rang with a sudden, dramatic insistence. Derek started apprehensively.

"If she has followed me here," he said in a hoarse whisper. "Listen, Arden, I'll do anything."

She ignored him and went to the door. She was not expecting anyone, but it occurred to her that it might be Brian. Instead Rachel stood on the threshold.

Arden had never been able to fathom Rachel. It was impossible to gauge either her mood or her likes and dislikes. She was pleasant, but wholly impersonal. A family association had begun the friendship between her and Arden and Derek which had continued during the years of their marriage. After the divorce, however, that friendship had ceased, without comment or communication. Arden accepted it as a sign of disapproval and made no attempt to effect any reconciliation. Even then, she could not—as she had previously told Derek —be sure how Rachel felt about the situation.

Looking at her, Arden realized anew how attractive she

was, and where, before her marriage, she had been smart by virtue of making do with inferior clothes to which she gave elegance, now, in a mink coat that shimmered like velvet, she brought with her an atmosphere of wealth and luxury.

"I hope," she said and smiled, "that I am not unwelcome, Arden."

Arden returned the smile.

"Not at all. Come in. It's getting on for two years since we met. Well, eighteen or nineteen months, anyway."

Rachel didn't avert her gaze or look uncomfortable. She said simply, "It was all rather difficult."

Arden was going to offer her condolences on her bereavement, but felt it would savour of hypocrisy.

No sound came from the lounge. Arden had the absurd feeling that Derek might have resorted to hiding, but when they reached the room she knew precisely what had happened. He had taken the fire-escape-staircase way out, going through her bedroom to reach it and avoid being seen. She could not say she was sorry, but her contempt increased.

Rachel took off her soft, suede gloves to reveal a magnificent square-cut diamond which Arden correctly assumed was not a gift from Derek.

"I expect you can probably guess why I'm here," she began.

"Suppose you tell me," Arden replied.

"The subtlety of evasion."

"Not at all, Rachel. I have nothing to hide and no axe to grind."

"I'd like to be sure of that. More than anything else on earth," Rachel added with sudden earnestness.

Arden gave her a cigarette and a cocktail.

"You can be sure. The past is past. No good purpose can be served by discussing it. And, in any case, I fail to see that it can concern you."

Arden was feeling sick with apprehension, for now her concern was for this woman sitting before her; a woman in love who obviously wanted the truth and even though the withholding of it would benefit Derek to an extent he in no way deserved, Arden prayed that she might not have to deal Rachel that final, humiliating blow.

"Listen, Arden: this is an unusual situation and my being

here like this isn't easy. Your life is nothing to do with me and I've no earthly right to pry. You know that Derek and I are going to be married?" She paused.

Arden said, "Yes; I know that."

"Derek told you?"

"Yes."

Rachel sipped her drink.

"Isn't it rather strange that after all that happened you should be seeing him again?"

Arden managed to look cool and controlled.

"I don't think so." Her sigh was eloquent of regret. "Just because a marriage breaks up is no reason why two people should be at each other's throats."

"I agree—in certain circumstances. What I cannot understand is that you always protested your innocence and Derek refused to believe you. If you had truth on your side it seems very odd that you could ever sink your differences with him unless, of course, you had remained in love with him and he still found an attraction in you."

Arden knew that to be a lucid summing up. She asked herself then whether a woman in Rachel's position would prefer to be disillusioned before marriage, have all her plans wrecked, or to discover afterwards by a slow process of heartache and misery, that the man she loved was a cheat and a liar. She said quietly, "I can assure you that I am not in love with Derek, nor he with me."

Rachel relaxed in her chair. Then:

"I've no right to ask you this question; it is an impertinence, but, somehow, I've an idea that you won't lie to me. We've never been enemies. . . . I know that you and Derek saw a great deal of each other while I was away; that he visited you at your cottage and here. In fact, I know he has been to see you this evening, Arden. I expected, to be honest, to find him here."

Arden was trembling, not for herself or for anything remotely connected with her own emotions. When it came to it she would have done anything to spare another woman the nightmare of a shattered faith. She said, "That is true."

Rachel stubbed out her cigarette before it was a quarter smoked; the gesture was one of nervousness and strain. Then, "Derek has sworn to me that at no time in my absence was he your lover; that there was absolutely nothing between you to which I could possibly object." She paused in an agony of fear before adding: "I'd give my soul to believe him. Oh *Arden*— can I?" She rushed on: "Is he telling me the truth?"

The silence that followed was filled with the drama of an unbearable suspense. And in that moment Arden knew there could be no further evasion. Her voice was shaken as she answered, pity and sympathy welling into her eyes, "I'd give anything to be able to say yes. But I can't."

Rachel's face paled. A cry escaped her.

Arden went on, "If there *is* any consolation to me it lies in the fact that unless there had been doubt in your mind you would not *be* here. You would have accepted Derek's word without question."

"I couldn't." The admission came in a whisper that echoed almost mournfully through the room. "There was just something that didn't ring true."

Arden went on urgently, "I'd no idea about your being in the picture. None. I'm not afraid you will doubt my word: I have fared no better at Derek's hands than you."

Rachel said, and there was grudging admiration in her words: "No, I do not doubt you. . . . Despite everything, you would have spared me if you could, where so many women would have told me gloatingly—if only to be revenged upon *him*."

Arden said in a hushed voice, "I'm so *sorry*, Rachel. So terribly sorry. I know the hurt, the sickening disillusionment. There's nothing quite so agonizing, but better it should come now than—afterwards." She added with a sigh: "Although I've been sitting here asking myself if it wouldn't have been kinder to let you go on in your fool's paradise—as I did."

Rachel shook her head.

"No," she said violently. "He wanted my money—just that. It's ironical, but true, that had I been poor I should have found it easy to accept his word. . . . I'd like to know about you—if you could bear to tell me. Perhaps the worse it is now the better I shall be able to bear it," she added bitterly.

"Very well," Arden said gently.

She told her story without embellishment of any kind, or undue betrayal of her personal reactions. It was a simple statement of facts and rang with sincerity. When she had finished, Rachel said, a stricken expression on her face, "I know it is true, but it just doesn't seem possible that any man could be so utterly false, so lacking in *all* integrity." She paused. "It's like a nightmare . . . you must have gone through hell."

"I did."

Rachel said, the urge to talk to someone washing over her uncontrollably, "I married without love. I wanted money and position. Derek always attracted me, but there was absolutely nothing between us until after my husband died. This is perhaps my punishment for my materialism. I'd built such dreams for the future and yet, all the time, there was that fear at the back of my mind. I cut my holiday short because a friend wrote that Derek had been seen with you. There was nothing spiteful about her telling me: she had no idea I was in love with him and hoped to marry him when I got back."

Arden nodded.

"He met you in Rome—didn't he?"

"Yes." She sighed. "And that's that. It would be easy to forgive him, but I could never trust him again and I'd rather suffer now and get over it, than live the rest of my life in the shadow of fear and doubt." She looked at Arden levelly. "Thank you for being so honest and for not being eager to disillusion me. I shan't forget that. . . . And what of you? Your future?"

Arden shrugged her shoulders.

"I just don't know, Rachel. The old platitude about living one day at a time. But that about sums it up."

Rachel asked in a strangled voice, "How long does it take for love to—die?"

In thinking of Derek, Arden realized the truth that her regard for him was not a fair analogy, but the possibility of her love for Lance dying seemed as fantastic as that she should suddenly stop breathing. She said evasively, "It must depend on circumstances . . . the cynicism that the cure for one man is another is logical, at least."

Rachel looked suddenly dejected.

"I haven't even the consolation that Derek *ever* cared. Or that it was a question of falling in love and out of it." She gave a bitter, little laugh. "I suppose I had it coming to me. I married for money—as he intended to do. But," she added fiercely, "I didn't *betray* the man who loved *me*."

Arden didn't speak; words were futile. Her expression conveyed both understanding and sympathy.

Rachel got to her feet.

"And that's that," she said harshly, glancing at the clock. "Derek is taking me out to dinner to-night." A sob caught in her throat. "He'd suggested our being married next week. . . . It just doesn't seem real that all the time——" Words choked in her throat. She looked at Arden in sudden appeal. "May I 'phone you sometimes?"

"Of course."

"I'm sorry I didn't keep in touch."

Arden said lightly, "That's all right. It wasn't an easy position."

Rachel was honest. "I liked Derek too much to risk his displeasure," she confessed. "That's the truth of it."

They went to the door. It opened and shut and once again footsteps echoed down the corridor. Arden felt that her life and all the drama associated with it was symbolized by figures moving up and down that long, seemingly endless tunnel.

Now only pity superimposed itself upon her own heart-ache. But it struck her, with shattering forcefulness, just how great was the wreckage and havoc that could be wrought by one man.

CHAPTER XIV

IT WAS inevitable that during the weeks that followed, Brian should insinuate himself once more into Arden's life, automatically constituting himself her escort and endeavouring as far as it lay within his power to enable her to forget yesterday.

Arden during that time gave herself up to whatever gaiety presented itself. She danced, saw most of the plays worth seeing, picked out the best films. Meadow View had been let for six months, so that, remaining in London at her flat, she was within easy range of entertainment. From solitude she swung to the desire for company. Anything to ease the agony in her heart. With spirit and determination she had set about the task of trying to forget Lance, telling herself that she was spineless, without courage, even a neurotic! But at the end of each day when she slid into bed and lay exhausted in the darkness, the thought of him was so intense that he might have taken shape beside her. Neither love, desire, nor pain lessened. She merely grew to bear it, to accept it as a ghost who walked beside her. She saw his name on the bookstalls; in advertisements. There were items of news about his activities and . . . he was still in England. In some strange way she derived comfort from the fact.

It was a week before Christmas when she and Brian attended Barbara Manning's cocktail party. Barbara was a star author of the firm; glamorous, generous and exceedingly clever, without either conceit or an inflated opinion of her work. At forty she had the charm, in the physical sense, of a girl of twenty, but with the additional asset of poise and experience. Everyone liked her; she brought an aura of excitement, zest and beauty to any gathering she graced.

Brian called for Arden just before six o'clock.

"For goodness' sake wrap up well," he counselled. "It's absolutely freezing, and going out of this warm flat . . . Can't have you getting pneumonia." He stopped and looked at her as she stood there in a dress of black velvet relieved only by a diamond clip; a dress that fitted her figure in long, slender lines, had tight, wrist-length sleeves and a low neck-line. "You look——" He caught at his breath. "Oh, *Arden*!" He invested her name with all the longing, the frustration that surged within him.

In turn, Arden studied him, asking herself in fury and impatience why she could not will herself to love him, to be *in* love with him. There was no man in the world whom she admired more, or to whom she was more attached. He had her absolute trust and merited it and was, in every way, the type of man to make a woman an excellent husband. But no breath of emotion touched her heart as she looked at him. She saw him with her eyes, appraised him with clear, perceptive powers; a mental appreciation that left soul and body untouched. Yet, in that second, reason dominated, and when he rushed on, "If only you'd marry me," she did not protest or change the subject, she looked at him very steadily and said, to her own amazement, "If I could convince myself that it would be fair to you, I would, Brian."

He gasped, amazed and almost incoherent.

146

"Fair to me?" he echoed and repeated himself. "But darling," he put a hand up to his forehead in confusion, almost afraid of losing his case through overstatement. "But don't you see? I know you are not in love with me; I've never deceived myself on that score. I just want the right to look after you—on your own terms," he added swiftly and significantly. "I know that you're not the type to fall out of love easily; I know what Derek meant to you. I have only one hope: that in time I may be able to ease that pain and make you happy again."

Arden's lower lip was not very steady as she whispered, "Oh, Brian! You're so good to me, so unselfish. You deserve so much more than I have to give."

He answered quietly, "I'd rather have your respect and affection than the love of any other woman, my dear." He took a step nearer to her. "If I could persuade you to marry me——" He rushed on: "And if ever you wanted your freedom . . . if you found someone else . . . I'd never stand in your way. That I swear."

Arden said shakenly, "If I promise to marry you, Brian, nothing in this world would ever make me go back on that promise. That *I* swear."

He held her gaze.

"I know. . . ."

Arden thought of the years ahead; the empty, barren years of loneliness; without reason, without purpose, because purpose lay in the service of others, in the adaptation of one's life to another's needs, not in the empty wastes of personal inclination which, in the end, dissolved into the negation of apathy. Could she say with truth that, just then, there was anything in the world she genuinely wanted that didn't involve Lance? Anywhere she wanted to go? Anything she wanted to see? Her every action was designed to kill the hours until sleep— even if fitful sleep—brought the mercy of oblivion. She took her body about, but her heart remained imprisoned and with it her thoughts that were so visual as to make it seem that every breath she drew had an affinity with Lance. Somehow she must overcome that, or it would drive her mad. The sick, aching need seemed to have a physical manifestation like a weight that pressed all the air out of her lungs and denuded her body of strength. . . . Wouldn't the knowledge that she was

147

responsible for Brian's happiness give her an incentive? Wouldn't she lose herself in *his* needs, *his* rights and, in time, build up something worth while for the future? She was not promising him a love that was not hers to give, and while he believed that the shadow of Derek still pursued her, she did not disillusion him. Lance and that brief interlude were a secret her heart would keep. To that she was entitled.

She put out her hands in a gesture of appeal and trust, the memory of the past sweeping over her as she recalled Brian's courage and integrity at the time of the divorce, his self-effacement and then his infinite kindness and devotion during recent weeks.

"I will marry you," she murmured gently; "and oh, I'll try so hard to make you happy; to make up to you for all you've suffered through me and for me. If loving you and respecting you can reward you even a little——" She stopped, her eyes suspiciously bright as they saw the dazzling joy in his and realized the depth of his feeling for her.

His kiss was deep and yet tender, a kiss that told of hunger and denial and the ecstasy of sudden possession; hers was a seal of dedication, a sacred resolve to go forward, leaving the past behind in her determination to live up to the promise then made.

He drew back and looked at her wonderingly.

"I can't believe it," he said tensely.

She smiled affectionately.

"You *can*."

"Darling—when? I mean, you don't want a long engagement, do you?"

"No," she said. "Let's talk that over after the party . . . we *must* be going."

"I feel that I've already been rocketed to the moon," he said boyishly. He shook his head. "You've never given me a moment's peace, young lady, since I first met you—four years ago."

"It comes to something when you have to marry a woman in order to get some peace," she teased, trying to capture his mood of exuberance and gaiety.

"May I tell everyone to-night?"

"Of course."

He said gently, "To be married in May would be rather

lovely, or if you are superstitious, very early June." He added, "Much as I want it to be to-morrow, I don't want to stampede you and by then I shall hope to have worked miracles."

Arden's heart seemed to lift a few inches. She had not thought in terms of months before marrying and yet could not ignore the relief that surged upon her.

"Bless you . . . June 1st," she said solemnly.

"That will give me time to find the right house and for you to furnish it as you wish," he said firmly.

Arden loved him for that. His was the type of sensitivity that would know of her reluctance to begin a new life in old surroundings and that Meadow View had come to stand for something that soiled her.

"That will be fun," she agreed. "I shall sell the cottage."

"And we'll keep my flat," he said stoutly. "Handy. . . . *Darling*——" He spoke in breathless, awed wonderment. "I doubt if I ever could be happier than at this moment, yet I know I shall be," he added almost humbly.

"We are both going to be happy," she promised.

Brian said with sudden gravity, "I wish I were a wealthy man, Arden."

She answered promptly, "I'm thankful you are not." She looked at him earnestly. "We've more than enough. I want to build a *home*, Brian, and all the money in the world cannot do that. It can merely build a house."

She spoke with great conviction, buoying herself up on the wave of a new enthusiasm. She had made a decision; a decision on which there could be no question of going back. She would be Brian's wife and the mother of his children. . . . She clenched her teeth because emotion poured through her heart like a river bursting a dam.

They went down to Brian's car. His swift glances were possessive and proud, he seemed suddenly to have acquired a new personality.

"I feel like a king," he said absurdly.

Icy winds clawed at their faces, the grim, damp December night hurled its fury at them. Street lamps threw uncanny shadows that lurked unexpectedly; rather, thought Arden, like life.

"The heater's on," Brian said as he tucked the fur rug around her.

149

"I'm beautifully warm," she assured him, telling herself that it was a joy suddenly to be cherished and taken care of again. Again. . . . Had Derek ever done that beyond the point where it came under the heading of good manners? Derek. His name meant nothing. All that might have happened in another life.

On the way to the Regent's Park house of Barbara Manning, Brian said, "I believe Lance Ashton is to be there to-night."

Arden's hands clenched as they lay in her lap.

"I thought he was due to go abroad."

"So he was—has been for months. Have you seen him lately?"

The question was purely conversational.

"No; not since just after we all had lunch together, as a matter of fact."

Brian nodded. The remark held no significance for him.

"I saw him about three weeks ago. He's taken a service flat in St. James's. Seemed to be rather tired of the country. Glad I'm not an author. Must be the devil sometimes."

Arden breathed deeply.

"Why?"

"Temperament; moods. Nothing *there* to do. . . . Blank sheets of paper to be filled with words! Ghastly."

"Not if it happened to be your job, or you had that particular mentality. With him the word 'gift' or 'talent' would be applicable."

"It still carries its penalties."

"And its rewards," she countered.

"Oh, true. I like my feet on the ground for all that. There's something solid about routine."

Arden smiled indulgently.

"I suppose so."

"But you'd like the other?" he teased.

"I can see the inward satisfaction, the sense of accomplishment in creating something. Something, of course, that is not merely ephemeral."

"You're dead right," Brian said. "To-night, however, I could not envy Lance Ashton, or any other man on God's earth, *anything*." He reached out and clasped her hand. "You're my world, Arden. Just that."

Arden sat there humbled by a devotion she in no way underestimated. She said impulsively, "Your attitude over Derek—my being with him again—had I needed anything to increase my regard for you, that certainly would have done so."

Brian said honestly, "You made my attitude simple, darling."

"Why?" Her voice was suddenly alert.

"Your honesty. You didn't pretend that he was other than your lover."

A knife stabbed at Arden's heart.

"But if I had, would it have made all that difference?"

He didn't answer her at once.

"It wouldn't have killed my love, but it would have lessened my faith, my respect."

In the darkness of the car she winced. That was precisely how Lance had felt.

Brian glanced at her uneasily. "What is it?"

"Nothing. Except that I realize how much easier it is to forgive infidelity than the deceit that all too often accompanies it."

"Without trust," Brian said resolutely, "there is nothing. When you lose faith in people's word you condemn them even when they are telling the truth. That is the tragedy of it."

"Or you refuse to listen to that truth," she said heavily.

He felt a sudden chill creep over him.

"You are not imagining for one second that you ever misjudged Derek?"

Her hollow, mocking laughter more than convinced him.

"Anything but that."

Brian heaved a sigh.

They reached their destination.

The Manning house stood out in the gloom, like a beacon on a dark night. Its bowed Regency windows, from which the curtains had been partly opened to let in fresh air to the centrally heated rooms, sent off beams of light across the roadway. Cars overflowed down side streets and an atmosphere of gaiety came on the wave of laughter and voices as they were admitted.

Barbara's parties were a tradition. They might begin as an affair for cocktails and end up as an informal dance. While everything was impeccably done, nevertheless, it was an unconventional pattern that followed in the wake of perfect service. She, herself, radiant in soft, misty blue which enhanced the lustre of her blonde hair, greeted them with a warm smile that was part of her personality. She was glad to see them and had gathered around her only those whom she considered friends or, being extremely precise, acquaintances whom she wished to cultivate as friends. Arden had known her and met her through Martin, who was her lawyer. Brian knew her both as a friend and because she was published by his company. She was the star of the "subsidiaries".

"You'll know almost everybody," she said gaily. "Arden, Martin's here. And oh, I got the lion, after all. Pleased about that, because I like him—not just his fame. You both know Lance Ashton, of course."

Arden tried to sound casual. She knew him.

"Don't go at the polite time . . . we shall dance afterwards and I've a special buffet laid on. Harry"—her husband who hovered adoring nearby and who had already grinned a friendly greeting—"says I'm crazy. But, I know that. Such fun, too!"

They moved into a large drawing-room, panelled in cream and blue damask, with a deeper gold-leaf beading. A parquet floor, adorned with priceless rugs, shone like a golden mirror.

Arden's gaze flashed across the gathering. It was not over-crowded and it was easy to distinguish the individual. And in that second she looked into Lance's eyes—eyes that met hers with faintly cynical directness that faded into swift, shattering emotion as he moved nearer and said finally, "Good-evening." His voice was smooth but, for her, it held a taunting note. "Quite some time since we met, Arden." He looked at Brian, arrested by something in his expression. "You are looking extremely pleased with life, Newton."

"I have," said Brian, "cause to be." He glanced at Arden.

In the tense second of silence that followed the temperature of the room seemed to Arden to rise to a degree so stifling that she felt she would faint. She saw Lance start almost in suspicion, then, "Really," he said promptingly.

"Yes . . . Arden has promised to be my wife. In fact you are the first person to know."

152

Lance stared at first incredulously, faint bewilderment clouding his gaze. Marriage!

"Congratulations." The word rapped out as he turned to Arden. "And may I wish you happiness?"

Arden's heart was thudding so painfully that it seemed to be choking her. An agony of misery washed over her; a longing for Lance, intensified by his presence, until control was a torture. He stood there challenging, cynical and withdrawn, his attraction never more potent or magnetic, and yet it would have been so easy to convince herself that beneath the cold exterior the flame of love still burned to torment him no less than her.

Brian laughed softly.

"I deserve the congratulations. . . . No man ever had a harder task!" The word slid off his tongue; he was too happy to be guarded, or even discreet.

Lance's smile was enigmatical.

"I can understand that," he said slowly.

Martin sauntered up, Heather at his side, and joined the group.

The necessary introductions were made and Martin said warmly, "None of your readers has enjoyed your books more than I."

Lance inclined his head in acceptance of the compliment and to his thanks, added, "This is an occasion . . . your sister has some news to impart."

Heather, her interest sharpened by the presence of Lance, looked blank and echoed, "News!"

Brian made the announcement, swiftly and with pride.

"No!" Heather gasped. *"Well!"*

Martin was both pleased and perturbed. He looked at Arden intently, made suitable remarks to both her and Brian, and then found himself watching Lance Ashton's face. An impressive, distinguished face . . . just the type of man he could imagine Arden being happy with. The thought flashed through his mind and he dismissed it.

Heather indulged in a string of banalities and then asked, "Are you being married soon?"

"June," said Arden swiftly. She avoided Lance's penetrating gaze.

Inevitably, the little group split up, but Lance remained

153

at Arden's side while Brian was dragged into a conference with two other men whom he had tried in vain to avoid.

Conversation beat around them like noisy wings, the chink of glasses—all became a cacophony.

"It reminds me of the first cocktail party we attended together," Lance said pointedly.

"Barbara's parties are always wonderful." Arden tried to sound blithe.

Lance said suddenly, tensely, "What are you thinking?"

His words took her by surprise, they fell stealthily between them like a ghost of memory pleading a lost cause. Her love for him surged and swelled within her, her body trembling with its impact, and she said, clutching desperately at a fugitive restraint, "Isn't that rather a superfluous question?"

His eyes widened.

"Superfluous?"

"Yes, since you wouldn't believe me whatever I told you."

He sighed and said ruefully, "I wonder." His expression changed as he sought to penetrate the mask she crouched behind in order to hide her own secret. "I suppose this is a fitting ending," he murmured cynically. "Devotion, tenacity and loyalty such as Newton has shown deserves reward."

Arden could not stay the words that rushed from her lips. "Particularly as all he has ever had in return from me has been friendship. I seem to remember that I told you that before— if not in so many words. My apologies for repeating myself," she said icily.

His pulse quickened, shaking him. There was something about her that tore at his heart. Now that time had brought the calm of reflection, the autumn of that first, sharp jealousy, the agony of fear lay upon him lest, after all, he had misjudged her. Yet there remained the deceit, the pretence. He said hoarsely, "Let's not hurt each other any more——" He made a helpless gesture, shrinking from the banality of his own words.

Their eyes met, emotion held them. Arden tried to speak but the muscles in her throat contracted.

"If only you'd listened," she said brokenly.

"Would that have restored faith?" he asked harshly.

Her gaze was suddenly steady and powerful in its honesty.

"Faith should not need *restoring*. If it had taken me on trust instead of condemning me unheard. *That* isn't *love*."

He cried, "And do you know love? Do you *profess* to know it?"

It seemed that every drop of blood in her body touched her heart like fire as she answered, "I don't profess—I *know*."

He winced; it was as though all strength went from him, making any feud, bitterness or cynicism, futile and empty.

"I see." He stared at her almost helplessly. "Strange how two people meet and, for a while, seem complete affinities and then . . . they end up talking to each other at a party—their worlds a thousand miles apart."

She said shakenly, "You set the distance, Lance."

He glanced to where Brian was coming towards them.

"In view of this important occasion and of your great love for Brian Newton—of which you left me in no doubt just now —that was perhaps fortunate for my peace of mind." His eyes became cold as the memory of the past crept back stealthily and insidiously to mock him. "To have been betrayed *afterwards* would have been far more shattering than disillusionment *before* you belonged to me."

Arden never knew just what prompted her words, but they came with a quiet impressiveness that stunned him.

"When the hatred goes from your heart you will understand, Lance. Perhaps it would better if that day never came. . . . If you'll excuse me," she added, and before he could speak, she had moved away, joining Brian and then finding herself in a little quiet patch with Martin.

He looked at her, conscious of the strain of her expression, the tension, and puzzled to a point of deep anxiety.

"This engagement is a little sudden, surely?"

"After all the years I've known Brian—all that has happened?"

"Neither is a reason for marrying him, Arden. Unless you are in love with him. Are you?"

Arden could not deceive Martin, or attempt to do so, and she answered, "I love him enough to be quite sure of making him happy and I am not cheating him. He knows exactly how I feel towards him."

"That doesn't set my mind at rest," he commented gloomily. "You were not intended for an existence of compromise."

She looked at him and her voice was gentle as she asked,

"Were *you*, Martin? Oh, don't you *see*? We cry for the moon——"

"Ah," he jumped in, "so there is a moon to cry *for*?"

Taken off her guard, the colour burned into Arden's cheeks, making it impossible for her to dissemble.

"If there were that moon, then it is as far out of reach as you are from Catherine," she murmured.

Martin looked disconsolate, but he was, also, persistent.

"Meaning that he is married?"

"I'd rather not talk about it, if you don't mind. There's nothing to be gained," she said quietly, "and nothing that can ever be altered. I'm going to marry Brian and no power in this world would ever change that decision now. He deserves so much and I'll never find anyone half so devoted, or so loyal," she finished shakenly.

Martin was making swift calculations. Whom did Arden know in the sense that was applicable to any emotional interest? It was an impossible question to answer, for he did not, naturally, come into contact with all her friends or acquaintances—many of whom were bound up with her work.

"Then there is nothing more for me to say beyond wishing desperately for your happiness, my dear, is there? And heaven knows, I feel deeply enough where you are concerned."

Heather joined them in that moment. "Martin . . . do we have to stay? I mean, haven't you had enough? I don't understand half that's said to me and you can't possibly talk about books you've never read and plays you've never seen. I'm quite certain that no one here ever does a stroke of work," she finished with unconscious humour.

Arden laughed. "They're mostly very successful people, Heather."

"Oh—*that*. I meant real work. I'll bet they've never cooked a meal or scrubbed a floor in their life," she said in the tone of one who considered that to be the ultimate achievement in any language.

"You'd be surprised," Arden countered. "It is merely that they are not interested very much in talking domesticity." She added swiftly, "Just a matter of taste."

"I never was one for this kind of thing," Heather said comfortably. "Far rather be doing my ironing and I left simply masses to do. Christmas is an absolute nightmare.

Nothing but work and more work. Not worth it. Just not worth it."

Martin asked, trying to curb his impatience, "And just what *is* worth it, Heather?"

She took affront.

"Oh, it's all very well for *you*. All you have to do is go to the office every day. You haven't to run a home and look after the children." She didn't quite know why she felt on edge unless it was that although Martin had given her the money to buy herself a new outfit for this occasion she had "made do" and, consequently, knew that she looked dowdy.

Arden, trying to be tactful, said—as is invariably the case—the wrong thing. "Oh, Heather! I knew there was something! How about my getting seats for you and the children for a pantomime? We could make a day of it. They'd love it and it would be a change for you, too."

Heather said swiftly, "Thank you all the same, Arden, but I hate coming up to London and hate London, too. Such a rush and it means getting back late and there's the evening meal——"

Martin said, "For heaven's sake, Heather, I can stay up here and meet you. We can have a meal out before we go home."

She said instantly, "I'd hate that. I always feel awful when I've been stifled in those ghastly hot theatres and restaurants. Gives me a dreadful head. I've got one now as a matter of fact. Can't stand central heating. Wouldn't have it as a gift."

Martin flashed Arden a meaning glance.

"I think we'll be getting along. Here's Brian to take over—if you needed it."

"Which she doesn't, really," said Brian. "A good party." He glanced at Arden. "Want to stay, darling? It's thinning out and there'll be dancing any minute."

"Dancing!" Heather made the word sound as though it were a penance. "How you people stand it beats me. I'm dog-tired *now*." She looked at Arden. "But I suppose you had a nice sleep this afternoon."

Arden laughed.

"I've been at the Advertising office all day, my dear. Only just had time to bath and change."

"Then you must be strong somewhere," came the retort.

"I should hope so," Arden agreed. She had never seen Heather in such a mood.

Brian tried persuasion. "Why not stay, Heather? Look here, I can put you up. . . . Arden could lend you all the things you need and——"

Heather protested vigorously, "I wouldn't dream of it. Not that I don't appreciate it, Brian. But I like my own bed and can't *bear* borrowing anything. Arden knows. She won't be offended." She glanced up at Martin. "If we go now we can catch the eight-forty and be home and in bed by ten."

Martin didn't speak, but his expression was eloquent of his utter indifference. Without Catherine, did it *matter* whether they went or stayed? He thought of her with a sudden desperate longing. She would have loved the gaiety of this night and entered into the spirit of it with the same zest and abandon with which she would have enjoyed a quiet walk through country lanes, or dining at an old hotel off the beaten track. He looked at Arden. Her marriage would never descend to the level of mediocrity, for Brian was too alert and vital a person to allow it, but, without emotion, without love, a dreariness would ultimately drain from it even the consolation of its stability and security. That was the tragedy. The best phases of human relationship soured without the impetus of passion.

In that second Martin intercepted a glance that flashed between Arden and Lance Ashton and for a second his heart felt that it stopped beating. Was it *possible*? Was that the answer? He had heard her speak of him, of course, and realized that their relationship was sufficiently friendly for them to have discarded the surnames. Yet, assuming they cared for each other, what had happened to keep them apart? His blood chilled slightly. *Derek?* He found no answer to the question and stopped conjecturing, telling himself that not even a brother had a right to pry too closely into the affairs of his sister. All he did know was that Arden's life, thus far, had been a tragic unfulfilment. She had married the wrong man—even though it was only now she would admit it—and she had added a second mistake to the original error. He said patiently —with that patience eloquent of absolute resignation—to Heather, "Very well, Heather. If you really want to go."

She brightened and, having got her own way, changed her
158

attitude as, sidling closer to Arden, she murmured, "Sorry I've been a beast. Don't know what got into me. I'm just not cut out for this kind of thing. Always on edge . . . you must come to us for Christmas."

Lance, passing by them on his way to talk to a friend, paused. "Not going?" He looked at Martin and thought that he had a characteristic and family charm. He turned to Heather whom he decided would make a perfect type for his new book. She stood for everything in life that was anathema to him. And she looked the part. The old *cliché* went through his mind: "What on earth made a man like Marchly marry *her?*" His eyes managed to conceal his reactions as he said: "The party hasn't really begun."

Heather replied nervously, "We're country bumpkins, Mr. Ashton. I'm just a housewife among all this glamour. Just a housewife," she repeated defensively, and gave a faintly inane giggle which grated.

"Then," he said quietly, "you are among friends. Ninety per cent of the women here to-night are, also, housewives."

Arden stepped in, watching the mortification creeping into Heather's eyes and aware of Martin's discomfort.

"You could include the men," she said gaily, "they do their share of the chores to-day—unfortunately."

Heather reacted violently and Arden groaned inwardly at her own *faux pas*.

"And why—unfortunately? Why shouldn't they help?"

Arden smiled.

"No reason; but I think it should cut both ways. Why shouldn't the man expect his wife to do half his office work? As I see it, both have their individual jobs and their obligations. However, everyone to their own pattern. Personally, I hope to find some vastly more thrilling pastimes with my husband than his helping me with housework."

Brian gave a little satisfied chuckle.

"Then I take it I've no need to buy an apron!"

"At your peril," Arden warned.

They laughed without being the faintest bit interested. It merely tided the conversation over until Martin and Heather left.

Arden watched them go and depression seeped into her.

Brian shook his head.

"There's a man making a damn fine job of living against his every instinct," he said solemnly. "Duty—plus. A worthy woman, Heather, but——"

"She never looks above the sink," Arden said regretfully. "They have absolutely no companionship, no community of interests whatsoever. If Martin hadn't his work he'd go mad."

Brian's gaze was intimate and adoring.

"How lucky I am," he whispered.

She forced a note of banter because, Lance gone from them, the room seemed suddenly empty.

"Don't be too optimistic," she challenged lightly.

He held her gaze.

"Don't forget that I've already seen you running a home, being a wife," he answered quietly.

"Which makes you a devil for punishment," she laughed. "You have been warned!"

Lance glanced back to where they were standing and Barbara Manning, who had just joined him, followed his gaze.

"I'm terribly pleased about those two," she said with genuine interest. "He's always adored her."

Lance became instantly alert.

"Meaning that——" He floundered.

Barbara said stoutly, "Meaning that the divorce was a scandal."

His brow puckered, his mouth felt dry, his throat constricted.

"I don't follow——"

Barbara stared at him in concern.

"I'm sorry; I didn't mean to give anything away."

"No; no," he corrected, suspense mounting. "I knew Arden had been divorced."

Barbara leapt in staunchly, "Yes, but it was a defended action, don't forget—just in case you don't know all the facts."

"*Defended*." The word escaped Lance's lips almost as if it burned them.

"Of course." Barbara spoke with absolute sincerity. "No one who knew either of them believed a word of it. Oh, not because Brian and Arden are saints, but because they aren't the types to sneak around corners and certainly not to perjure themselves in order to escape any consequences. Arden was far too wrapped up in that wretched husband of hers to look at any other man. But he was a petty, jealous humbug if ever there was one." She rattled on at terrific speed: "I did hear that they'd been seen together recently. . . . Thank heaven it was only a rumour. Brian has been a wonderful friend. His loyalty never wavered. He's stood by her magnificently. We all hoped that, in the end, he'd win."

Lance stood there, stunned. Oddly enough, insanely enough, he told himself fiercely, it had never occurred to him to consider the possibility of the action being defended. The thought leapt at him: *Janet must have known.*

Barbara exclaimed, "My dear man, you look very surprised. Glad I mentioned the subject." Her gaze was warning. "Don't you go getting any wrong ideas about Arden." A smile broke from her lips. "Not that you would: you're good friends—aren't you?"

Lance felt suddenly denuded of strength.

"Yes," he said dully. Obviously, Barbara did not know the facts of Arden's subsequent relationship with Derek. He knew that he was glad.

"Divorce laws in this country!" She made a little sound of disgust. "Biggest hypocrites in the world. Better not let me ride that pet hobby-horse—this is not the time for such luxuries!"

With that she sailed away, flinging him a gay smile over her shoulder.

Lance stood there, unable to explain his reactions. On the face of it was the information so vital? Did it change the position from his point of view? Arden's words came back to haunt him: *"I have a story to tell . . . you would not listen to it, or believe it."*

Impatience gripped him. That chapter in his life was ended. He told himself fiercely that, having suffered as he had at the hands of his former wife, it was not in him to take any other woman on trust, or to endure anything—tolerate anything—in the nature of deception. That he could not forgive. Suppose Brian and Arden had been innocent at the time of the divorce? What of all that had happened since? Had there been no attraction between them, she would hardly be engaged to him now. It suited him to build up the case in order to escape from the tormenting sensation approximating guilt that lurked in his subconscious mind.

It was later that evening, when only intimate friends of the Mannings remained, and dancing was in progress, that Lance managed, after much effort, to get Arden to dance with him.

Arden had made it obvious she had no wish to do so. She had avoided him deliberately, dreading the intimacy of his arms about her, struggling against the desire that tore through her body.

Lance guided her, with almost masterful determination, to the centre of the floor. His hold was firm and close, his eyes met hers in seeking, unconscious appeal.

"For once I win," he said deliberately. "You had no intention of dancing with me."

She sought frantically for an excuse, but she was aware only of his nearness and of his overpowering effect upon her; of her love that seemed to take shape as her heart thudded madly against him, so madly that, in unison with his own, it became one giant pulse between them which neither could ignore.

"I had no intention," she managed to say swiftly, "of discussing the past, or ourselves, again."

"Nothing is solved by ignoring the issue."

She nerved herself to meet his dark, passionate gaze.

"There is no issue." Her lips twisted wryly. "You made that abundantly clear the last time we met. *I* emphasize that now by my engagement to Brian."

"Why didn't you tell me that you defended the divorce case?" He had not meant to mention it, but the urge was stronger than his will to resist.

Arden tensed.

"I assumed you knew." She said forcefully and deliberately: "It is strange how the knowledge of your own innocence makes it perilously easy for you to imagine that others take it for granted, also. There is no perfect alibi—for the guiltless. And since your informant against me was so exceedingly well versed in the art of distorting certain facts, I am not surprised that such an important item in my favour was withheld. It makes perfect sense to me. But that still does not mean I wish to discuss it, Lance."

She could see that he was wavering, torn between the conflict of warring emotions, at the mercy of a temperament volatile and not wholly without prejudice inspired by the disillusionment of his marriage, and she fought tenaciously to stave off any point of compromise.

"As you wish. I thought you might welcome the opportunity——"

She cut in sharply, "The opportunity of vindicating myself?" Her laugh was suddenly low and hollow. "If you knew the irony of that. I have done with vindication, *or* the desire for it."

A knife was turning in her heart as she spoke, but only anger and hostility could prevent her from betraying the love, the yearning that surged within her.

He didn't speak for a moment, then, "It is not a habit of mine to misjudge people, Arden."

She flashed him a challenging look.

"Don't tell me that your confidence has been shaken merely on account of the divorce being defended. I had so many other vices to account for. It was a long list, if I remember rightly. And I collected scalps." Her voice taunted him, it came from an anguish, a terror of her own impulsive action in agreeing to marry Brian. Lance's arms emphasized the enormity of her decision and the desperate emptiness that lay ahead.

He wrestled with his own shattering thoughts, swayed first one way and then another, striving to form some conclusion that would set his mind at rest.

He could not freeze the words that rushed from his lips. "Will you answer one question?"

Again her eyes met his and then her gaze fell before the unspoken longing that was unmistakable.

"No," she said shakenly, "because no purpose could now be served. You would not believe me . . . I'm sorry, Lance. I suggest you ask your secretary anything you want to know about me." She drew in her breath sharply as she added: "I've an idea that she and my ex-husband had one idea in common at least. To damn me in your eyes."

Lance stared at her, almost stupefied.

"Are you seriously suggesting——"

"I am 'suggesting' simply and solely on my woman's intuition," she said honestly. "Now, if you don't mind, I'm rather tired. Would you excuse me?"

He inclined his head like an automaton and politely

returned her to Brian's side. He knew in that second that there was nothing more he could say to which she would listen. And never had he loved her so well as in that moment of final and irrevocable loss.

CHAPTER XV

LANCE began work on a new novel and found that at the end of each day as Janet handed him the typescript, his dissatisfaction increased. Within it was betrayed the turmoil and instability of his own mind which was haunted by the ever-growing fear lest he had misjudged the one person in the world he loved. That fear crystallized, eating its way into his every thought, his every hope. And while he detested himself for the weakness, he was nevertheless paralysed by it—mentally, physically and spiritually. And the date of delivery of the new book crept uncomfortably near. It did not matter that he could easily obtain an extension of time: his principles rejected taking advantage of his position and success. He had promised the MS. That was enough.

And as Janet handed back the day's work one evening she said anxiously, "It isn't going well—is it, Lance?" She was concerned and sympathetic. "Personally, I think you are very foolish not to do something about getting away for Christmas. You need a break—a complete break." She added casually: "I don't know why the thought suddenly came into my head: but I notice that Arden Marchly and Brian Newton are engaged. Did you know?"

He looked at her with an unnerving gaze.

"I knew," he replied grimly. "It was announced at the party the other night."

She said with a faintly aggrieved air, "You didn't tell me. Well! That will come as a surprise to people."

Lance had waited for just that opening, for he had been assembling all his facts, and now they were complete.

"On the contrary," he said, and something in his tone arrested her attention, making her catch at her breath.

"What do you mean?" Fear lurked beneath her smile, an empty, foolish smile calculated to hide her feelings.

"Just that, Janet." He looked at her very levelly. "Could

you tell me why you omitted one rather important detail from your vicious damnation of Arden?"

"My damnation of her!" Janet echoed the words as though he were mad. "I don't know what you mean. As for omitting anything——"

"The little matter of the divorce action being defended," he said slowly.

Her heart regained a more normal pulse rate.

"Well, really, Lance! I assumed you knew."

"And why should I know since you took such delight in imparting the news?"

She covered her confusion by adding hastily, "I mean that it was a thing anyone could find out. I showed you the cuttings."

"You—*what*?"

She covered up her mistake hastily.

"I'm sorry. Derek showed them to me."

"*Derek.* . . . So you are friendly with him?"

"Nothing of the kind. Honestly, Lance! I don't know what has come over you lately."

"I do," he said grimly. "I've come to my senses."

There was a second of tense, electrical silence. Janet felt that she was being walled into some airless cubicle peopled with grotesque, fearsome shapes. Unsure of her ground, of how much he knew, there was little she could say.

"Then," she snapped, "there is no reason to be hateful to me. What does it matter whether the wretched divorce action was defended or not? The woman's engaged to marry the co-respondent and as far as I'm concerned——" She broke off impatiently. "Honestly, Lance! Anyone would think the matter was important."

"It is," he said with a forbidding quietness, "to me."

She paled.

"When did you see Derek Rayne last?"

Her eyes widened in her pale, hard face, she smoothed a shaking hand over her shining, black hair—a nervous gesture.

"When? . . . The day I told you that Arden was his ex-wife."

Lance was sitting in his chair and he leaned over the arm of it to take a cigarette from a box on the table nearby.

"That isn't the truth." His voice was stern. "You've seen

him many times since then . . . no, don't get up; I've not half
finished yet. And that day you were supposed to have met him
'in the village'. That wasn't true, either. You met him at
Tring after he had telephoned you."

"How—how could you possibly know that?"

"Partly deduction; partly discovery. A friend of mine
happened to have lunch at the hotel near there that day. He
mentioned seeing you. At the time it didn't register. Later, in
fact as I began to piece things together, it had significance. He
was able to pin-point the occasion because it was his wife's
birthday."

"Well! Is there any law against my having lunch with
a man?"

"None whatsoever, my dear; but you must have had a very
good reason for lying about it. And that reason provided
a common purpose to you both," he added fiercely.

"I think," she ridiculed, "that you should see a psychiatrist, Lance. You are really behaving in a most extraordinary
manner."

He ignored that.

"You and Rayne were both intent upon achieving the same
objective—to damn Arden in my eyes."

Janet tried to keep control of her emotions and she said
gently, "Lance, you don't know what you are saying. Why on
earth should I want to do that? It is true I suspected Arden
—and my suspicions were correct. But, beyond that, she
wasn't involved in your scheme of things. Oh, I know you
were friends——"

"You knew," he said, and his voice rang through the silence,
"that I was in love with her. I would add, just in case there can
be misunderstanding, that I still am."

He did not misjudge Janet as he made that statement, for,
instantly, her attitude changed, the tigress took the place of
the lamb as her eyes darkened in the fire of jealousy that was
like a flame burning within her.

"So!" she cried. "After all that happened, she fooled you,
too! Why——"

"I don't want to hear anything you have to say and I will
not listen to any vituperation. For your own purpose you told
me a story—I congratulate you on the manner, the convincing
manner, in which you told it—that seemed irrefutable."

"It is irrefutable," she burst out triumphantly. "There's nothing you can say or do will change that! She was his wife; she was his mistress and Brian Newton's, too. And she fooled you. She wasn't one scrap better than your wife. Did you imagine I was going to sit back and watch you wreck your life for the second time?"

"I'm sorry," he said grimly, "that I cannot appreciate your solicitude."

Urgency crept into her voice.

"Listen, Lance . . . I've not lied to you. It's true I didn't stress the defence angle of the divorce. Why should I? Frankly, I knew it carried no weight and I knew what she was to Mr. Newton."

"You *knew* nothing of the kind. And the very fact that your meeting with Rayne was no accident proves he had some ulterior motive for telling you the story he did. That was why you were so careful to talk of a casual meeting, an unexpected meeting. It made sense and rang true. But it doesn't any more."

She cried fiercely, "Do you mean to tell me that you disbelieve——"

"I disbelieve everything except the facts that are indisputable: that Arden was Rayne's wife and that their relationship at Meadow View *was* as you were so happy to suggest."

"And isn't that *enough*?" She sneered. "Or do you like being taken for a ride, deceived and fooled? You, of all people! It isn't possible."

Lance studied her and a feeling of disgust surged over him.

"I thought," he said regretfully, "that you were above anything like this, Janet. I would have staked my life on your loyalty. At best I can try only to make excuses because you were actuated from the start by a fiendish jealousy."

She stared at him, the blood seeming to be impacted in her veins, her head throbbing mercilessly. Just when she had congratulated herself that victory was hers; when Arden's engagement had removed the final barrier and she had felt completely safe and secure.

"Loyalty," she cried, her voice rising. "When everything I said was for your benefit; because, because——" She stopped.

"Suppose we leave it at that?" he said more kindly.

She made a gesture of despair.

"But, when it comes to it, what has happened? ... If I was wrong about Brian Newton's part in the story, then it was the only thing I was wrong about," she added violently.

Lance looked at her very steadily. "I suggest to you, Janet, that you knew you were wrong and that part of your story was nothing more than a vile slander backed up cleverly and subtly by an unfortunate but convenient truth. Just sufficient truth to make it all a horrible distortion. You know and I know that such truth can sometimes be the biggest lie of all."

"And you would believe *her*?"

He said, and a sickening sensation engulfed him, "I'd give my soul for the privilege of being allowed to do so. It's strange, that. Your story filled me with a fire, a jealousy that was fed, unnaturally, by the past. You didn't overlook that—did you? Every word you uttered was calculated to hit at a wound. I wouldn't hear reason. I wouldn't see beyond facts which I realize now probably told me very little."

"Too bad all this wonderful faith you've suddenly acquired has come too late. You'll never marry her. Never." A homicidal gleam came into her eyes. "And I'm glad. Glad! You men are such blind *fools*. What does devotion and loyalty and service mean to you—nothing! Along comes a pretty, empty doll without principles or morals and——"

"That is enough," he thundered.

In that second, reading her doom in his cold, contemptuous gaze, she lost every vestige of pride and courage as she cried brokenly, "Lance . . . you must listen . . . I was wrong. I'll admit that, but I was in love with you—you knew that, too. I prayed you might come to care for me, built the hope up in my mind, and then *she* came into the picture. I knew that first day when you were so eager to take back the drawing. . . . I knew that she was the one woman who could wreck all my plans, my dreams, and I vowed that, somehow, I'd——" She stopped, aware of the enormity of all she was saying, horrified by the fact that she had been capable of it, and yet still goaded by the passion that tore at her body reducing her to a pitiful, dejected state of ignominy, as she covered her face with her hands and burst into uncontrollable sobbing.

Lance got to his feet and going to the cocktail cabinet poured out some brandy which he offered her saying quietly, "Drink this . . . you'll feel better, then."

And even in that second when his mind was seething with emotion as the thought of Arden brought a hunger almost unbearable—even then, it struck him how curious human nature was, how absorbing were human types. Janet, cold, elegant, authoritative, dominating. . . . Yet when it came to it, there was no strength, no control. While the more sensitive woman, delicate, sympathetic . . . she would be precisely the reverse, without it even being expected of her!

Janet drank and mentally searched for a way out. She'd allowed herself to be stampeded into this scene, whereas, had she kept quiet . . . What was the use of arguing like that? Her only hope was to appeal to his pity. Lance was the soft-hearted type who couldn't bear tears. Somehow there must be a way of winning him over. He had lost Arden. . . . She saw the folly of clutching at that fact, for he could only hold her partly responsible for that tragedy. She was in no doubt that Arden reciprocated his affection and but for the carefully contrived story would have married him. A flash of triumph momentarily pierced the gloom of her reflections. In that at least she had succeeded, whatever happened. She looked up, her expression appealing, "I'm so sorry." Her voice was hushed.

"That's all right." He took the empty glass from her.

"If you'd just bear with me, Lance."

"Well?" He looked down at her, remaining standing and leaning against the mantelpiece. "I'll try very hard to be patient, Janet. But I refuse to go back over old ground and I am not seeking information."

She said softly, "I've been wrong, wicked even. Nothing you could say would be too bad, although, in all honesty, I cannot retract the story I told you. It stands as the truth as I know it. In that, at least," she said effectively and without scruple, "be fair. Any wrong I may have done you lay in my ulterior motive for telling it." She hurried on: "We've been friends, Lance. Your work has meant everything to me; your success——"

He stopped her with a deadly finality.

"I'm sorry, Janet, but this is the end."

Her face went grey.

"You mean——" The rest of her words were lost in an unnatural sound that seemed to come from the base of her throat.

"I mean that I couldn't go on working with you," he said quietly. "All these weeks—ever since, in fact, you began all this—I've lost the mood. And it isn't wholly my own feelings that are responsible. Suffering can provide impetus. Conflict—*that* is the death of any creative effort. And there has been that conflict. I've absorbed your mood just as any writer absorbs the mood of those about him—alas!"

"Are you telling me that my work as your secretary is—over?"

"I'm afraid I am." He looked at her very steadily. "In view of my feelings for Arden and the knowledge I have of your conniving with Derek Rayne, anything less would be an insult to her."

"To her! And what does she know or care for your actions?" she burst out, anger mingling to increase the fear and horror that lay upon her. "All her thoughts are for someone else; someone she's going to *marry*. Marry," she repeated. "And deny if you can that she refused *you* before any of this happened!"

She knew then that what had seemed her trump card was, in reality, the death knell of her hopes.

Wordlessly, Lance walked to his writing-desk and took out his cheque-book. He filled in a form for one hundred guineas, tore it out with precision and, returning to her side, handed it to her.

"This," he said with an impressive dignity, "is in lieu of notice. I shall be pleased to give you any necessary reference. I have no fault to find with your work." His gaze became more steely. "I merely suggest that you do not interfere in the private life of your next employer. I don't think there is any need to prolong this unpleasant scene."

She took the cheque without looking at it. Then she stammered, "But your book . . . Lance, be reasonable. There's so *much* on hand."

"Don't worry," he said grimly, "I'm quite capable of typing my own book, if necessary. I used to do so even after my so-called success. It has its virtues," he added icily. "If not I can soon get someone. Secretaries are not hard to come by and efficiency is not at a premium—even though loyalty may be." With that he reached for the telephone and ordered a hire car. "I even," he said, the bitterness within him wiping out mercy, "remember some telephone numbers."

The instinct of years overcame the drama of the occasion as she cried, "You are going out! But, what about the weather? It's bitterly cold."

He gave the necessary instructions. The local garage would send a car immediately. No, driving conditions were perfectly reasonable. A bit of ice, nothing to worry about.

Lance replaced the receiver.

"I can drop you at your cottage, Janet," he said politely.

She stood there tall, forbidding and, to him, the epitome of an unlovable woman—and nothing more damning can ever be said than that. Not all her perfectly chosen make-up, her elegant clothes, her poise could atone for the fact.

"Thank you," she said stiffly, "I'd rather walk." She stopped as she realized anew all that had happened. "All the things I've got here . . . personal things." She referred to make-up, her own pet note-books, a dozen little oddments that would need collecting from her working-room.

"Come back for them," he said quietly.

She brightened.

"To-morrow?" Hope surged again.

"Yes; I shall stay in London to-night."

"But Baker could have driven you up——" She stopped as she saw the irritation on his face.

"Baker is not on duty and, in any case, his wife is not well."

"You let him get away with murder. His wife is only expecting a baby and as she already has two——"

"Suppose you leave me to know my own business best, Janet?"

She coloured and moved to the door.

"I can't believe all this," she said chokingly.

"Neither can I," he replied. "All I ask is that you do not make it doubly embarrassing for us both by imagining that I shall ever feel any differently." He reached her side. "Now, if you'll excuse me, I have things I want to do before I leave."

He opened the door. They went out into the hall. The next second he turned and mounted the wide, spiral staircase. She watched him until he was out of sight.

No word was spoken.

CHAPTER XVI

ARDEN came out of the bathroom and looked around her with a certain longing for the luxury of an evening alone. To have relaxed, gone to bed early with a book, would, in that moment, have represented a semblance of happiness. Everywhere she looked there was evidence of Christmas and a pang shot through her because no spark of enthusiasm stirred within her, only the growing hunger which nothing seemed to assuage. A hunger for Lance which, far from decreasing, had become more acute with the passing of time. Was it only four days since the night of Barbara's party? It might have been four centuries.

She went to her wardrobe and drew out an evening dress of silk georgette which she stepped into and appraised. It was a colour that suited her fair beauty—a pale orchid that shaded to pink and moulded her figure, while flaring out into innumerable yards from her minute waist. That night she was going with Brian to a private dance given by his great friends, the Porters. Allan Porter had made a fortune on the stock-markets and spent it as he made it. He and his wife Cherry were a gay, irresponsible couple, with a house at Ascot and a flat in Brunton Street. The party was being held at the Savoy. The Savoy . . . and Lance. It didn't matter, there was no escape for her.

She stood before the long mirror in her bedroom, pinned a diamond clip on her left shoulder, drew a comb finally through the front, careless wave in her hair and thanked heaven she was ready. It would be an hour before Brian called for her and in that time she could relax, without worrying if he should decide—as was too often the case—to reduce his time limit to half! She had been caught before when resting without having finished her toilette!

Christmas! The cards had piled up and she began to open them. People whom she held in great affection, and from whom she heard no more than once a year, thrust themselves actively into her thoughts, almost as though, spiritually, she were visiting them. She sighed. She loved Christmas almost with a childish love of gaiety that broke the monotony of prosaic routine. The prospect of spending the holiday with Martin and Heather did nothing to revive her spirits, but since Brian, also, had no parents and Martin had begged them to go, she felt that to refuse would have been churlish. Christmas with Martin and the children, without Heather, or with Heather forced to take no part whatsoever in the domestic affairs . . . that would have been pleasurable. As it was, the house would be in domestic chaos, the turkey would be overcooked until it fell off its bones in protest, and they would be forced to listen to Heather telling them what a beautiful and wonderful meal they were fortunate enough to be eating! Arden smiled; a smile that faded as tears stung her eyes. How would Lance spend Christmas and with whom? . . .

She lay back in her chair, cards discarded, and rested her head against the cushions, feeling a wave of longing sweep over her which she did nothing to combat.

The ringing of the bell set her nerves tingling. Brian! Fifty minutes early! Just as she had anticipated, she thought with a loving, indulgent, but regretful, smile as she went through the hall and, flinging the door open, cried, "Early . . ." She stared aghast. *"Lance!"*

He said hoarsely, "This is almost where I came in, only the first time it was 'Darling——' "

"You have," she said, drawing upon every ounce of restraint, control and reserve, "an almost indecent memory, Mr. Ashton."

"Mr. Ashton," he echoed. "How many hundreds of years is that ago?" He changed his attitude. "I'm sorry to bother you, Arden, but if you could spare me ten minutes, I'd like to talk to you."

Something in his voice tore at her heart, freezing the arrogant words of dismissal that leapt to her lips.

"Of course. I'm expecting Brian at any time. We're going to a private dance, so you will have to excuse me if anything you may be saying is interrupted." She nerved herself to look at him. "Although I cannot understand why you should imagine there is anything further *to* be said between us. I thought I made that quite plain last week."

"You did."

He followed her into the sitting-room and a wave of sensuous perfume was wafted subtly to him as her dress swayed out softly.

"Perhaps I can offer you a drink," she said politely, feeling that he must hear the wild beating of her heart. "It's bitterly cold out, I believe." She went to the cabinet and pulled down the flap, giving him a whiskey without asking—an automatic gesture.

"I see that, at least, you remember my taste," he said significantly.

His expression disarmed her and she fought back as she said cynically, "All my scalps happen to drink whiskey. So *convenient.*"

He winced, his gaze holding hers masterfully, possessively, and inescapably as he said, "You couldn't possibly hurt me half as much as I have hurt myself since that ghastly night, Arden." He took the glass she extended to him and remained standing, almost dogged, while she sat down, thankfully, for her legs had lost all strength to support her. "That is why I am here."

She pitched her back against the cushions of her chair, and because her hands were trembling violently, held her glass cupped within them for a second before saying, "There is still nothing further for us to discuss, Lance. I am in no doubt of your opinion of me, but I would remind you that I am engaged to be married, therefore I cannot see that anything you have to say can concern me."

"It doesn't," he replied gravely, "in that sense. I just wanted to apologize—humbly and sincerely," he added.

She was taken completely off her guard.

"*Apologize!*" Scorn lashed her words. "To *me!*" She tortured herself as she added: "Me, the woman who——"

"*Please—*" His cry silenced her. "I ask no quarter, Arden. You were right when you said the other night that when hatred went from my heart . . . well, it has gone. A hatred based on the past, directed through you at a woman who betrayed me. The psychiatrist would love that angle," he added. "I'm here to tell you that I'm ashamed—yes, ashamed. I behaved damnably."

"So," she whispered and her heart choked her, making every word an effort, "you know the truth at last."

"The truth?" He looked at her with a tenderness that gave way to a passion so intense that she dared not keep her eyes on his. "If I do, then it is embodied in that faith you were so insistent was a part of love. If I'd not been half crazed with

174

jealousy, with the viciousness of the story that appeared to have every fact to support it, I should have known you were incapable of the things of which I accused you."

She put a hand up to her throat almost as though she could not get her breath.

"You mean," she gasped, "that——"

"I know no more than I did last week at this time, with the exception that I am convinced you were right about Janet. I have dismissed her to-night," he added as an afterthought. He looked at her steadily. "You told me that you had a story to tell . . . I believe you. Just that. But, if it were possible to win your love, to marry you to-night, I would not even ask you to tell it," he finished fiercely.

Arden tried to speak, but could not. Emotion swirled and eddied about her, tormenting, ecstatic and desperate, in turn.

"Oh, *Lance*," she murmured.

"My dear . . . it's your forgiveness I want. I know that whatever the past holds, you did not set out deliberately to deceive me. I know it through my love for you—a love that when last I was here was a poor counterfeit of all I feel for you to-day. I've lived in hell from that moment; tormented with doubt and conflict; and when I saw you at Barbara's party . . . I *knew*; I knew that even had you been guilty of all I accused you, I should still want you," he finished roughly.

The silence held them as it held the drama and irony of life, the tragedy of an understanding that had come too late. Arden tried to think of an answer when the only answer she ached to give was to rush to his arms and pour out the passion of her love for him, his kiss the only reward for the defeated hopes, the disillusionment of yesterday. But a loyalty to Brian held her fast within its grip. She could not use him, accept his steadfast devotion, promise him the future and then, for the sake of her own happiness, discard him. Her promise to him in the circumstances had been more binding than a marriage, so that, once again, indirectly she was the victim of her own codes. Her own words to him echoed through the silent corridors of her tortured mind: "*If I promise to marry you, Brian, nothing in the world would ever make me go back on that promise. That I swear.*" She could not escape on the wings of her own desires. Honour and decency were involved and if she went back on them she would never know either peace or happiness. She said, nerving herself to meet Lance's gaze, "It isn't easy to find the right thing to say, Lance. To know that you believe me incapable of all that horror—I can't tell you," she said brokenly. "It is a dreadful thing to be unjustly accused of anything—no matter what," she added. "And so strange that twice in my life I should be a victim of that injustice. Just as twice in *your* life you imagined that you had been betrayed. I know, I can see why you felt and reacted as you did."

"Your generosity humbles me."

She shook her head.

"It isn't that. When one has been hurt there is a defensive attitude that makes it so easy to jump to conclusions, to believe the wrong thing. You've almost seen me as you saw your wife, re-lived the misery of those days of broken faith. . . ." Her sigh was deep. "Thank you for coming. You'll never know what it means. We were friends and suddenly——" She shuddered. "It was horrible—horrible."

He took a step forward and stopped.

"Oh, my dear——"

"I'd like you to know the facts," she said swiftly. "I wanted to tell you, but there are some stories that can only be told in sympathy—stories that seem fantastic if jerked out coldly in the face of opposition. Almost like a newspaper report of a life which, while presenting the truth, makes it look so utterly sordid."

"How well I know that," he agreed.

She looked up at him and then lowered her gaze as she began the details which covered the period of her marriage and afterwards. Lance listened, transfixed and groaning inwardly to think he had been so intolerant in his judgement of her deception. But for that angle, he thought desperately, this crisis would never have arisen. Every now and then he gave a stifled exclamation of disgust, a comment of angry condemnation, and when at last she finished she added, "There is nothing more to tell, Lance. Nothing. But I shall never cease to regret—bitterly—that I did not break one promise in my life. . . . If I had done, you would have known the truth of my relationship with Derek from the very beginning." She spread her hands in a gesture of helplessness. "But as I saw it then there was nothing that concerned you in any dishonest way."

"I appreciate that." He sighed deeply. "It is a sad fact that love can be blind to reason or tolerance. . . . You have suffered—haven't you?" His words, simple of expression, nevertheless held a great understanding which in no way minimized all she had been through.

"Disillusionment—as you so well know—denies one even the peace of loss by death. It is so difficult to believe the worst of anyone." She added quickly: "After that first emotional shock is over and one can think calmly."

"You loved him, Arden?"

She said tensely, "I believed I did and I would not belittle the fact because of all that has happened. Love is such an elastic word. It can mean so many things. But I know, now, that I loved in self-deception. I wanted vindication and from that I built up an illusion. I valued marriage, took it seriously." She managed to meet his gaze. "As I imagine you did."

"Yes; you don't have to tell me how you felt." He added, "I was always doubtful of your love for Derek and, of course, Brian Newton did not come into it from my point of view."

"Or mine," she said truthfully, "until after all this happened. As I've already told you."

Lance willed her to meet his gaze.

"May I ask you just one question?"

"I cannot stop you. I will answer it if I can."

"Then that night—the last time I was here"—a grim regret sharpened his voice—"before we'd discussed anything . . . I could so easily have convinced myself you returned my love. Suppose——"

Arden made a last superhuman effort. She knew that one word now and nothing could stem the torrent of her yearning, her aching longing to tell him the truth. She said, catching at her breath, "Once before you kissed me, Lance. I gave you an honest explanation. Emotion is strange and our friendship —oh, I can't explain."

He helped her out.

"You were in the twilight of discovery—hardly knowing what you felt."

"Yes," she lied, thinking of Brian.

Lance looked at her with a passionate earnestness.

"And now you have found your answer. You left me in no doubt of that last week when you spoke of being in love—

knowing love. I couldn't deceive myself then, or dispute it as I was able to do when Derek was in the picture."

Arden's gaze faltered and then, again, met his.

"No; there is no doubt now. I've learned that when one really loves it is beyond all question and as much a part of oneself as breathing." She found some outlet in the statement.

Silence fell; the silence of defeat and desperate longing for Lance; and of absolute renunciation for her. It seemed that her heart was being wrenched from her body as it thudded so fiercely that it choked her: a physical protest at its imprisonment.

"He is blessed," Lance said hoarsely. "And if I may say so without being unctuous, worthy. I like him even in my envy." His voice was unsteady. "He will make you happy, Arden."

Arden heard his words with the anguish of irreparable loss. For she knew that she had so twisted the truth in her loyalty to Brian that this time Lance could not possibly doubt her word. There could, she thought, be no greater irony than that. Now she sat there, cold to the point of shivering—despite the warmth of the flat—facing a future that suddenly terrified her, for Lance would have no part in it—even as a friend. Her thankfulness at this reinstatement, and his restoration of faith, made her exult, but at the same time destroyed her. The exultation came from the knowledge of his understanding; the destruction because she was now left without any weapons, any cynicism, any bitterness whatsoever. She said in a whisper, "And you?"

"Too restless to have any idea what I want," he said honestly. "I've work to do . . . *work*." He sighed. Then irrelevantly: "Will you go on with yours?" A strange light came into his eyes. "I asked you that before—didn't I? Is the answer the same?"

"Yes; my views haven't changed."

It all seemed so futile, so meaningless. A succession of follies, mistakes, that were irremediable. If only she could have known the repercussions attendant upon her decision to take Derek back into her life, what an agony of misery would have been saved.

"That all seems a very long while ago," he said solemnly.

"Yes. . . . Are you going away for Christmas?" She resorted to triviality—anything to avoid prolonging the personal note.

178

"My mother is expecting me," he said wryly. "And you?"

"We are going to my brother."

"I liked him very much," Lance said warmly. "In different circumstances we could have been friends."

Womanlike, weakly, Arden cried, "Why not now?"

Masterfully and penetratingly his gaze met hers.

"We are back where we were the first time you rejected me," he said roughly. "I could not stand seeing you, wanting you and knowing you were out of reach. And this time, Arden, I can read my sentence in your eyes. You do not mention friendship as you did then."

"Because I'm more adult," she admitted. "I know it wouldn't work. The platitude that nothing teaches like suffering is grimly true. We've been through most phases of it, you and I."

The clock struck eight-thirty. And memory struck with it. Coffee. Midnight . . . and the first breathless excitement of the Fleur d'Argent.

Suddenly, the words wrenched from him, he cried, "And even knowing that, being left in no doubt whatsoever of your feelings, I still dare to say, to repeat my former words, my darling, 'There is a part of you that no other man will ever possess: a part that belongs to me—some spark of affinity, some mental fusion.'"

Arden felt that she was struggling to reach the safety of a distant shore, swimming through gigantic waves of terror, sickness and desperation. She said in a whisper, "Friendship, Lance. I mention the word now. *That* regard cannot die."

"And puts me in my place. I'd no right to say any of that."

She got to her feet because she knew that will-power was ebbing and that he must go.

"I think we are both privileged on this occasion," she murmured. "I've said little I wanted to say" (Oh God, how true that was, she thought frantically), "but to know you understand—that you know the truth . . . It's been——" She broke off.

The old sympathy, closeness that needed only a minimum of words, flowed between them.

"It doesn't have to be said," he broke in tensely. "I know I'm forgiven . . . no misunderstandings, Arden. Be happy, my dear, and remember sometimes."

"I will." It was the merest whisper. He was so close that she had only to put out her hand, only to raise her lips, and draw the veil—the mask—from her eyes. Desire mounted on a wave of passionate need, of love sharper and more insistent than anything that had ever touched her heart before. "Oh, Lance, I'm so *sorry*," she said with a stifling regret. "I can't bear to think of your——"

A wry smile touched his lips.

"It's a hell that oddly enough I would not escape from," he assured her. "Tennyson's words were so true. I don't know what time does to unrequited emotion, perhaps it blunts that first, sharp anguish; all I do know is that you have become a part of me that I shall never lose, or want to lose," he added.

Her eyes were suspiciously bright as they met his and for a second he started as he saw the stark appeal within them.

"*Arden . . .*" Her name fell passionately from his lips.

Arden recovered and dashed a hand across her eyes, realizing that she could not conceal her tears. Then, "I'm sorry," she whispered, "but all this suddenly overwhelmed me, Lance. Everything . . . and my own utter inability to change things."

He accepted that, disgusted because he could still hope, when every instinct warned him of his own defeat.

"I bless you for caring that much," he whispered. His voice changed. "And now I must go. No loose ends this time; no threads left untied."

They walked—oh, the familiarity of that for her—out into the hall together and in silence. She could hardly bear him to go and yet longed for escape from the torment of a restraint that imposed a will-power almost superhuman.

"I shall," she said huskily, "read all your books."

He paused at the door and looked at her—in a lingering, passionate farewell.

"They will always send you a message," he whispered. "No, just stand there . . . don't come to the door." His gaze burned down into hers.

His name was on her lips, but no sound came from them. The silence held only the mad throbbing of her heart. . . .

She knew that he had gone, although her vision was too blurred to see. Panic gripped her. She tore open the door and thrust her body forward into the corridor.

A voice said blithely, "Now that is what I *call* timing."

Arden stared, almost stupidly, at Brian, and in that split second gained composure, thankful for the subdued lighting which would make it impossible for him to see her tear-filled eyes. It was obvious to her that while Brian had come up in the lift, Lance must have walked down the stairs, otherwise surely they would have met.

"I knew you'd be early," she said in a rather high-pitched voice as she felt his arm about her waist and managed to manoeuvre so that, the moment they stepped into the hall, she darted into the bedroom, saying as she went: "I need only a last coat of powder and I'm all ready."

Brian chuckled. His heart sang; he was blind to everything but his own incredible happiness.

"Why bother? I shall probably kiss it all off. We don't need to leave for twenty minutes."

Arden, hands shaking, face tissues going in all directions, managed to repair her make-up swiftly. If only her heart would stop thudding and her limbs stop shaking. She stepped back from the mirror, lifted her head and took a very deep breath.

Brian said, as she joined him, "Ah, now I can see how lovely you look."

With a little laugh she switched one light off.

"If we've twenty minutes to spare we can well do without all this electricity!" She could not have faced his scrutiny and now the room was in shadow; kindly shadow that would conceal her haunted, glistening eyes.

"I've no quarrel with that."

He drew her down on to the settee beside him and she managed to lie so that her head was beneath his chin, raising it only to receive his kiss.

"Arden . . . your heart—it's thudding! Oh, darling . . . You do care, don't you? Just a little?"

She said shakenly, "More than a little; I want your happiness, Brian." She tensed. "You are happy?"

He answered honestly, "Happy to the point of fear."

The bad moments over, she nerved herself to look at him, her eyes asking the question.

"Fear lest all this is just some fantastic dream," he murmured. "Say it isn't."

She replied evasively, "Aren't I real enough, solid enough?" She forced a note of banter into her voice.

"And Derek?" He hated himself for the question, but the thought of the past still tormented him. Before his engagement his whole heart and soul had been concerned with the fugitive hope that one day he might still persuade her to marry him. That accomplished he was, contradictorily enough, swept out of his emotional backwater.

Arden was thankful—fearlessly and honestly—to answer his question.

"Derek has left me nothing for him but contempt and even that has no part in my thoughts. He is dead, Brian. Absolutely dead. All that might have happened in another life."

Brian stared at her and gasped, "I'd hoped and prayed . . . Oh, my dear . . . if you knew——"

He was shaking and she could feel the impact of his emotion like some vital force thrusting itself between them. In that second the tumult in her own heart died down. He was her sacred trust and her duty, not the lesser part of which demanded that never for a second should he suspect the gnawing hunger within her, the passionate love which she knew would never die. Anything less would be a mockery and a crime against him.

Gently she put her lips to his. It was a kiss of dedication and she clung to him drawing courage and strength from his need of her. Conflict died. This was her destiny.

CHAPTER XVII

For the first time for several years snow fell on Christmas morning. Arden looked out upon it as it lay dazzlingly white, turning the countryside into a frosted picture-postcard. Trees, heavy with its burden, sagged and lowered their branches like garlands swung against the smoky grey-blue sky. Giant firs rose darkly, their greenness piercing the opal mantle in defiance and triumph. This was their season.

Martin's house lay between Egham and Chertsey and was humped at the top of a hill which gave views twenty miles distant. After London, the silence made Arden's head feel curiously heavy, almost as though the incessant roar to which she was accustomed still reverberated within it.

Despite the cold, she leaned out of the window—still open, after the habit formed in childhood, during the night—and breathed deeply of the icy air, tanged with the earthly fragrance which no perfume in the world could recapture. And even as she did so it was as if a hand clutched her throat, while her vision dimmed to wipe out the scene before her so that only Lance's face was visible.

She banged the window angrily, bit her lips and dashed a hand across her misted eyes. She hated the weakness she could not overcome and feared the betrayal of her emotions unless she could master them. And that, she found impossible. The mind was deaf to all appeal; it was like a film which projected only the heart's image.

The stillness made her pulse seem audible. She shivered and realized for the first time just how low the temperature was as she flicked on the electric stove.

Heather appeared—a strange shape in an old tweed skirt and short-sleeved jumper.

"Happy Christmas," she said. "I've brought you some tea. It's early yet, but we don't want the day half gone before we get up. My, it's cold in here. And no wonder, if you will persist in having your windows open. No pity for you."

Arden laughed.

"I don't need any." She moved forward and kissed Heather's cheek. "Bless you for the tea. I was just kidding myself that I'd be able to forestall you."

"Couldn't sleep," said Heather, not unkindly. "We were mad to agree to let the children go to stay with Gail's friends. But Martin was so insistent. The Wetherbys have a vast house, pots of money, and there were to be fifteen children in all there over the holiday. You know the kind of thing . . . daughters and their children. Family reunion plus friends. Gail was mad to go and it is dull here, I suppose." She rattled on.

Arden said sympathetically, "I'm sure you were right to let them go. Only young once." She found that with Heather one continually fell back on platitudes.

"Maybe . . . if you drink your tea you can get your bath

in before Brian. That's one advantage of two bathrooms—even if they do have to be kept clean."

"This," said Arden, "is a sweet house, Heather."

It was. One of those old-world places, discreetly modernized. Heather had done a good bit with it, but the furnishings lacked imagination, although the furniture was good.

"I suppose I'm too busy keeping it clean to notice. . . . In the old days we'd have had two maids here."

"But now the children are at school——" Arden spoke tentatively.

"I haven't Nannie. She used to help in so many ways . . . ah well! I must be going or we'll never have any breakfast." She added: "Don't forget. Nine o'clock. Far too late, but Martin was positively aggressive about it."

"Well, he does have to get up pretty early in the normal way, doesn't he?"

Heather smiled. Nothing she had said had been pointed or ill-tempered, just a betrayal of an attitude of mind.

"At precisely the same time as I do," she retorted. "Can't say you look particularly well. Does being engaged suit you? Or aren't you happy? I told Martin last night that I didn't think you were," she said with forthright inflection.

"*Please*." Arden panicked. Once Martin started on that track, she was doomed. "Of course I'm happy."

"But you're not in love with Brian—are you?"

Arden countered banteringly, "Look who's talking. I thought you didn't believe in love."

"I was speaking for myself, then. I'm not the type to get all emotional over anything, or anyone. Way I'm made," she said, cutting her sentences short as she did on occasion. "For all that I'm not blind—not half so blind as people think." She studied Arden intently. "I know you: soft, sympathetic, feminine—it's stamped on you."

"Sounds positively revolting," Arden laughed, striving to change the conversation.

"And I like you," Heather added more gently. "We've always got on together even though we've not a great deal in common. All I say, my dear, is: don't be a fool. You won't spare Brian anything this way. Mark my words. So if you're up to some high-falutin' burnt-offering stunt." She tightened her lips, then: "I'm warning you."

Arden thought of Martin. Was it possible that, after all, Heather *knew*?

"Don't you agree with—burnt offerings?"

Heather poured out Arden's tea and handed her the cup.

"If you were already married to Brian—yes. Not now."

Arden dared to say, "Would you ever divorce Martin?"

Heather didn't prevaricate.

"No. He's my husband. I'd be hopeless on my own. And I'd miss my home and all it stands for. Thank heaven he's never had any romantic notions in his head. That's why we're so suited and get on so well. Never quarrel. Never. We don't always see eye to eye and he'd like a more social life. But not having it doesn't worry him. Couldn't have a better husband than your brother. I'll say that."

She moved to the door.

Arden got in a parting shot. "And why shouldn't your formula for marriage suit me?"

"Ah, that's different. Brian adores you. He can't take his eyes off you. Martin isn't like that with me. Oh, don't look so shocked. I've never deluded myself. Just because I like housework and have no interest in sex doesn't mean I can't *think* and see what is in front of my nose. I'm thankful things are as they are. I couldn't stand the kind of married life you want. That's why I chose Martin. Being practical has its advantages and spares a good deal of suffering. It may be dull. Well! I like it that way."

She bustled out, leaving behind her a suggestion of wisdom far beyond that with which Arden would have credited her. And, also, a concern which Arden knew was utterly sincere.

Breakfast was a pleasant, domestic scene—on the surface. Arden watched Martin with an increasing absorption. She knew where his thoughts were. It struck her how fantastic life was. In a house not very far away, at Ascot, Catherine would probably be sitting over just such another breakfast table. . . . At least her body would be there. Only that. And, somewhere—her heart missed a beat—Lance, also, would be beginning the day, probably with his mother and a country house party. . . . Was this pattern stability, the upholding of the marriage tradition? Or was it the desecration of every human ideal? She found Brian's gaze intently upon her.

He said, "Darling, you looked very sad and pensive. What was that all about?"

Colour mounted her cheeks. Heather flashed her a knowing "I told you so" glance.

"Happiness can be just a little sad," she countered.

Heather helped herself to an incredibly large portion of ham.

"Thank heaven I'm not bothered with all this fanciful stuff." She smiled at Martin. "Oh, I knew what I was going to say: Lance Ashton is on television tonight."

Arden's cup rattled and the contents spilled over in her saucer and on the tablecloth. She felt that every nerve in her body was exposed and that her heart lay bare for everyone to see. The mere mention of his name was a fierce emotional shock—particularly as she had not expected to hear it. And as she looked up, making a little exclamation of disgust, she managed to say carelessly, "Lance? What is he *doing*?"

"Telling a story—you know, that intimate type. We must listen." She looked at Brian and Martin. "Don't forget."

Martin's gaze rested upon Arden.

"We won't forget," he said thoughtfully.

To which Brian added, "By the way, have you seen Lance lately, Arden?"

"A day or two ago, as a matter of fact." She tried to make her voice impersonal without knowing if she succeeded. She added swiftly, before any further questions could be asked: "He wanted to know if I were going to continue my art work after I was married."

Brian continued to eat his toast.

"And what did you tell him?"

"I told him no."

Brian smiled.

"No more book jackets for him—eh? Too bad. No one else can produce those landscape scenes and bring them to life as you do, darling."

Arden forced a note of almost high-pitched gaiety.

"My first was my swan song," she said.

Martin put in, "Isn't that rather foolish? Surely you could keep your hand in and do *his* work. Hang it, one jacket a year isn't going to rush you."

Brian said lightly, "That occurred to me."

Arden managed to say composedly, "All or nothing!"

They lapsed into silence.

It was later that morning when Martin, alone with Arden, said, "You're behaving like an absolute fool, Arden."

She started, shocked.

"What do you mean?"

"Lance Ashton," he said briefly. "I knew there was someone—almost on your own admission. But I did not know who he was."

Arden moved to an occasional table on which rested a dish of cashew nuts. Slowly, and with what was intended to be casualness, she picked one up, put it in her mouth, ate it and then said, "I think you've had too much to drink, darling." She nerved herself to look at him. "Whatever put that idea into your head?"

"You."

"Because I happened to spill my coffee when his name was mentioned?"

"Ah," said Martin, "so you can point the occasion." He groaned aloud. "Is he in love with you?"

Arden faced him.

"Listen, my dear: no purpose can be served by this conversation."

He looked at her with great earnestness.

"You," he said, "are my sister, but far more important than that, you are my friend. I trusted you with my secret; are you going to deny me yours?"

His words fell upon the silence and upon Arden's heart, bringing a rush of emotion she could not stem. There was a poignancy about them that shattered her so that she cried weakly, "No . . . no! You're right. So right. But it's a long story, Martin, and it has only one possible ending—*this*—this situation as you see it now. In that you must trust me to know my own business—as you know yours with Catherine."

Martin was continuing his task of arranging glasses in the cocktail cabinet, and bringing forward the necessary bottles. The scene hung before them like a tapestry which they were destined ever to remember. Christmas morning; the snow; and a log fire crackling in a wide chimney corner . . . oaken beams garlanded with decorations; a floor-to-ceiling Christmas tree glittering and still, its lights sending off prisms of amber, red, blue and green. . . . The smell of a turkey cooking; the thought of champagne on ice. . . . But a Christmas muted, without music either in the heart or the house. . . . Loneliness isolating them from a love they craved as a drug addict craves a drug.

He answered her simply, "He is not married. Has he ever asked you to marry him?"

Arden rested a hand on the wide beam of the fireplace which formed a mantelpiece. She looked down into the white-hot fire, remembering.

"Yes," she said, and the quietness of her voice was a requiem to resignation. "Then there was Derek and I refused. The next time, there was Brian—or shall we say, the next time——" She broke off incoherently. "It's such a long story. Please, Martin, if you've any love for me, don't talk of it now."

He turned, trying to master his own fierce emotion, as he held a glass to the light to make sure of its cleanliness, then:

"Do you want your life to be like mine?" he demanded fiercely. "If that will not sway you, influence you——"

"Nothing on God's earth would influence me now," she said solemnly. "It's odd, Martin: I'm the kind of fool who does everything wrong in life, but for the right reason. My engagement to Brian is no *ordinary* obligation. If it were, there would be no problem."

Martin leaped in, "Meaning that Lance *would* marry you?"

"Since you put it that way—yes."

"Then in God's name——"

She raised her gaze.

"I turned to Brian when Lance would not have been prepared to marry me," she said quietly. "I gave him my word after he had waited for years and been dragged through the divorce court for my sake. I may be wrong; I may even be wronging him, but I could no more discard him now than I could jump into that fire—that is, not for my own ends, my own happiness. There are some ties quite as great as marriage. This, to me, is one of them. If I were deceiving Brian about my love for him, pretending *to* love him—— But I'm not. I've made him happy and——"

"I *wonder.*"

At that she started.

"*How* can you say that?"

188

"Don't underestimate him, Arden. Love has a sixth sense."
She shook her head.

"If I believed that where Brian was concerned, it would be wishful thinking," she said shakenly.

"And if I told him the truth?"

She recoiled and cried out, "I'd never—*never* forgive you." Her eyes met his—dark, appealing and yet deadly in their steadfastness.

Martin heaved a deep sigh.

"You mean that—don't you?"

"Would you forgive me if I told Heather about Catherine —how you feel about her?"

"Isn't that rather different?" he suggested quietly.

"Not to me; as I see it, my obligation is as great. We have to live by what we feel, Martin. Not what others feel for us."

He said gently, "How true that is. . . ."

"And you promise?"

"Yes," he agreed. "I promise." He made a violent gesture of protest. "The criminal waste in life, the futile striving, the frustration!"

"We're travellers," she said reflectively, "and if we mistake one sign on our way, there is only a wilderness to await us at the end of our journey." She stopped abruptly as Heather and Brian came into the room.

"I helped to get the turkey into the oven," Brian said, looking from face to face. "What are you two up to? Getting in an extra drink before we've a chance of joining you?"

"Just that," said Martin jocularly. "Now——"

Heather glanced at the clock.

"I can sit down for half an hour. . . . Hot in here, isn't it? Martin, none of your champagne cocktails for me. Just a gin and orange—and very little gin."

"Why not have a glass of water?" he suggested comically.

"I wonder what the children are doing," she said. "It isn't Christmas without them somehow. I'll never let them go away again. I didn't *want* to. Our first Christmas apart."

Martin avoided her gaze. A sensation almost of guilt surged upon him. Knowing the children were happy and where they had chosen to be had, momentarily, put them from his thoughts. Arden looked at him and as he turned back to attend to the drinks a wave of understanding flowed between them. Never

189

had she loved him so well as in that moment. In the darkness the light of their relationship, their friendship, burned steadfastly and in sympathy.

Only one thing was real to her that day. The moment when Lance came on television that evening. It was as though her heart pulled away from her body in order to reach him and the screen that kept him from her became a sudden enemy. None of his magnetism was lost as he turned and smiled at his audience. He sat in his armchair as she had seen him so many times, utterly natural, relaxed and with a friendliness that could not be assumed. His alert, resonant voice began firmly, conversationally, and they knew that television had discovered a new personality.

Brian said, "So Gorton Main's efforts have been rewarding. This will be a feather in his cap. Ashton's got just the right touch for this kind of thing. Don't you think so, darling?"

Arden could not bear the interruption and she merely glanced at Brian and nodded in the semi-darkness.

It was a simple story Lance had to tell, but it bore the stamp of greatness in its dramatic content. Impossible for Arden to dissociate herself or his love for her from it—even though it might not have been considered a romantic contribution. And no man could have put more feeling—as distinct from sentimentality—into it, and as his voice died away, his vast, unseen audience was hushed in curious homage.

Heather moved briskly and before Martin could stop her had switched on the light.

"I like him," she said; "but there wasn't much to the story, was there?"

Martin gasped, "Not much to it!" He stopped. How futile to argue.

"I prefer a thriller myself," she said. "Or something like Mrs. Dale's Diary."

"Not," said Brian, "surely to-night!"

Arden managed to control her emotions, thankful for any opportunity of avoiding further discussion about Lance.

"What about The Archers?" she asked Heather. "They're terrifically popular and human, too."

"I like Mrs. Dale better," Heather insisted. "I'm always having arguments with people."

"Good for Mrs. Dale and good for The Archers," Arden

said, listening to herself mouthing the banalities as she tried to still the wild beating of her heart and stamp Lance's image from it sufficiently to allow her to get through the rest of the evening.

Heather had turned to the door.

"We'd better have some supper now, or I'll be washing up at midnight. Rather a silly time to have a story if you ask me." She looked at Martin. "You can give me a hand," she said pleasantly, "and let Arden and Brian have five minutes on their own."

Martin was already at the door. It closed on them both. And silence fell. There was neither happiness nor unhappiness in that house—only negation.

Arden said, "I'm afraid all this is very dull, Brian."

He was honest. "It would be without you, darling. Heather's a good soul but——" He sighed. "I'd loathe this kind of life dedicated to inanities and routine. Martin must get to screeching point. I should."

Arden said heavily, "There comes a time when if one kept *on* screeching I imagine one would go mad. The alternative is acceptance and resignation. And as you said: Heather's a good soul. That tightens the bars around the cage."

Brian started.

"Darling! You said that so harshly. You don't think of our future marriage like that?"

Arden cursed herself for not realizing how her words might be taken. Impulsively, she put out a hand and clasped his.

"I was talking, or thinking, of Martin."

"Of course. And you couldn't find a finer person than he."

"True—even though he is my brother."

"Ashton made a damn fine job of that story—didn't he? Excellent publicity, too, and while he doesn't need it . . . it certainly can't do any harm. He'll pull in thousands of new women readers. Would have done well as an actor. I'm rather surprised. Agreeably surprised. The firm will be pleased. Darling, are you listening?"

Was she listening? . . .

"Of course. I agree with you, but I'm not in the least surprised. I always thought he'd be good on television and in that type of thing."

Brian gave a little laugh.

"I'll have to watch you, young lady. You're a fan enough of his already."

Arden tried not to get tense, not to be on the defensive.

"I must certainly stand up for the firm's authors," she retorted banteringly.

He reached out and drew her into his arms.

"How about giving some attention to the firm's employees first?" he suggested, as his lips found hers.

Arden ached to be alone, away from the intense loneliness of being loved without loving. She did everything within her power to meet Brian's mood and respond to the passion of his kiss, but her lips and her body might have been made of wood, for no emotion stirred within her and even affection failed her. It was as though a part of her were already dead . . . dead. . . . Not that. Given away. The part that was heart, soul and mind, belonging only to Lance, impervious to all other forces and which nothing and no one could tempt back from his keeping.

With a gesture calculated to hide her feelings and as Brian's lips left hers, she buried her face against his shoulder and rested there.

From the kitchen, Heather's radio blared out carols.

Brian asked almost sharply, "Does your sister-in-law never turn that thing off?"

"Not unless she is forced to do so." She sat up jerkily. "It gets on your nerves, too?"

"Destroys all sense of peace," he said. "If there's anything to listen to, that you want to hear—listen. But that background noise with conversation turning into a shouting match. It was the same this morning when we were doing the turkey."

"I'm sorry, Brian."

"Nonsense, nothing to do with you. . . ."

"I promise," she said with a smile, "that I shall not inflict that misery upon you."

"I'm not afraid," he retorted. He got up from her side and went to the windows, pulling on the cord so that the night was revealed. Arden switched off the lamp and, gradually, the sapphire darkness revealed moonlight on snow. "How about a walk after supper?" he suggested.

"I'd love it."

Lance would, she thought, paint that scene with words; words holding all the magic of jewels set by an expert hand.

He would have captured the deep shadows, the frozen white-
ness, the pure, omnipotent moon.

Brian's arm encircled her shoulders.

"We must decide about that cottage we looked at last
week-end," he said enthusiastically.

"I loved it, but I still feel the journey is too much. You've
enough strain in these days without adding a fifty-minute run
to it night and morning."

He was touched by her solicitude.

"Darling! I'm not an old man!"

"And I have no intention of your becoming one. To say
nothing of the fact that it would be a cross-country journey
by train. No, main line. No argument." Her smile was warm
and gentle. "I can bully you, too."

He picked her hand up and kissed it.

"I'd like nothing so much as to be bullied for the rest of
my life," he said huskily.

The rest of my life. . . .

To Arden, then, the future seemed eternity.

CHAPTER XVIII

THE months slid away, each one beginning with a new
significance for Arden, and when she tore the sheet of April
off the calendar and put the red square to May 1st, she faced
the fact that she had exactly four more weeks of freedom.
Her heart quickened its beat. Five, for May was a five-week
month and even that seven-day respite counted.

Brian said, "Darling, I'm going to have a special gathering
—I've got to get one in before you take over! I shall expect
you at the flat on Wednesday at eight! No arguments."

She looked at him reflectively.

"And no mystery?"

"Absolutely none. No, being serious: I've an aunt and a
cousin coming down from Cheltenham whom I want you to
meet." He laughed. "You cannot say I've plagued you with
relatives, at least."

"Nor I you," she flashed back lightly. "We're sadly lacking
in them, in fact. I wish my parents *were* alive. One misses such
a lot with not having them to visit and be interested in one's

life." She looked at him steadily. "That is why we must have a family. An only child—particularly if it is a girl—is such a mistake unless circumstances make it inevitable. I'm warning you, that's all."

Brian held her gaze.

"A family," he echoed wonderingly. "You really mean it, too—don't you?"

"Of course. You've always liked the idea, I know."

"It's my idea of marriage," he admitted simply.

She gave him both her hands.

"Mine too," she managed to say breathlessly.

He kissed them both in turn.

"Have I told you before that you are a very wonderful person?"

"I can bear the repetition," she promised.

"I'm serious, Arden. You'll never quite know what I feel, or how passionately I want to make you happy."

She lowered her gaze and then raised it to the level of his own.

"I think I know, my dear. And I can echo your words just as deeply."

"I'm quite certain of that." He added, resorting to banter to hide his emotion: "Now how about giving some attention to our honeymoon plans?"

Arden instantly had a mental picture of the Crag Hotel, Maenporth, near Falmouth. To her it stood out among every hotel she had ever visited as combining all the charm, dignity and comfort with a setting unsurpassed for beauty. But at the very thought of that perfection, that beauty, her heart contracted. To go there without Lance would be to thrust a dagger deliberately into her own heart. She said swiftly, fearing lest he would suspect she had some place in mind which she was rejecting:

"Let's be gay and go to Spain. I leave what part to you. I know my own country so well and it would be wonderful. That is if you are in agreement."

"Spain," he said firmly, "it shall be. I think Madrid as a centre. We can go to Toledo, Salamanca, Avila. And we could spend a day or two visiting the Balearics. Yes, I like that."

"I've not been to Spain," she added.

"I like it the more for that fact," he answered. "No past, only the present and the future."

"Just us," she said gently, then: "I'm going down to the cottage this afternoon, will you join me there? We could have a meal in Richmond."

"I'll be there. . . . You're happy about the place?"

"Very; it's tucked away, secluded, near the river and, at the same time, not *on* it to be a nuisance. Above all it is an easy journey for you."

"You'll be content—really content to live there?"

"You know the answer to that. What is more, I'm quite ready to give up the London flat—my flat, I mean——"

He hastened to say, "That wouldn't be practical. My lease is running out as you know and we mustn't be left without a mouse-hole in London. Quite probably, we shall live there for weeks in the dead of winter."

"I know you are right . . . I just didn't want you to get any ideas into your head about my wishing to be independent and——" She broke off. "Oh, you *know*."

"I know: I know you pretty well, my sweet."

Inwardly Arden groaned. The tragedy was that he didn't and never at any time would be able to do so.

The days passed and Wednesday evening arrived without any interest awakening within Arden as she set out for Brian's flat to meet his relatives. She dreaded the idea of having to simulate happiness, possibly talk about herself, while yet being determined that Brian should not have any cause for complaint in her behaviour.

She reached the flat which was tucked away in a rather old-fashioned street near Victoria. It was dark and part of a private house which had been converted, with the usual attendant inconveniences and lack of amenities. Brian, how-ever, had made it bright and attractive, his sitting-room walls were book-lined and a coal-fire created an atmosphere of home.

"You look beautiful," he said, appraising her dress of misty blue that was perfect in its simplicity with its tight, long sleeves and short, slim skirt.

"I hope they'll like me."

"They will," he said with conviction. He held her gaze. "I like you, Arden. And it isn't always a man can say that of the woman he loves."

"Oh, Brian . . ." Her voice broke, her heart ached because she could not love him in return, only feel that deep respect and affection that was as calm and serene as a river flowing gently on a summer's day.

He patted her hand and urged her forward into the room.

And even as she entered it, Lance sprang to his feet.

She stared at him aghast, the colour mounting her cheeks as her heart knew a sudden exquisite relief. Just to look at him, to feel his dark, searching gaze upon her, was balm. She managed to say with deceptive casualness, as she held out her hand in greeting, "I thought you were in Austria."

"I was; I returned only two days ago."

Arden's brows puckered. She couldn't quite understand why Brian had not mentioned the fact that Lance would be there. And where were the relatives?

Brian explained lightly, "My aunt and cousin are coming along later. I persuaded Mr. Ashton to look in early." He paused before adding: "I'm afraid that I used subterfuge and the elastic term 'business'."

Arden's gaze was drawn to Lance like a magnet. An agony of longing swept over her that seemed to be crushing her heart until every breath was an effort.

"Subterfuge?" The word escaped Lance in sharp inquiry. "I don't understand."

"No," said Brian crisply, "but you will."

The room became heavy with drama; drama that created a suspense they could not ignore. Eyes met eyes and flashed silent interrogation. Arden sat down, her hands clutching the edge of the chair's arms. She stared at Brian, bewildered and apprehensive. His manner was subdued, his expression hard and forbidding.

Lance remained standing by the fireplace. He glanced swiftly down at Arden and back again to meet Brian's contemplative gaze.

"I shall," he said with some authority and incisiveness, "be glad to."

In that moment Arden cried, "Brian! What's the matter?"

Brian moved forward and took up a position between them.

"There are just one or two questions I would like to ask you both."

Lance tensed. Arden felt physically sick as a dozen possibilities raced through her mind.

Brian looked from face to face. Arden said in a puzzled,

restricted tone, "Questions? But I don't see the connection." She floundered, "I mean——" Coherency failed her; emotion silenced rational thought.

Brian said briefly, "I don't think any good purpose can be served by prevarication." He shot them an unnerving, almost accusing glance. "Am I right in believing that you are in love with each other?"

His words fell upon the silence with an uncanny, shattering impact. Arden gave a little gasp of horror. Was it possible that Brian, too, had misjudged her? Imagined that between herself and Lance was some guilty liaison? If so . . . She recalled his words to her just before they entered that very room. Had they been a sham to lure her into this situation? Her tortured brain could not see beyond the disillusionment of such a possibility.

Lance said with a curt emphasis, "You are perfectly right in assuming that I am in love with Arden. But I strongly resent the implication that she is in any way involved or that she has, in any shape or form, been disloyal to you. I don't know just what is in your mind," he went on grimly, "but——"

Brian interrupted him. "I want the truth," he rapped out. "Just that, and I mean to have it."

Arden gave a little cry of alarm: *"Brian!"*

Lance's voice rose stridently as he rushed on: "For God's sake, man, don't be the fool I was. Hasn't Arden suffered enough from suspicion and injustice without your adding to it? *I* can tell you all you want to know." His expression was dogged. "Believe me, had I felt that Arden had any regard for me I'd have put up a fight—openly and be damned to you! Engagement or no engagement. As it is: I mean nothing to her—nothing. You can hardly object to our former friendship, which my feelings for her indirectly ended."

Brian was adamant.

"Suppose you let Arden speak for herself," he said coolly. He looked at Arden, his expression almost hostile. "Why didn't you tell me all this?"

She stared at him stupefied. It was true. He, too, *was* accusing her, imagining her disloyal, unworthy of trust.

The tension was almost unbearable. Lance's gaze burned down upon her, adoring, baffled and apologetic.

She said shakenly, "Because I saw no point in doing so.

Lance asked me to marry him and I refused." Her voice broke. "Since it was obviously before our engagement, doesn't that tell you all you want to know?"

He answered her with quiet deliberation, "It tells me what you consider it best *for* me to know," he replied. He paused imperceptibly, then: "When you became engaged to me you said these words: 'If I promise to marry you, nothing in this world would ever make me go back on that promise. That I swear.'"

Before Arden could speak, Lance rushed in. "Damn you, Newton! This is too much. What are you trying to prove? I've *told* you: Arden is in love with *you*—you! God knows I thought you deserved her. Now I'm not so sure. You must be mad."

"That remains to be seen." Brian looked down at Arden as he went on relentlessly, "You've heard what Lance says. Is it true? You are in love with *me*?"

She cried desperately, "I'm going to marry you! Isn't that enough?"

"No," Brian answered and his voice rang with a determination that stung her to action.

She faced him defiantly almost.

"I've given you absolute loyalty. Are you accusing me of deceiving you? I've never pretended. I could bear this better if I had. You knew how I felt."

"I thought I knew," he countered. "No, you've never pretended. Until *now*."

Lance stepped forward angrily. "What is behind that remark?"

Brian relaxed a little.

"You insist that Arden is not in love with you," he said quietly.

"Regretfully—I insist," came the steady reply.

Brian looked down at Arden.

"I want the denial from you," he persisted adamantly. "I want it given to me on your word of honour. *Are* you in love with Lance?"

The silence that followed his question was so heavy that it was like pressure bearing down on them. Arden saw Lance start, incredulously and still grim in his anger, and then she watched the sudden blinding hope that leaped to his eyes as they met hers and it seemed that in a look they became one—

like two halves of a circle suddenly miraculously joined. And nothing, no power on earth, could have stayed her words.

"Yes; *yes*, I am."

The tension, the drama made comment impossible as her voice died away into stillness. In one sentence all was changed; the structure of each life reshaped.

Brian spread his hands in a gesture of appeal. His voice was thick as he murmured, looking at Lance, "I'm sorry, but this was the only way I could ever have forced her hand. God knows it has been hard." He put an arm around Arden's shoulder. "Forgive me, my dear."

Instantly she responded.

"You mean that you—*understand*?"

He moved and sat on the arm of her chair.

"Of course I understand. I knew you'd sacrifice yourself, your happiness—everything, rather than break that promise to me. If I'd asked you for the truth calmly and quietly when we were together, you would have been evasive—as you have been evasive on so many occasions. I'm a pretty simple sort of person, but love has a sixth sense and while I could accept your not being in love with me, I couldn't bear the knowledge that you were in love with someone else and unhappy. So! I had to be sure and I knew the only way was to confront you with Lance." He looked up at Lance. "To say nothing of wanting to make certain you would be prepared to stand by your regard for her, defend her, if necessary. Now I'm satisfied." As he finished speaking he moved from her chair, ruffled Arden's hair and whispered unsteadily: "Be happy."

And before either had time to speak he had gone from the room.

Arden raised her eyes and seemingly without volition got to her feet.

"Oh, *Lance*."

His arms went around her, but before his lips met hers, he looked at her wonderingly, like a man gazing in disbelief on paradise.

"You love me . . . since when, my darling? . . . I can't believe it. I hardly dare to believe it."

"I think I loved you from that very first moment, but I *knew* the night you came to take me to the theatre . . . that ghastly night. I was going to tell you——"

"My darling . . . what a fool, a blind fool I was. Can you ever really forgive me?"

"If adoring you and wanting you so desperately means forgiveness . . ." she began.

He silenced her with a kiss that took from her every scrap of resistance, a kiss passionate, unending, and even as their lips left each other so they returned convulsively as though afraid of further denial.

And then, suddenly, they broke away and eyes met eyes in all the wonder of revelation as happiness saturated them, like warming sun seeping into the body on a cold day.

"Brian," she said meaningly.

Lance understood. This was neither the time nor the place to prolong their reunion. He went to the door and opened it, calling as he did so.

Brian came back. He was calm and composed again, like a man who has fought and won a great battle and knew the peace of victory.

CHAPTER XIX

It was a quiet wedding. No word of it had leaked out to the Press and Lance was determined, at that stage, that it should not do so. After the ceremony, he and Arden returned to a simple buffet meal which Heather had willingly and miraculously produced. There might have been other ways in which the marriage could have been celebrated, but Lance understood and appreciated Arden's desire to give Martin and Heather the pleasure they sought.

Less than a fortnight had elapsed since their dramatic scene with Brian. For Arden, time had appeared to stand still. Her heart had wings and the ground beneath her feet was light as air. The face that looked back at her in the mirror almost made her self-conscious, so obvious was its radiance, its glowing, vital happiness.

She had seen Brian during that time. At her request he visited her and at the sight of him she said swiftly, "Oh, Brian, I had to talk to you. . . . I couldn't just let all this pass without further comment. I hope you don't mind."

"I'm glad," he said gently. "You look—*different*," he murmured. "That makes me happy."

She said, her voice unsteady, "You were so wonderful. I can't *tell* you——"

"You don't have to. I *know* you."

She smiled at that.

"How well, apparently." Her eyes darkened and became grave. "Where did I fail you . . . give myself away? I *tried*. I never for a moment intended——"

"You don't have to tell me that. . . . I think my first suspicion came on Christmas night, after Lance's broadcast as we stood together at the window. Remember?"

"So well."

"I knew that I could never reach you; never make you love me as I'd hoped. The realization stunned me and I tried to dismiss it. But I couldn't. I looked back and recalled the day when you and I and Lance had lunch together at the Fleur d'Argent. And the suspicion grew. Oh, I knew you'd not seen him, apart from the instance you admitted. And I was no happier than you," he confessed.

"I'm so *sorry*."

"My dear, you're a person whose loyalty is probably almost a fault. There is such a thing as committing suicide in order to keep a promise and half killing the person for whose sake you keep it!" He shook his head in indulgent devotion. "Indirectly, your loyalty to Derek, to marriage, sent you back into that misery and mess; love always feeds on emotions of that kind."

"You're so right," she agreed humbly. "And I've been so wrong—so misguided is the word. But, oh, I was *sincere*."

"Do you know your greatest vice?"

"Tell me."

"No self-preservation. You need someone to keep you in order." He added: "Lance is the right man. I realize that. I never was. Too soft. You'll revel in coping with his temperament whatever it may be; my pigeon-hole mentality——"

She protested, "*No*."

"Arden . . . you're not just in love with Lance, you're interested in him, the way he thinks, his intellect, his whole make-up. If ever two people were suited to each other—you two are."

She lowered her gaze so that he should be spared the triumphant happiness within her. Then, "Our future is your gift. We shall never forget, or overlook, that."

He said more briskly, "But there's another angle. I had a point of view, too. I'd lived with the ghost of unhappiness. The difference between suspense and knowing is that you can live with *knowing*, but you can never live with, or make friends with, suspense. I shall not be half so unhappy now, as I should have been watching your secret misery, your struggle. You must, in your fashion, know this as well as I can tell you."

She didn't protest.

"I do," she agreed.

"That is why half the sacrifices in the world are the greatest of all follies. Conscience, the desperate effort to do the right thing, so often makes a mockery of genuine honesty." He laughed. "I'm getting positively pompous."

She moved nearer to him.

"It is the very height of self-preservation when I tell you that I ask only one thing—that you shall find happiness, Brian."

"I probably shall," he said comically, "now that I've really settled the problem of what to do about Arden!" He added reflectively, "I know now that your life is settled. I'll promise you one thing: I'll do my damnedest to remould my own. I can't do more than that," he added jerkily. "And I shall come to see you both later on. Meanwhile I am going to live at the Richmond cottage. . . . Yes, I like the idea, so don't worry!"

That scene flashed through Arden's mind as Martin raised his glass in a toast. And Lance, looking at her, said quietly, "To Brian."

No word was spoken. Brian's telegram was the only one they had received, just as he was the only one who knew the time and place of the wedding—as was, they felt, fitting.

Arden stood in that oak-beamed sitting-room and remembered Christmas morning and the fantastic change that had come about since. Could anyone have told her, then, that five months later she would be standing in that same room, as Lance's wife, she would have regarded the possibility as no more than a madman's dream.

She had only a few seconds alone with Martin before she and Lance left for their honeymoon . . . Maenporth and the Crag Hotel.

"Now," he said huskily, "I'm content. I don't have to ask you how you feel—it shines from you like that blazing diamond on your finger." He glanced down at the magnificent solitaire engagement ring now resting above the chased, platinum band.

"I suppose one *can* grasp the fact that it isn't all a dream? At the moment I find it terribly difficult, Martin." Her anxious gaze met his as her mood changed. "And you?"

"If there was anything that could have helped me, this— your marriage—is it. I shall have Lance's company—we're in harmony—and yours. Those things make a difference. Your unhappiness and your damned stubbornness have given me a headache," he added with mock admonition. He glanced over his shoulder. "Your husband is getting impatient."

Your *husband* . . .

They left and as the car turned out of the narrow drive and the last wave had been given, Arden murmured, "Thank you for that, darling. . . . It meant a great deal to Martin." She added: "And you've taken Heather by storm. I shouldn't be a bit surprised if the next time we see her she isn't wearing a Dior model and dancing the Samba!"

His hand closed over hers.

"I've found a friend in Martin and that means a great deal. I value friends. . . . Arden, I'm not really hearing a word of this, because I still cannot quite accept it as being true. I feel I must be wandering in some Alice-in-Wonderland world and that a knock on the head will send me straight back to my misery!"

"I know. . . . But I'm an awfully solid dream."

"At least seven stone . . . ten," he hazarded, banteringly.

"Seven-eleven," she corrected. "And I don't take sugar either in tea or coffee!"

They laughed—that carefree laughter poised on the edge of emotion that flamed to life whenever their eyes met, and kept their pulse rate high no matter how composed they endeavoured to be and to look.

"I must remember, although I don't mind in the least being taken for a bridegroom! I am one, and having been a bachelor——" He stopped abruptly. "You know, that's strange. . . . It seems that so far as I am concerned, this is utterly and completely new—the *first* time."

She stared at him. She had not thought of Derek.

"I believe," she said quietly, "that we are reborn with every new experience. One learns and matures in the shadow of one's mistakes. That is progress."

He turned the car in the direction of Sunningdale.

"All this from a book jacket," he said, held by the memory, inspired by a sudden rush of ideas that not even happiness could stem.

"*Mrs. Ashton.*" She gave a breathless, passionate significance to the name.

"*Dearest.* . . . Oh, Arden! There's so much ahead. So much I want to show you—so many parts of the world. And to have your companionship." He stopped abruptly. "That above all is beyond describing. There are no empty places of the heart and soul when I'm with you. You *fill* my life—utterly."

They drove in silence that was but the muted passion of harmony. Then, "We'll go to Stockbridge, Sherborne—that route," Lance said.

"I know only the Ilchester, Ilminster way."

"Just as it should be," he said pleasurably. "I can show you Sherborne on the way home. We can break our journey there and stay at the Digby."

"Sherborne was your old school—wasn't it?"

He gave a low laugh.

"Yes. How did you know?"

"*Who's Who,*" she answered blithely. "I can check up on you far better than you can on me."

"But I can look into your eyes," he teased. "They betray you."

"But not now, darling. I do want to get to the hotel in one piece."

"You shall. . . ."

She sighed, a rapturous sigh.

"It was about a year ago I stayed at the Crag—on my own. I promised myself that if ever I were happy again I would come back to it—but not alone."

The car sped on. Through the pines and silver birches of Berkshire, the rhododendrons of Hampshire, on to the rolling downland of Wiltshire, where they had lunch at Salisbury and, afterwards, travelled through the Dorset pastures to Shaftesbury and Sherborne—Sherborne with its golden stone houses and ancient Abbey. On to Crewkerne and Chard where the scenery spread to heights of panoramic magnificence, as they climbed to what seemed to be the very top of the world and looked down on views breathtakingly lovely in the full, golden light of that May day. Soft, blue mists hung in the valleys, touching the bright, young green of newly-awakened trees and the apple blossom that festooned their branches, like pink snow.

And so they slipped over the border into Cornwall, lying—particularly at that time of year—peaceful, untouched, in the magic of Yesterday, its bays like opals carved by nature as the rocks glistened in shimmering hues. And the world with its traffic and turmoil was left behind as they recaptured all the tranquillity and serenity of another age.

Down through St. Austell, Probus, Truro. . . .

Lance pointed to a turning to King Harry Ferry and said:

"Restronguet is up there, my darling. I shall take you there and to the Pandora. You will see for yourself how perfectly you recaptured my word-picture of it." His fingers closed upon hers. "There's romance in the thought of all that. . . . Here we are less than a year later—*together*." He added: "Fiction can never be so strange as life, so fantastic."

They hugged the Penryn river to Falmouth and then some three miles out of it—towards Helford Passage—they reached the Crag set, proud and impregnable—an old Manor House—lying in fifty acres of sub-tropical gardens and woodlands, and looking down from its great height on the secluded Maenporth Beach.

Lance was amazed.

"And I thought I knew Cornwall. This is—heaven."

"It had to be," she whispered, her eyes shining.

They wound their way up a steep—but simple—drive, banked by bluebells, primroses, rose campion that formed a solid wall of colour which, later, spread out into woods that lay like blue seas, cradled in green as expanses of bluebells blotted out all save their own beauty. The smell of freshly turned earth, of bracken, poured into the clean, fragrant air. And at last they reached the summit where the hotel itself—built of Cornish granite in Tudor-period style—stood on what was a plateau set against the sky. Around them the country rolled, to east, north and west, and south, below them, lay the sea.

"Elysium," Lance said as he helped Arden out of the car, and kissed the top of her head as he did so.

They went inside, where antiques and close-fitting carpets preserved all the beauty and colour of what was once a gentleman's residence. Flowers, artistically arranged, reflected themselves in highly polished surfaces and whispered of home.

The owners, remembering Arden, greeted them with a friendliness and charm which made it easy to appreciate just why the hotel bore the stamp of dignity and perfection, and having made certain that all their needs had been catered for, discreetly disappeared.

And, so, at last they stood in the large sunlit bedroom overlooking the sea. Arden raised her eyes . . . and the next second was in his arms.

He held her with a passionate and yet tender closeness, almost as though, with the sensitive appreciation of the artist, he could not precipitate that final, ecstatic surrender; as though every moment leading up to it was like the slow movement of an exquisite symphony, needing that rapturous crescendo before reaching its tumultuous climax. Instinctively, as eyes looked into eyes, Arden understood; her woman's soul enthralled by a restraint that, far from shattering desire, intensified it.

Lance said hoarsely as they stood and looked down upon tiers of trees, gardens, woodlands, to the white-capped, turquoise waves surging on to the shore below, "These moments must be set in time, my dearest. . . . We can never *quite* recapture them even though, in fulfilment, we may know a deeper happiness. I want you desperately and yet . . . I want these brief hours to hold a magic because we haven't to say good-bye to each other at the end of them."

"Only you," she whispered, "would be able to wait on the breath of ecstasy." She curved back against him, lifting her lips, feeling the surge and throb of passion and . . . drawing away from him.

"And only you," he said tensely, "would understand that mood."

"*Mood*." She caressed the word. "How few people appreciate moods." She sighed. "All they confuse them with is being moo*dy*—which is as remote from them as the stars from the sun. Oh, Lance! It is just as though I had ceased to be me—as though I were physically a part of you as I am mentally, we're so in harmony." Then as desire mounted, she stepped away from him. "Now to unpack, bath and dress."

"With interruptions," he warned her.

She flashed him a provocative smile.

"Yes, please."

Later, they went down for cocktails into an intimate little bar leading out into a carpeted conservatory, holding two lighted aquariums. At one spot, through the actual floor, a sub-tropical tree was growing, spreading out to give originality and charm. Through the open door, the grounds stretched into infinity.

Lance ordered the drinks and then raised his glass, his eyes passionate as they met hers.

"To my wife," he said softly.

She drank a second later and it seemed to him that she sat there in all the radiance of youth and beauty, as though there were something not quite of this world about her—or his own happiness.

They dined in the oak-panelled dining-room, with its shining polished tables and deep, mullioned windows giving panoramic views of sea and country.

"I'm glad it is a little out of season because we have the added joy of privacy," he said softly. "I'd like to book every room in the hotel and have you to myself!"

She thrilled to his words.

"I'd like to come here for Christmas," she murmured. Then: "But not our first Christmas. I want that at *home*— our home—the Manor House where we first met." She stopped abruptly.

"What is it?" His gaze deepened.

"I'd forgotten something." She looked at him wonderingly. "I'd forgotten *someone*."

"Who?" He tensed.

"*Lance Ashton*," she said quietly. "I'd forgotten him completely, seeing only my husband—the man I love."

His hand closed over hers surreptitiously.

"Keep on forgetting him," he begged. "And yet, oh darling! When we get home there's a new book clamouring to be written. Something that will hold the very essence of you and all you mean to me. No," he added, with a wide smile, "I'm not going to break out into light, romantic fiction, don't worry! I'm just going to write with more of my heart—that's all." He looked at her with earnestness. "Thank you, my darling, for all your generosity which was so much greater than mine, for your understanding and . . . for loving me."

His words became almost stern lest she should think them too sentimental. But she knew that in them lay the very soul of all he felt for her.

The meal was everything they could have desired. The champagne soft as velvet, and the atmosphere breathed the romance that touched their heart like magic wings. They sat there talking, so close as to be indivisible, so aware of each other and so utterly in unison.

Their coffee drunk, they went out into the still fragrance of the spring night. The grounds were a sanctuary, where the branches of trees, meeting overhead, formed a vast, shadowy world of light and shade and every now and then they caught a glimpse of rolling countryside, of sea and woodland. A round golden moon rose in the heavens, gentle, serene. The first star shone, like a dream held in space.

"*Arden* . . ."

His arm was around her; their lips met and instinctively they turned back. . . .

The silent, waiting room absorbed them and now a soft, mysterious dusk filled it, throwing rose-hued lights upon the furniture and upon the pastel-shaded sheets that gleamed invitingly.

Lance's arms went out and as he drew her to him it was as if the universe stopped, while from a moment in time they took a kiss so different, so passionate in its expression of adoration, as to fuse them into one being. . . .

"I love you, my darling," he whispered.

Her eyes met his, her body curved against him, her lips parted in a sudden exultation that merged into a frenzy of emotion as desire rushed between them like a fierce tide that nothing, now, could stem. . . .

As darkness crept stealthily out of dusk, she lay in his arms, the rapture of surrender—absolute and triumphant—holding all the wonder, fulfilment and ecstasy of marriage.

THE END